The Tender Summer

JIM JOHNSON

HARVEST HOUSE PUBLISHERS
Eugene, Oregon 97402

Other books by James L. Johnson:

Code Name Sebastian Series
The Death of Kings
What Every Woman Should Know About a Man

THE TENDER SUMMER

Copyright © 1985 by Harvest House Publishers
Eugene, Oregon 97402

ISBN 0-89081-426-0

Printed in the United States of America.

In Dedication To

*All the God-fearing and God-loving pioneers—
men and women—who in the past and present
still go in peace and give all mankind the taste of
the true "tender summer."*

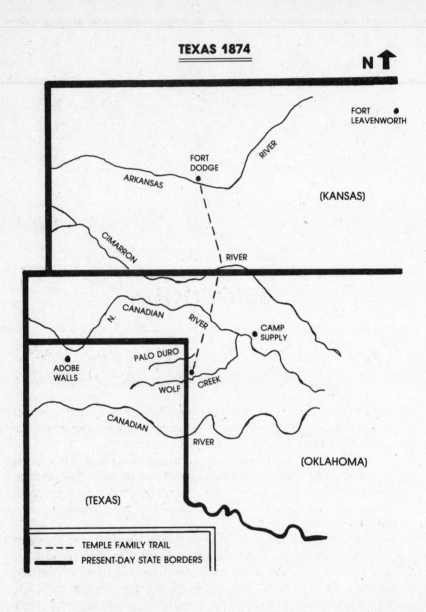

TEXAS 1874

N

FORT
LEAVENWORTH

FORT
DODGE

ARKANSAS   RIVER

(KANSAS)

CIMARRON

RIVER

N. CANADIAN   RIVER

CAMP
SUPPLY

PALO DURO

ADOBE
WALLS

WOLF   CREEK

CANADIAN

RIVER

(OKLAHOMA)

(TEXAS)

- - - - - TEMPLE FAMILY TRAIL
━━━━━ PRESENT-DAY STATE BORDERS

PROLOGUE

The summer of 1874 found the United States in a continuing expansionist mood as thousands of pioneers joined the rush across the Western prairies looking for a "place to grow."

But in the midst of this exploding migration, both settlers and the government ignored the rising anger and resistance of thousands of Indians. Treaties with the Indians, repeatedly broken by white men, created distrust and growing hatred even in the most respected peace-pursuing chiefs.

The previous summer, 1873, and again beginning in the spring of 1874, the Indian treaty lands in Texas, south of the Cimarron River and west to the Panhandle, had been breached by white buffalo hunters. Driven by the high prices for buffalo hides in the East, hunters slaughtered thousands of the animals, stripping them of their hides and leaving their carcasses to rot on the prairies. Frustrated, angry, and frightened by this senseless carnage, the Indian tribes gathered to face their most desperate hour. Buffalo meant food, clothing, shelter. Without them, the Indians were doomed to extinction.

As a result, furious bands of Kiowa, Comanche, and Arapahoe began forming alliances to attack unsuspecting settlers, government surveyor parties, even small army supply trains—anyone white— throughout the northern and middle sections of Texas on up through Oklahoma and Kansas.

In spite of the danger, hunters and settlers continued to encroach on Indian treaty lands. By the spring of 1874 a war was brewing behind the government's assurance of "business as usual." By the end of the summer the history books would record the time as "The War of '74" when all the fury of the Plains Indians was unleashed on uninformed, unwarned, naive pioneers who stepped over the line. It would end in the late summer of 1876 with the Battle of the Little Big Horn and the demise of the famous General George Armstrong Custer in South Dakota.

Into the tormented land of North Texas in 1874 came the family of Jeremiah Temple, a family of seven—Jeremiah, age 46; Elizabeth, his wife, 38; adopted daughter, Joanna Danforth Temple, 20; daughter, Marcella, 19; and sons Andrew, 17; Paul, 16; and Timothy, 15.

Their experiences demonstrated the courage, fear, faith, and tenacity—and even presumption—that many pioneers knew who felt the call of the land and obeyed that call. For the Temples, it would also become a unique journey, one that would prove that the long, hot, killing summer of 1874 carried a taste of something else: the kiss of tenderness.

One of them in particular, Joanna, would come to know a different kind of touch, one she never dreamed she would ever know or ever accept.

1

She opened her eyes and stared at the wall only a couple of inches from her face. The rough, weather-beaten boards turned gray with age were mortared with a hardened stucco between the cracks. A feather touch of early June air came through those fissures, tickling her nose. But it carried no hope of new life. It was a dry breath, smelling of sand and a season that would not or could not break loose.

She was in Fort Dodge, Kansas. The year, 1874.

She reckoned it to be near dawn with just a trace of light coming through the small window across the room. She heard no stirring outside, but a fragile, clinking sound from downstairs meant that Mrs. Temple was up, poking up the fire, getting ready to make the porridge. Mr. Temple, if habit prevailed here, had been up earlier to haul in firewood from the wood store outside.

She felt a stirring in the bed beside her and Marcella leaned in closer to her. "Joanna?" her muted voice came in a half whisper, still heavy with sleep, reaching out in the dim light. Joanna did not respond, content to keep her face to the wall, pretending sleep, feeling some comfort in that soft puff of air on her cheeks.

"Joanna?" Marcella whispered again, her voice rising slightly. "Joanna, I'm scared..." Her breath was warm on Joanna's neck. There was a frightened tone to her voice, childlike, as if she were walking into a dark room calling to someone for assurance.

"What for?" Joanna finally answered, not moving, keeping her voice smothered by the blanket pulled up around her mouth.

"Well..." and Joanna felt Marcella rise up on her left elbow to lean over her, "I heard that Colonel McDonnel, you know, commander of Dodge? He was talking to another officer about trouble with Indians in Texas...aren't we going to Texas?"

Joanna hesitated, a bit irritated. Marcella was the queen of the ball back in Northfield, Minnesota, a strikingly beautiful blonde with soft blue eyes that carried provocative lights of mischief. She turned the heads of all the men when she walked into a crowded room. But she could be so incredibly dense about facts that did not apply to her shape or coiffure. It particularly annoyed Joanna now, even as she thought of something short and quick to put her at ease. It was more difficult now because she did not feel comfortable about Texas either. Yet, she was older than Marcella by a year, older than her three stepbrothers as well. And she was looked on in the family as one not easily afraid of anything or anyone.

But thoughts of returning here to Kansas unnerved her. It brought back those terrible memories of another night when there was fire, screaming Indians, and death. None of the Temple family knew— except perhaps Mrs. Temple—what this return was doing to her insides.

"Of course, we're going to Texas," Joanna finally said, a bit too abruptly perhaps, but impatient with Marcella's lack of understanding. "You face Indians when you have to," she concluded, feeling that the soft flutter of air coming through the wall was unusually warm.

"And that Mrs. Browning who fixed our beds up here in the loft?" Marcella continued, ignoring Joanna's attempt to assuage her fears. "She said that the Indians are killing buffalo hunters...and surveyors...even settlers...she said she wouldn't go fifty feet from

Fort Dodge. Papa says we're going straight through Indian country, northeast Texas, to the Canadian River country. Didn't he say
that in Northfield? Mrs. Browning, when I told her, her eyes got
big-like, as if she was terribly afraid for us..."

"Your father did not say 'straight through,' " Joanna countered.
"You read too much into everything. He said 'through if I have
to'...there's a difference. Think positively. Good things. And the
goblins will go away. Try to get back to sleep."

The sound of more light clatter of dishes and the snap of logs burning in the fireplace came from downstairs. She felt Marcella slip down
on her pillow again, sighing. A horse whinnied somewhere outside
in the fort. Then the bugle sounded, blasting the quiet dawn with
sharp, jabbing sounds.

When they faded, Marcella said, her voice coming up from a
whisper to a hoarse sound, "Joanna, did you see that officer who
rode in with his troop last night?"

Joanna sighed, resisting what was coming but deciding she had
better get up. "What about him?" she asked, in a tone of resignation.

Again she felt Marcella's body turn toward her. "Joanna!" she
said, exasperated.

"Shhh! You'll wake your brothers next door..."

"But, Joanna," Marcella went on, lowering her voice to a whisper
again, "he's—well, he's so handsome in a—well, a gloriously rug-
ged sort of way. Tall, riding so straight on that big bay quarterhorse.
Captain Tom Brainerd. I heard him introduce himself to Colonel
McDonnel on the porch of his office."

"My, my, you are indeed knowledgeable on everything in this
place," Joanna said dryly, turning from the wall then and pushing
the blankets back from her face. "Did you also notice that all his
troopers are Negroes?"

"What difference does that make?"

"Well," and Joanna kicked the blankets back as a signal to
Marcella that she was more interested in getting up, "no white army
officer leads a Negro troop lest that's all he's got left to command.
Anyway, Negroes are not known as fighting men in the army."

"How do you know that?" Marcella challenged, her voice stronger
now, disregarding her brothers sleeping in the small room behind
them.

"I've done my reading, Marcella, while you were being courted
by every freckled, pug-nosed army officer back in Northfield.

Anyway, I'm older than you, remember, and have lived considerably more than my years...your father told you that.''

"Just because you settled in Kansas with your family once doesn't make you an expert on Negro soldiers or officers who lead them," Marcella insisted, not even trying to keep her voice down. Her tone carried hurt and anger because of Joanna's attempt to puncture her fantasies about the officer.

Joanna hiked herself out of the blankets and slid down the bed to put her feet on the cold, wooden floor.

"Well?" Marcella insisted.

"Well what?"

"Oh, forget it!" Marcella said, giving a low, deliberately agonizing groan of frustration. "Don't you ever see anything besides guns and horses and wild game—jackrabbits and elk and deer or whatever? Don't—don't you ever think of loving a man, romance, marriage? Don't you ever feel anything inside you?" Marcella always went into that silky muffle whenever she talked about love and romance, Joanna thought. "A warm feeling, your blood racing, your cheeks hot and getting hotter, your pulse clattering like your heart is about to burst?"

"Had that once when I had the grippe back in Minnesota."

"Oh, Joanna," and Marcella drooped back onto her pillow with a long disgruntled sigh.

"Hey, will you two stop yakkin' in there?" a voice growled from behind them. That would be sixteen-year-old Paul who loved his sleep. "It's still the other side of midnight for cryin' out loud!"

Joanna stood up and glanced out the window at the first red tinges of morning sun. Pulling her white cotton gown over her head, she felt the sticky dampness of the room. As she glanced quickly down the length of her body, she felt for her clothes. Joanna knew she did not have the curvacious form of Marcella. Her legs were too muscular, as were her shoulders. That came from long walks and hunting—activities Marcella avoided with extreme care.

Despite the promise of another hot, dry day, she pulled on long bottoms, then a light cotton shirt. After that, her familiar leather Levis went on with the wide brown belt pulled tight around her small waist. She lifted her long, raven hair into a pile on her head, pressed it down flat, and pinned it into place.

"No ," Marcella said glumly, watching her, "why should you think about men? Long underwear, Levis, hair piled on top of your head..." Then her voice shifted to a note of pity. "You *are* a beautiful woman, Joanna," Marcella appealed to her. "If you'd only look at yourself once in a while, dress like a woman more often...when was the last time? I can't remember. If you'd let your lovely dark hair stay down, instead of stacking it on top like that...many a man would look twice at you. Sometimes your brown eyes carry a sparkle that brings color to your cheeks and there is something about you, Joanna, something fascinating, a mysterious beauty that seems to jump out from you—"

"Careful, Marcella. You keep that up and I might give you competition for that officer of yours," Joanna said teasingly, uninterested in Marcella's concern for her. "Anyway, when you ride a horse for any distance you appreciate longies and Levis... something you wouldn't know." She buttoned up her brown buckskin top shirt, then sat down in the chair to pull on knee-length wool socks and boots. Walking over to the small nightstand, she poured water from a pitcher into a porcelain bowl, cupped two hands full, and slapped her face, snorting against the bite.

"Don't forget this," Marcella said, reaching up to take the brown brimmed trail hat from the peg on the bed and tossing it across the room. Joanna caught it. "Put it on, Joanna...make yourself a complete picture of a man."

Joanna placed it carefully on her head, tucking up stray wisps of her dark hair underneath the brim. She glanced once at Marcella through the mirror. There was a small, amused smile on her soft mouth, a smile that had a trace of cynicism in it.

"You could join the army if you wanted to," the younger girl said, her voice lilting with mockery. "They'd never know until you took a bath...and then maybe not even then." She gave off a tittering laugh.

"I've thought of it," Joanna replied, refusing to yield to Marcella's jabbing. She pulled the hat lower over her eyes. "Now...you lie there if you want to and dream of your officer, that Negro leader Brainerd or whoever. I'll go find us a jackrabbit for lunch."

"You and Buffalo Bill would make a marvelous pair, Joanna," Marcella teased again through that cynical smile, and she giggled as Joanna turned to back down the ladder leading from the loft. "Buckskins and buffalo guns, eating dry beef and rabbits...and maybe even living in Indian lodges."

Joanna paused abruptly on the ladder, her eyes turning quickly to fasten steadily on Marcella's face. Marcella knew that look, and her self-satisfied smile faded. She sat up quickly, lifting a hand toward Joanna. "I—I'm sorry, Joanna...for that, really...I—"

"Your mother needs your help," Joanna replied crisply and moved on down the ladder. She paused at the bottom and glanced over at Elizabeth Temple bending over the black porridge pot hanging over the fire, stirring patiently. She turned her head and smiled lightly at Joanna.

"Bright and early as usual, Joanna," she said in her usual quiet tone. There was gentleness, beauty, patience, and persistence in Mrs. Temple. Joanna felt strong love for her, because of that deep abiding capacity for feeling. There was certainly more feeling from her than her husband, Jeremiah, whose mind stayed locked between land speculation and the Scriptures, a mix Joanna often found hard to reconcile. "You slept well, Joanna?"

"Yes, ma'am."

Elizabeth Temple was her aunt, the sister of Joanna's father. At thirty-eight only the slight fade in her blonde hair and the trace of tired lines under her pale blue eyes gave any indication of age. She still carried that aura of grace and breeding that came from her Bostonian heritage. She had been a schoolteacher back in Northfield and had taught Joanna since she had joined the family when she was twelve years old. After the massacre of Joanna's family in South Kansas in 1866, Joanna alone survived after hiding in the brush near the soddy cabin. Elizabeth insisted that the girl come to live with them. Jeremiah Temple concurred out of what Joanna believed was his "Christian duty," even though she did not want to judge him too harshly in that.

The adjustment had been slow for Joanna, but it was Elizabeth who helped heal the wounds and finally led her out of the terrible darkness and loneliness that she felt.

Joanna glanced at her again. The lines of beauty showed in the fine, delicately-shaped face. Elizabeth was at the age when she should have been back in Northfield surrounded by a familiar home and mementos of a life well-spent. But she was loyal to her husband; when he said go, she went.

"You ready for breakfast?" Elizabeth asked, looking toward her.

"May I take it later, ma'am?" Joanna asked. "I'd like to run Pointer and maybe get a jackrabbit...if that's all right? May I help you with breakfast?"

"No, dear...it's Marcella's turn. Marcella?" she called toward the loft above.

"In a minute, Mother," Marcella responded.

Just then Jeremiah Temple came through the door with an armload of wood, walked past Joanna, and dropped it into the box by the fireplace. He brushed his hands and turned toward the young woman.

"Well," and his voice carried the usual booming cannonade of optimism, "the early riser, eh, Joanna? I like that in you, girl. Dawn's the best time to get your thoughts together and talk to the Lord. Then to a good breakfast...how does that set, eh?"

"Joanna wants to ride before breakfast," Elizabeth said.

He turned to look at his wife, who kept stirring the porridge, then back to Joanna, a look of puzzlement coming across his face. He was a big man, well over six feet tall, broad-shouldered, salt-and-pepper mustache emphasizing the downward slant of his long hawklike nose. He had a full head of hair that billowed in shades of black and white, like frozen ocean surf. In Northfield he was an awesome figure at social functions, a man of means who had speculated on many businesses and made the kind of profits that brought bankers from all over Minnesota.

"Well...you can't ride outside the fort by yourself, Joanna," he said, that familiar frown of disapproval cutting between his eyes over his nose.

"I'll be all right, Mister," she said confidently. She had never called him "Father" or even "sir." When she had first come to the Temple household she asked if she could call him "Mister," a term of high respect to her but not equal to the love for her own father. Jeremiah had accepted it after some pause, but only after Elizabeth told him it was proper and right that he allow it. Joanna felt he never had become used to the term, however.

"What do you mean 'all right'?" he asked. "The tree line is less than a mile from the fort...but it's a long way. You'll be alone, unprotected. Who knows how many marauding savages are waiting?"

"Jeremiah," Elizabeth put in quietly in her patient tone, "Joanna knows what she is doing..."

"How? Anyway, they'll never let you ride out of the fort alone," he insisted.

"Mister, I talked to the corporal of the guard last night—"

"You what?"

"He said I could go out if I did not go into the tree line. I'll stay close, I promise."

"Well—" he sounded a bit uncertain, a bit grumpy still about it. "I hope the corporal of the guard knows what he's talking about ...you'll be back soon?"

"Yes."

"So," and his voice came up in that optimistic tone again, as if he had decided for her after all. She moved to the door and picked up her Sharps carbine leaning against the wall. She preferred the single-shot Sharps to her Henry repeater because it had more accuracy at shorter distances. "You just take care out there, Joanna. We don't want any trouble now that we're just about ready to move on out to Texas. You stay in sight of the fort, you hear?"

"Yes, Mister."

As Joanna turned to the door, he said, "Joanna?" She waited. "Colonel McDonnel is giving a special officers' dinner for us tonight in our honor. There will be a party afterward. I expect you to be there in proper attire."

She hesitated. He knew she hated "proper attire" affairs. But he also knew that she did what Elizabeth had taught her to do out of respect for him. Anyway, there was that familiar note in his voice that did not allow for argument.

"I will be there," she replied. After a pause, she added, her face looking at the closed door, "And in proper attire."

"Good! Long's you're out there, bring us a jackrabbit, Joanna. Hey? What say to that?"

Joanna opened the door, glanced back at him, then to Elizabeth, and smiled.

When she was gone, Jeremiah took to pacing across the small room, his heavy steps beating like drums on the pineboard floor.

"I'm worried about that girl, Elizabeth," he said, running his right hand though his bushy hair. "She's been different since we left Northfield. Every mile down the Mississippi, then even more so as we made Leavenworth, now here. She's tense, fidgety, oiling that rifle of hers over and over. That girl should be putting together a trousseau; instead she collects awards for shooting contests. Not right...not right at all."

"Well, you taught her all she knows about rifles and shooting contests, Jeremiah," Elizabeth replied lightly.

He paused in his pacing and glanced at her. She did not smile. "Maybe so...but I didn't teach her that ungodly vengeance that seems to have come to a head now. She's back to that terrible time in 1866 here in Kansas...and she acts like she's replaying it. Only, it's strange. It's like she's calling the tune this time..." Elizabeth gave the porridge another stir. "This thing, this strange drive she has about that incident, it will poison her in the end, Elizabeth...or kill her. God help her."

"She has to make her journey, Jeremiah," Elizabeth said conclusively. "Everyone has some journey to complete. Joanna has hers too."

"Well, I don't hanker to hers," he insisted, pacing again. "Dressing like a game trapper all the time. I mean you can't deny your sex forever, can you? Anyway, it's not Christian. One thing to defend yourself, quite another to lay plans to take someone's blood. I don't want judgment on this house, Elizabeth...I don't want to open the door for the devil to jump through."

"You brought her here to the place where she remembers even more. Marcella!" Elizabeth called again. "You get down here and do the table right now. And get your brothers up or your father will come up with the strap!"

"Oh, Mother," Marcella groaned from up in the loft.

"Remember," Elizabeth said, turning back to Jeremiah, "she's part of the family and we pray her through like we have with all the rest."

"You think I should have left her back there in Northfield?" Jeremiah asked, perplexed.

"Of course not...it would have been cruel, heartless. Whatever she finds here is what she will need to ease the torment of her soul and heart. But we must not plague her with it, Jeremiah."

"She should listen to the Scriptures more," Jeremiah grumbled. "I don't think she hears a word of it most of the time."

"Don't be hasty in judgment, my dear," Elizabeth replied calmly. Just then Marcella came down the loft ladder, dressed in a bright blue calico dress, the white petticoat showing in sharp contrast.

"Well, now," Jeremiah boomed. "Look at our lovely daughter here! Now there's a beauty, eh, Elizabeth? Would you look at her now! Hardly sun up and here's our darlin' Marcella lookin' ready to go to the ball! Why, you'll have every officer in the line standing at your door today, Marcella!"

"There's the cutlery, Marcella," Elizabeth said to her. "Best be hurrying...I hear the stampede of your brothers upstairs."

Elizabeth lifted the black pot of porridge from the fire and placed it at the head of the table. Her mind went again to Joanna while Jeremiah continued to fuss over Marcella. "God keep her safe," Elizabeth prayed silently, "and may her journey be complete soon!"

2

Joanna walked briskly across the fort parade ground toward the stables. Off to her left, the troopers of the Sixth Cavalry housed at Dodge were lined up for morning parade, horses snorting, saddle gear clanking, some short guttural laughs or irritated growls from sleepy men trying to keep their mounts in line. The troop band was already waiting a short distance from Colonel McDonnel's quarters.

"Get in line there!" a burly sergeant bellowed as two horse soldiers fought to get their mounts settled and in place. Joanna paused, fascinated by the cavalrymen snappily dressed in their best blue, finally sitting their mounts straight, holding for the order.

She glanced toward McDonnel's quarters, noticing the open door. Then the colonel stepped out onto the porch with two officers. He was a short man, a bit heavy in the middle and broad in the chest with a heavy dark mustache and short goatee. He did not pose the kind of figure a commanding officer of a fort should be, but then she wasn't sure what that was anyway.

The band struck up with trumpets and flourishes and then broke into "The Girl I Left Behind Me."

"By the right, column of twos!" the lieutenant on horseback shouted to his troops. "Yo!" The long line swung to the right in an easy, well-coordinated movement and began moving down toward the fort gate, turned to the left and to the left again to come up the fifty yards or so to where Colonel McDonnel and his aides were waiting. The music filled the morning air with the blood-surging melody, and Joanna felt her heart trip as she watched the lieutenant turn his head and salute Colonel McDonnel on the porch. All eyes in the long column snapped right with that salute as they passed the porch. McDonnel kept his hand up in salute until the column had passed. The horsemen then wheeled their mounts to the left, came back, and stopped ten yards in front of the porch.

"Troop!" the lieutenant's voice was loud and crisp in the morning air. "Single up! Parade! Yo!" The troops moved their mounts to the left, stringing out into single file, forming a long, blue line.

The music stopped on cue and the young lieutenant walked his horse toward the porch, stopped ten feet from it and said, "Sixth Cavalry all present and accounted for, sir! At your pleasure, sir!"

McDonnel hesitated a moment as if he were studying that long, blue line in front of him, perhaps savoring the glory of the moment himself, then said dryly, "Very well, lieutenant...dismiss your troop to the duty roster of the day."

"Sir!" The lieutenant turned his horse around and faced his troop again. "T-R-O-O-P!" his voice snapped in the rapidly warming morning air. "Prepare to dismount! Dis—mount!" Again, in a perfectly timed move, the troopers dismounted and stood to the bridles of their horses. "Sergeant Black, dismiss the troop and see to the duty roster of the day!"

"Sir!" the bearded sergeant responded. "Troop...dismissed!" he shouted, and the parade was over, the troopers turning to lead their horses back to the stables.

"What duty roster?" Joanna heard one soldier grumble to another as they passed. "I done cleaned my rifle, my barracks, served in the kitchen so's I hate the smell of buffalo meat, polished my boots so's I can see the veins runnin' in my nose in them. When we all gonna go out on patrol lookin' for Injuns?"

"You got a camp fire war here, boy," the older soldier replied, disgruntled.

"What's that mean?"

"It means you tend the fire and spill no water on it. In other words, we are on stand-down at Fort Dodge. We let the buffalo hunters have the fun with the Injuns."

The two men passed by, and Joanna moved along to the stable across from where the troopers kept their mounts. She came alongside Pointer, rubbed him on his flanks and back. He nudged her affectionately with his nose, and she gave him a sugar lump in return. He was a strong, beautiful gelding, a saffron-tan color with a ginger-colored mane. She saddled him quickly, anxious to get out on the prairie.

When she approached the fort gate, she saw the corporal of the guard, the one she knew as Jake, who had told her the previous evening that she could ride outside if she wanted to.

"Jake?"

He turned from talking to two other soldiers and looked at her. He was a sunken-cheeked man who looked more like a boy, a chaw of tobacco forming a lump under his lower lip.

"Ya?" he said, frowning at her.

Joanna pulled her hat brim down lower over her eyes. "I'm Jo Temple, remember? You said I could go for a ride outside the fort this morning..."

Jake rubbed his cheek, not sure he remembered, and then shrugged. "Okay...ya...watch it out there, sonny. I don't need the colonel dressing me down for allowing guests in this here fort gallawaggin' around the prairie out there. You stay in sight of the fort, ya hear?"

"Right," Joanna said shortly, aware of the eyes of the other troopers on her.

"Open the gate there," Jake ordered, and two soldiers lifted the heavy bar and swung the huge post doors open. Joanna nodded her thanks to Jake, who continued to watch her intently, still unsure. She touched Pointer's sides with her boot heels, and he jumped to the prod and was out of the gate in two long strides.

Joanna felt the power of the gelding under her and let him out in a gallop for a hundred yards, feeling the warm, muggy air slap at her cheeks, tug at her hat. There was something about rushing air around her that was exhilarating, the feel of the horse under her giving her a sense of total freedom. She finally reined him in and walked him, but felt the urge to run again. It was too warm. The sun was orange-red, burning down on brown grass that had not yet burst into green. The tree line ahead of her appeared to have no green buds. It looked scraggly, bare, and withered, the dust boiling up in small puffs under Pointer's hooves. It was too dry. If it didn't rain soon, nothing would grow and the land would remain withered, locked in dust.

Her mind drifted to the remark of that one trooper about a "camp fire war," but not really understanding what that meant. If it did mean that the soldiers here at Dodge were not taking to the field, then how would settlers be protected from Indians? How would the Temples survive? How would she?

She reined in Pointer then and dismounted, bending to look at a single bluebonnet sticking up from the edge of a pine stump. The only sign of spring. She reached down to pick it, then changed her mind. She was sensitive to solitary life fighting to emerge, no matter what form it took. Maybe she was like that, Joanna thought. She had been like a root out of dry ground for so long. No, it deserved to be there, to suck what life it could from that old stump, to give this tormented, dry land some reason to hope.

She reached back and took her carbine from the scabbard on the saddle. She felt the easy, balanced weight of the gun, a weapon she felt at home with. Guns and horses had made up her life since she was fourteen—ever since Jeremiah had taught her how to shoot and ride. The eight sharp-shooting target medals in her trunk were her pride. But they were not the totality of significance either. Those medals said she could shoot and shoot well. And that meant that one day, maybe soon now, she would fulfill what all the practice and shooting awards were meant to accomplish.

She felt a pocket of sweat on her upper lip as she pondered it. There was a combination of excitement and a little fear mixed in. Anticipation of that future moment when she would get her revenge mingled with the cotton paste in her mouth that came with the thought of facing an Indian she had to kill. Not just any Indian. But that *one*. The one she remembered charging his horse around her parents' sod home here in Kansas, shooting into the cabin, then killing her dog Cricket. And then the end of it—the last long scream from her mother inside. When it was over, only the ashes remained, the bodies of her father and mother and two little brothers in the ruins...

That one Indian—maybe a year or two older than herself, riding a pinto pony, yelling and screaming the savage song of death—she had kept that image in her brain for eight years. Now she was on home ground again, drawing closer, she hoped, to relieving the torment of that image.

She led Pointer along in a walk, her eyes roving for sign of a jackrabbit jumping out of his hole. But there was no sign of life here. She felt a dryness within herself that matched the smell of the dust and mold that held the earth prisoner. Marcella's remarks always dug deeply under her skin even though Joanna managed to ignore her barbs. She had no sense of anticipation about the dinner party at Colonel McDonnel's that night. She knew no greater waste than having to put on feminine mannerisms when she had other matters in mind. Anyway, no matter what she wore, it never seemed to do anything for her; Marcella could wear any old cotton thing and look like a queen.

"You are beautiful," Marcella had said to her this morning, as she had said so many times in the past few years. There were times when she wanted that beauty to desperately show, to be seen and recognized by others...but it would not come. Marcella saw what others did not see, what Joanna would not let them see, what she did not believe about herself anyway. But Joanna had no time to dwell on the younger girl's comments.

She paused once, Pointer nuzzling her neck, sweeping the tree line with her eyes, feeling the hard, dry prairie earth crunch under her boots. Her heart beat erratically now. This land had taken the life from her, wiped out the true music of any spring, locking her into the winter of her soul.

She stopped then, not really understanding why. Her mind had been finely honed to the instinct of a hunter, an instinct she had taught herself and learned from Jeremiah and his oldest son, Andrew. He was the quiet one, the thinker, but also the one who was the hunter, who tracked like a hound and could sense the movement of a honey bee fifty yards away. She had learned to sniff, to watch, to compute when something was near.

This was one of those times.

Her eyes darted to the right and left, sensing a rabbit maybe, ready to make a run for the trees not more than a couple hundred yards ahead. There was nothing. The feeling remained, however. A sense of something not right here, beyond her past nightmares.

She turned slowly and mounted Pointer, holding the carbine in her right hand, the stock against her thigh. She took the time to check the breech, cocked the hammer back, and prodded Pointer toward the tree line. She knew that Jake was probably watching her from the fort, probably getting more alarmed as she walked Pointer toward the forbidden grove of scraggly cottonwoods.

She stopped not more than twenty yards from it, peering through the transparent cover of leaves. Pointer snorted and pawed the ground with his right foot so that the dust came up and gagged her some.

Then she saw him.

For a long, silent ten seconds when there was not even the sound of a bird, she sat very still. He was sitting on a gray horse just inside the tree line, perhaps twenty feet back, a tall Indian in full ceremonial battle dress, feathered warbonnet and all. He was old, his hair unkempt and almost white hanging down to his shoulders, his face, behind the garrish yellows and reds of war paint, looking wizened and sunken. Across his saddle he had an old muzzle-loading musket. In his right hand was a round buckskin shield, in the other a long lance decorated with colored feathers.

In those endless silent seconds, they stared at each other, and she saw it all again...the burning soddy, the Indians yelling and killing...her heart jumped with the memory, and Pointer felt it and shifted his weight around, snorting nervously again. She held him at tight rein, keeping her eyes on that almost phantom figure sitting there stoically.

The impulse to run was strong in her throat, the fear thumping in her chest, her limbs turning to mush, a paralysis setting in on her that kept her frozen. But then something snapped within her, and all the past eight years of remembering welled up in a spurting geyser of revenge. In place of fear came calculation, cold and decisive.

She felt the sweat slide from under her hatband, down her left cheek, the bitter salt taste forming on her lips. Slowly she raised her carbine an inch at a time, pressed the stock back to her right shoulder, her cheek tight to the walnut, her finger reaching slowly up to the trigger. He did not move even then, just sat there and stared at her, as if he did not understand.

She had begun to squeeze on the trigger now, the whole scene in front of her frozen in time, her sights dead on the round, brass medallion hanging over the Indian's heart. She disregarded the warnings of what trouble this would make for Jeremiah and Elizabeth Temple. Right now she was reacting out of years of instinct, a mind honed to just one reaction when confronting an Indian, the years of nursing this moment when she would deliver some of the burden of hate that had held her prisoner for so long.

Suddenly Joanna heard the sound of a horse's hooves almost on top of her, even as she prepared to make the final squeeze on the trigger. Then she felt the blow on Pointer's rear end, knocking her off balance in the saddle, almost spilling her off. Before she could right herself fully, Pointer was jerked around and pulled into a gallop away from the tree line.

Glaring at the horse and rider next to her, his hands on Pointer's bridle, Joanna fought to an upright position in the saddle. He yelled, "Yah-ah! Yah-ah!" and dropped behind to Pointer's rear and slapped the horse with his quirt, sending him on a jumping gallop. The dust was a choking curtain, shutting him out of her sight, and she began coughing and spitting against it while a searing pot of rage rose in her throat. She tried to get her rifle around on him, but he crowded her again, so that she was shoved off balance.

When she straightened, Joanna turned to see him up close, his brown army trail hat with the crossed swords stitched over the brim, the brown buckskin trail shirt bearing the blue officer epaulets on the shoulders. Then she saw the yellow line down his tight blue trousers tucked snugly into his boots. An officer, all right.

She yanked on Pointer's reins, pulling him to the right away from the officer. The dust boiled up again, putting him behind the cloud. She reined the horse in, coughing and gagging on the dust. He too had stopped behind that veil, but she could only make him out as a shadow through it.

The dust settled slowly, and she saw him more clearly. He was the captain of the Negro troop, and this made her all the more furious. He sat there and waited.

"What—just what do you think you're doing?" she screamed at him. "What—what right have you to drag my horse, whip him and interfere? Of all the gall-dangdest manners I've ever run across!" She shoved the carbine back into the scabbard with an angry thrust. "You put your hands to my horse again, mister, and you'll get a bullet through you, officer or no officer!"

He did not smile, but his blue-water eyes had shafts of amusement flicking across them, angering her all the more. His face was long, angular, with strong high cheekbones, all accented by a short line of dark mustache bringing out a wide mouth with thin, softly shaped lips. His dark hair ran down to the nape of his neck.

"You were aiming at that old chief out there—"

"I know what I was aiming at!" she snapped back, trying to get control of herself, yet still trembling inside at how close she had come to delivering that bullet.

"He's an old Arapahoe chief come back to die in his old hunting grounds out there in that tree line," he continued calmly, his voice sounding almost as if he were teaching her.

"So? I could have dispatched him in a hurry if—if you hadn't been so stupid about it!"

"There were ten of his young braves right behind him in that grove, not more than twenty or so feet," he went on.

"Oh?" she challenged belligerently. "I have good eyesight, and I didn't see anybody but that old Indian."

"I was downwind of you coming up around them...you couldn't see them from your position. Surprising they didn't take you before you even raised your rifle. But if you had shot, you'd be dead by now or dragged off to their lodge somewhere to live a hell you wouldn't even want to think of."

"Well," she coughed on the dust again, still angry at him, even more so in knowing she had not seen the other Indians, "if you are quite through with your Prince Valiant rescue, do you mind if I proceed?"

Only then did she sense that her trail hat had fallen back to her shoulders, held only by the buckskin bonnet strings around her throat. She felt her hair around her cheeks and coming down the back of her head. She glanced at him quickly. But his expression had not changed. A flush of heat ran from her ears across her face.

"If I were you, I'd get that hat on before you go back through the gate," he said. "The corporal of the guard won't feel so good when he sees what he let out to wander around the countryside." He pulled his hat down lower over his eyes as a kind of nod of respect to her and galloped off to the fort gate without a look back.

As Joanna took a deep, shaky breath, she coughed on the dust again, cleared her throat, and rubbed Pointer's neck to let him know she was sorry for it all. She fumbled with her hair and finally, in frustration, jammed it under her trail hat, tightened the buckskin bonnet strings, and urged Pointer on to a slow walk to the gate.

3

Captain Tom Brainerd followed the sergeant into Colonel McDonnel's office, stopped a few feet in front of the desk, and waited. McDonnel did not acknowledge him or the sergeant. After a full minute of waiting, the sergeant turned his head toward Tom and lifted one eyebrow to indicate his puzzlement, then turned and walked out.

Tom continued to stand in place, looking down at McDonnel's head bowed over the papers he was signing. There was a widening bald spot on top, and the darkness of the hair was streaked with light strokes of frost. Tom knew that McDonnel realized who he was by now, since Tom had reported earlier to his sergeant major when he had arrived at the fort. McDonnel's ignoring him now was part of his distaste for past events surrounding both of them.

The room was very quiet, almost like a sealed tomb with both windows shut. It was a typical commanding officer's room like the larger forts had. The smaller forts had offices that were no more than ten by ten feet. This was fifteen feet wide and twelve feet deep. Over to the right, in the corner, was a potbellied stove. The hot, sultry air in the room perpetuated the smell of wood ashes probably still in the grate of that old stove. Behind the desk on the white stucco walls were pictures of McDonnel posing with various generals during the Civil War, the larger one with General Ulysses S. Grant himself, now President of the United States.

Over to the left on the wall was a huge map of Kansas, dotted lines indicating Texas to the south and blocked-out areas outlining the province of the army of Missouri. Yellow-tagged pins represented the forts across the frontier.

A large painted portrait of a woman showed her to be thin and sallow, sags of exhaustion under her pale gray eyes. That would be Colonel McDonnel's wife, Alicia. Tom was shocked at the age that showed in her face. He remembered her five years earlier as a vivacious, bright, outgoing lady who had caught everyone's eyes. Now she seemed ravaged, starkly bony and carrying a look of despair behind her false smile.

McDonnel continued to ignore Tom, scratching signatures, sounding like a mouse eating through a plaster wall. Then he reached for his official seal and stamped each signature with a loud, thumping sound. Finally, not looking up from his work, he said, "Your orders, captain," and the emphasis was on "captain" as if to challenge the rank.

Tom put the leather pouch down on the desk in front of McDonnel. He stamped his seal a few more times on papers, put the seal into the desk drawer, and only then reached over for the pouch. He glanced up briefly at Tom. He still had those large brown eyes, except now they seemed veiled by fatigue or preoccupation with deeper matters of his soul. What had happened to his wife seemed to have happened to him, at least in the visage of faces. His face was fatter, almost puffy, his body more obese. He sat like a buddha in his chair, hunched down under his own weight. There was a time, five years ago, when Colonel McDonnel, then a major, was a figure of power, all muscle, no fat, trim and ready for command. Now he was like bread dough, expanding in the heat of the oven which was Fort Dodge.

"Impossible, captain," he said with finality, pushing Tom's orders aside as if they were contaminated.

"Sir?" Tom asked politely, feeling a burning shaft run up his spine at the tone of McDonnel's voice, one of disinterest and sarcasm. "Sir, those orders, if you'll pardon me, are signed by three generals at Fort Leavenworth..."

"And your father-in-law, Colonel William Potter, I see," McDonnel countered with an acid tone. "You are supposed to be under house arrest at Fort Abraham Lincoln, captain." His voice sounded like a bullwhip in the sealed room. "I have no reason to honor this—this piece of paper under those circumstances which I have not been informed have changed."

"Colonel, General James McClelland, commander of the Tenth Cavalry is also on those orders—"

"And how your father-in-law managed to get a respected general to sign a paper like that, recommissioning an officer under house arrest for dereliction of duty five years ago—which resulted in the deaths of twenty troopers and five civilian families, including his own wife—is beyond me, captain."

McDonnel pushed his chair back and stood up. He walked to the window behind him that faced the blank walls of supply sheds.

Tom paused, picking his way carefully now, yet burning to make the point. "Colonel," he said, keeping his voice controlled, "I have my orders."

McDonnel grunted in some disdain, then leaned against the wall beside the window and stared out. "I know you and your father-in-law, Colonel Potter, have been waiting to dig this thing up again. But it won't work, captain. The court-martial already determined the verdict...you are guilty of dereliction, abandoning Fort Morrow to a Cheyenne attack five years ago..."

"Sir, I am not here to challenge that finding," Tom replied, feeling the urgency to do so, however.

"And the very idea that you would insinuate I gave the order to that courier to ride off to tell you to pursue those renegades, leaving your fort with only twenty men to protect those civilian families and your wife is a matter of deep resentment to me, captain!" McDonnel went on.

Tom knew he was not going to contain it after all. "Sir, if you insist on going over it again, I have my resentments too. My father-in-law was with you at Fort Lyon when you told that courier to ride to Fort Morrow and tell me to pursue—"

"There was no such order! What courier are you talking about? He did not appear at the court-martial because there was no courier!"

"Sir, I would know him if I saw him—"

"Silence!"

"Sir."

Tom noticed now that McDonnel's face had turned a shade paler. He moved away from the wall by the window and began pacing behind the desk, his hands behind his back, eyes on the floor, collecting himself.

"After your house arrest at Fort Lincoln, you come here and expect me, the commander of Fort Dodge, to allow you to go into Indian country with that—that sorry excuse of a command you led in here?"

"Yes, sir," Tom said, letting out his breath slowly. "Those are my orders."

"To do what, may I ask?" and McDonnel continued pacing, his voice still heavy with reprimand.

"Well, sir, if you read those orders, they say that I am to lead a troop into the Indian treaty lands of North Texas, especially around the Panhandle and particularly the Adobe Walls area where Quanah Parker and his Comanches are raiding."

"Ha!" and McDonnel's voice exploded with a gust of air that hit the low ceiling with all the derisiveness of a cannon shot on steel. "Captain, you should have been hanged long ago for what you did at Fort Morrow. When General Sheridan hears about your being out of Fort Lincoln with phony orders like this, you can be sure you will hang! I don't know how you got those signatures on that order, mister, but you can be sure I'll find out!"

"General Sheridan is in Washington, sir...."

"Which you and your father-in-law undoubtedly knew beforehand when you two concocted this document—"

"Colonel—"

"Captain, you will speak when I give you permission!" He turned toward Tom then, his clouded, brown eyes widening to show the bloodshot whites and the pupils now hard with his anger. His heavy breathing pushed unevenly against the tight folds of his uniform across his chest. "Now, then, captain," he went on, turning to pace again, his voice coming down an octave but heavy yet with incrimination, "the army of the Missouri is not patrolling North Texas under the orders of General Sheridan and General Sherman.

The buffalo hunters are taking care of the Indians very well..."

"Permission to speak, sir?"

"Proceed, captain," the colonel said with impatience in his voice.

"My orders are to show some force in the Panhandle," Tom explained, keeping his voice even, unhurried. "I realize the strategy of Generals Sherman and Sheridan, along with Secretary of the Interior Delano, that the army is to lie back and allow the hunters to kill off the only means of survival for the Indian, the buffalo—"

"Then you understand why there is to be no show of force," McDonnel countered. "The strategy is a good one, and I intend to follow it. Of course, I recognize that all those papers you wrote while at Fort Lincoln about the white man's mistreatment of the Indian and broken treaties has given you a twisted view of the issue. An Indian is an Indian, captain, may I remind you? He has no sense of treaty obligations; he has no civilization. He has no instinct but that of an animal. In light of all that, you come in here with orders to show force to the Indian with that rag-tag troop you command? Do you know anything about Quanah Parker, captain?"

"Yes, sir...I studied—"

"Studied?" McDonnel turned away from Tom and walked again to the window, leaving the sound of an incredulous laugh hanging in the air. "Parker is a raging savage...if you think you can go out there and talk him into a reservation, then you might as well consider it a seal on your death." He paused, as if a sudden thought had commanded his attention. He turned slowly and came back to his desk and Tom's orders. "Try being peaceful to the savages," he continued, his eyes glancing over the orders, "you should know better than that. After what those Cheyennes did to you. You sound more like them than us, captain..."

"Sir, I still have my orders—"

"So in this peacekeeping show of yours, you will shoot buffalo hunters who encroach on Indian treaty lands in North Texas as well as Indians who attack the hunters, correct, captain?" McDonnel went on, ignoring Tom's attempts to get to the issue.

"I will do what I have to do, sir, to prevent the war building up in Texas...the hunters are encroaching on Indian treaty lands and forcing Quanah Parker and the other chiefs to retaliate."

McDonnel did not say anything for a long time, his eyes still on those orders. "Captain," he said, his voice calm now, "perhaps you should go on your journey. But I will not supply you. I have no orders from higher up to do so. You will have to go to Camp Supply for provisions.''

"Sir, that is a three-day ride at least, and away from the Panhandle..."

"Captain, until those orders are clarified by General Sheridan, I owe you nothing.''

Tom knew it was done then. He had come here to smoke out McDonnel, true, about what happened that terrible day at Fort Morrow. Instead, he felt himself in disarray. It was obvious, however, that Colonel Mark McDonnel was not resting very well over that incident, judging by his defensive behavior. That gave Tom reason to believe that the colonel was covering up. He remembered then what his father-in-law had told him three days ago at Fort Leavenworth after he had ordered Tom out on his patrol to North Texas. "Don't try to get even with Colonel McDonnel, Tom. Your folks brought you up, taught you to avoid vengeance. They were God-fearing people, taught you well. In God's own time, He will bring justice...remember that."

Now he watched McDonnel as he took the pen and scrawled his name on the orders. "There you are, captain," he said, dismissing him. "You are free to go out and meet Quanah Parker in your— your mission of peace with that scallywag Negra troop of misfits you call a command."

He gave a small, tight, crafty, leering smile. The fat face and large brown eyes, the mustache and goatee, the buddhalike body, seemed to fill the room now. Tight, airless, lifeless.

"And what about the settlers, sir?" Tom asked. "Are you escorting them or leaving them to themselves out there?"

"The settlers are warned not to go into that territory. If they choose to do so, they take their own risks."

"And the buffalo hunters?"

Another sly smile, but the eyes remained lifeless and hard. "The same for them, captain."

The colonel extended the leather pouch with Tom's orders inside. Tom looked at the freckles and the hair on the back of the man's hand, and all of that only increased his revulsion for McDonnel.

"By the way, captain," McDonnel added, his voice rising a bit to a forced tone of pleasantness, "I am giving a dinner party and reception tonight in honor of Mr. and Mrs. Jeremiah Temple and family heading out to North Texas. I expect you to be there."

Tom caught the note of irony in the colonel's voice. "Very good, sir..."

"Dismissed, captain," McDonnel said with that acid snap to "captain," which sent another flush of heat through Tom.

Tom saluted, turned, and walked out. The sun was past two in the afternoon now. It was hot, heavy, stifling. He stood on the porch looking across the parade ground. Nothing moved. The corporal of the guard was standing his duty at the gate, mopping his face with a red bandanna now and then. The watch was in place on the walls, but the troopers took turns sitting in what shade they could find up there. A fly droned now and then, sounding tired in the heat. Nothing more.

He tried to take a deep breath to ease the heat in his lungs and the rage in his brain. The words of his father-in-law came to him again: "...you will not get justice until you find that courier McDonnel sent to you with the message to pursue those hostiles out of Fort Morrow. Only God knows where he is or even if he is alive now. Right now, though, some of us are going out on a limb to commission you to take a command into the field and keep Quanah Parker contained and get those buffalo hunters back over the treaty line. Some of us happen to believe in what you wrote about the unjust treatment of those Indians; and we don't believe, as Sheridan or Sherman or even Ulysses Grant, that the best way to exterminate the Indian is to destroy his one means of survival, the buffalo. A war is building out there, Tom...do what you can to prevent it. God be with you!"

None of that assuaged fully the nagging sense of bitterness in Tom's mind. Justice was not being served. Colonel McDonnel had lied, yet now he commanded one of the most prestigious forts in the army of the Missouri, the command that he—then Major Tom Brainerd—would have inherited five years ago.

So where was God in it all now? Tom leaned against the rail of the porch and gazed into the powdery dust, trying to quiet the rumbling pocket of hot lead in his stomach.

Death and destruction was in his path now. But he was bound to face it. He had at least been given a command by trusted officers, even though it was done without General Sheridan or Pope's knowledge. Those officers believed, contrary to the general's belief, that there had to be some kind of army show of force if the buffalo hunters and Comanches were to think of calling off an inevitable war. Tom knew, though, that it was close to a "lost command." Many of his troopers were former cooks, livery men, and horse groomers. A few among them could use a gun well enough, some had field patrol experience. But except for a very few, none of them had come up against Quanah Parker's Comanches or the likes of them. And after five years of being out of the service, Tom wasn't sure if he could handle it successfully either. But he was committed. Better to go out with a sense of honor than to rot at Fort Abraham Lincoln.

He walked down the steps and across the dusty parade. Amos Chapman, his scout, approached him. Chapman, a half-breed, was married to a Cheyenne woman and served as interpreter at Camp Supply. His face was brown from his mixed blood, the sun and the smoke of lodge fires, his black hair long and straight with a red band around his head. His eyes were dark and small, squinting most of the time as if he were doing a lot of thinking.

"Are the hunters gone to Adobe Walls?" Tom asked him.

Chapman nodded. "Fifteen, mebbe sixteen..."

"Whiskey?"

"Plenty..."

Tom glanced down at the hard, red clay of the parade between his feet. "That means they'll try to trade off that firewater to keep the Indians off them. All that'll do is make the Indian crazier and more murderous. They still don't understand. Is Billy Dixon among them?"

Chapman shook his head. "Didn't see him...mebbe he go early with smaller group. I hear Comanche dance big medicine down at Palo Duro. A new prophet said to have strange powers...he says summer will be very dry, but it will be a summer of honor for the Comanche in war."

"Hmmm," Tom said. "Not hard to predict the dry summer. Not the way it smells right now." Chapman nodded, but Tom knew that when Indian prophets say it will be dry, as far as Chapman was concerned, that was final. Tom glanced at Chapman. He didn't know why the scout had chosen to ride with him. Chapman knew well enough that fifty untrained Negroes were not fit for the field against Comanche. Tom had come to know Chapman six or seven years previously during the captain's Cheyenne chasing days on the Colorado. He happened to be lounging around Fort Leavenworth just as Tom was leaving for Dodge a week ago. Tom asked him, "You want to come for twenty dollars and your keep, Amos?'' Chapman was squatting by the stable wall. He looked at the scruffy-looking Negro troops.

Then he shrugged. ''Twenty dollars will keep my squaw in beads,'' he said and vaulted onto his painted sorrel and fell in alongside Tom.

Now Tom said, ''Chapman, there's a family of settlers planning to head out to North Texas in the morning. Find out how many water barrels they are carrying on each wagon. If only one, see if you can talk the quartermaster into an extra one for each, fill them and rig them on the wagons tonight. Here's my request in writing. Sergeant Winters owes me one from years back.''

Chapman took the paper and put it into his faded blue denim shirt pocket. Then he turned and walked swiftly toward the stable area and disappeared around the corner.

Tom continued to stand on the parade, debating whether to inspect his troop or mosey over to the post canteen and pick up any gossip on the buffalo hunters heading for Adobe Walls. He took off his trail hat and wiped the sweat from his forehead with his sleeve. It was going to be a very tough, hot, dry summer. There was the smell of death in the air already. He did not relish the thought of the days and weeks ahead. Nor was he looking forward to dinner with Colonel McDonnel.

He looked up at the mean, brassy blue of the sky and the magnesium sun that glared in white heat. He thought of Martha then, the shaft of loneliness grabbing him. He slapped his hat against his leg as he walked toward his quarters, trying to shake the memory of her and that awful day five years ago at Fort Morrow. He had beaten off the attack by the Cheyenne with the 100 men he commanded at the fort. When the Indians retreated across a range of hills, dragging their dead and wounded with them, a cheer went up among his troopers. They had ridden with him, A and C Companies of the Twenty-first Regiment, Third Cavalry, for a year. That day they paid tribute to him for his leadership and his tactical sense that had routed the Cheyenne band away from the fort. Tom knew, however, that his ''tactics'' were simple—putting the right men and the best shooters in the right places on the walls, no more.

He had sent a courier immediately to Fort Lyon, a half-day's ride south, to inform Major McDonnel of the victory. Five hours later, just before sundown, a courier returned, not his own, from McDonnel informing him: ''Major McDonnel's orders, sir...

pursue the Cheyenne war party...search and destroy, sir!''

Tom was baffled by the order. By now the Cheyenne had a full day on him and by morning they would surely be out of the area altogether. ''You have it in writing, corporal?'' he had asked the courier, who had a blonde scruffy beard and a brass bugle hanging on a strap over his shoulder.

The bewhiskered tobacco-chewing trooper who looked more like a renegade Indian himself than a soldier shook his head. ''No, sir, the major sent me flying as soon as he got your message....''

''You a bugler, corporal?'' Tom asked, curious about the man now.

The soldier spat and gave a half-smile. ''No, sir...handed on to me by a sergeant out of Fort Stark once who had lost his bugler in a brush fight with Apaches. I just toot it now and then, sir...''

Tom had taken his time about the order. He asked the courier's name. Jack Davison. He debated whether to send Davison back to get a written order from McDonnel which army regulations required or get on the march. But by the time he returned, the Cheyenne war party would be long gone into Wyoming territory. Not wanting to create what would look like an insubordinate move, he organized his two companies for the pursuit but with no particular hope of catching up to them. He told Martha that he would be gone in the morning just for the day. He remembered how she had clung to him that night as if sensing the danger he would be facing or what she might face without him. He assured her that he would not be gone long. Anyway, he would take eighty of his command and leave twenty behind—his best men—to protect the fort.

He left the fort the following morning at sunup. He had one scout, Buffalo Traigert, an old trapper from up Colorado way. They picked up the Cheyenne tracks a mile out and continued to follow them for most of the morning. At noon Traigert noticed that the tracks swung south. They followed them for another hour and Traigert pulled up his horse to study the ground.

''Them tracks is heading back east, major,'' he said solemnly. ''I think they be doublin' back on us toward the fort.''

Tom ordered his troop on a gallop back to Fort Morrow praying all the way that his hunch was wrong. But when he saw the fort from a distance, dark smoke boiling up from it, he knew, with a stab of agony, that the worst had happened. The Cheyenne had indeed doubled back, stormed the fort, overwhelmed the remaining troopers inside, and killed all of them, including the five civilian families...and Martha.

He buried her himself in a small grave outside the fort and stumbled through the days and weeks following her death. The investigation by Fort Leavenworth led to his court-martial charging him with dereliction of duty. His father-in-law, Colonel Potter, was at Fort Lyon when McDonnel gave the order to his courier. "I didn't hear it all," he testified. "But I saw that courier ride out." McDonnel denied under oath that he had ever given such an order. When the court asked Tom why he had not insisted on a written order, Tom simply said that he had no reason to doubt Major McDonnel. Meanwhile, the courier named Davison was not found listed on the roster at Fort Lyon. A Corporal Davison was on the record as having served there a year before but had been officially listed as a "deserter" for months. But without the written order nor the courier to testify to the truth of the message, the court ruled it had no choice but to find Major Tom Brainerd guilty of negligence, reduced in rank to captain and confined to Fort Abraham Lincoln "pending final sentence at a time the court saw fit."

Afterward, Colonel Potter had received permission from General Pope's office to mount a five-man patrol to hunt for the courier named Davison. They searched for a month but came home empty-handed.

In those first two agonizing years at Lincoln, the burning hatred for the Cheyennes and Major McDonnel threatened to destroy the captain. After awhile he forced his mind to look at it all as objectively as he could. McDonnel, he knew, wanted the command of Fort Dodge more than anything else in his life. Driven by his own social-climbing wife, who kept prodding him to go for higher rank, he had obviously decided to get it by a blatant act of dishonesty. There was nothing Tom could do to alter what McDonnel had done—unless somehow the courier showed up.

As for the Cheyenne, he realized that building hate for them was not going to honor his dead wife. So he took instead to studying the Plains Indians in those long hours of house arrest when he was confined to quarters. He was intrigued by what he read of their behavior, their history, their genius at hunting and at war, but mostly their peaceful nomadic life. He talked to reservation Indians at Lincoln—the Sioux, Cheyenne, Blackfoot—through interpreters. Their view was simply that they wanted to live in peace, hunt buffalo, and roam the prairies that they had known since time unremembered. Their war, they said, was only in defense of that dream; and since the white man would not sit down and talk with a "straight mouth" about treaties and continued destroying the Indian's livelihood—the buffalo—they had no choice but to fight back.

Tom wrote voluminously about the issue, insisting that the white man could live peaceably alongside the Indian if he worked at it. But his papers were dismissed as "idealistic and not founded on experience by army and civilian personnel."

Tom realized the impossibility of making his point while under house arrest. And then came the order from Fort Leavenworth lifting his quarantine temporarily and ordering him back to Kansas where his father-in-law issued new orders for active service in the field.

Now pausing on the parade ground of Dodge, the sun beating heat through his brain, he knew that he was in a no-win situation. When Sheridan found out he was in the field, against his orders, there would be a patrol out after him. God only knew what would happen to Colonel Potter and Generals McClelland, Seager, and Hook for signing that order. Colonel McDonnel might yet have another laugh over the fate of Captain Tom Brainerd.

But those officers had believed he had a chance in keeping Quanah Parker's Comanches off the buffalo hunters, and, in turn, talk those hunters out of Adobe Walls and Indian treaty lands. But he knew now that the task was beyond the possibilities of success. All he could do was try.

He put his hat back on his head, slapped at the sweat itching down his face, and headed for his quarters. He needed time to think, plan whatever strategy he could. If this was his last command, then he intended to make the best of it.

4

Colonel McDonnel made certain when he took command of Fort Dodge that he would have a proper guest dining facility and party reception area in which to entertain dignitaries.

The dining room adjoined his office quarters, a large room with a dark mahogany table in the center that could seat twenty people or more when fully opened. The room was paneled with mountain cedar and decorated with Early Renaissance and American paintings. Curios of elephant tusks and tiger and leopard skins decorated the walls. The colonel often explained the mementos as "gifts from President Grant's African hunt, in remembrance of our time at Bull Run together." McDonnel would also point out a cluster of framed photographs on the wall showing him with the President a year earlier when they had gone on a buffalo hunt. The chandelier that hung down over the table was made of glass crystal with Bangkok brass ornamentation, which McDonnel took time to point out, mounted with sixteen candleholders. In each holder was a large white-and-blue candle burning with a small flame reflected off a glass mirror mounted in the ceiling above. It gave the room a soft, warm brightness, creating an elegant atmosphere for dining.

Joanna overheard Jeremiah telling Elizabeth about rumors that McDonnel had high taste, indulging it more recently from the cash percentages he took for all the buffalo hides the hunters brought back to the fort for shipment to the East. In exchange, McDonnel allowed the hunters to cross the Indian treaty line into North Texas where the buffalo were still plentiful. Jeremiah, however, concluded, "All of that is probably bandied about by sour-grapes troopers."

Yet, looking around the room now, Joanna had to believe that no army officer—not even a general, let alone a colonel—could afford such taste on his monthly pay. But she dismissed it as irrelevant to her and concentrated on getting through this dinner and the reception afterward as quickly as possible.

Colonel McDonnel had gone through formal introductions, and it was time to sit down. Joanna looked for her place at the long table where name cards had been put on the plates. She felt uncomfortable in the light blue cotton muslin dress which was too tight around the waist and neck, making her feel as if she were sealed in cement.

Earlier Marcella had insisted on helping her choose the dress and primp up properly. Joanna had been in no mood, however, and refused until Elizabeth intervened and told Joanna, "Do it for Jeremiah...it is his big night."

So Marcella combed out Joanna's long, dark hair. It tumbled down over her shoulders in natural waves which led Marcella to exclaim in wonder and delight. Looking at Joanna in the mirror, Marcella said, "Joanna, you have the most beautiful hair and the darkest brown eyes...look at you!"

"You said that once already today," Joanna snapped. "Get on with it, Marcella."

Marcella continued and then, looking at Joanna's face, she said, "Listen, Joanna, don't let Father know, but I am going to put a little touch of color on your cheeks—"

"Marcella!"

"Shhh! I know Father is deadly serious on what he calls paint, but this is a very light pink powder he will never notice. It will bring out the lights in your eyes.''

Joanna protested again, but finally gave in to get all of this fuss about dress over with. The powder did something all right, and Joanna now was silenced by what she saw of herself in that mirror. Her eyes were more the color of dark chestnut with a luminosity enhanced by her naturally long dark lashes. Her mouth was softer looking in the full curve of her lips, slightly tinged pink as she ran her tongue over them.

Marcella glanced at her in the mirror again and simply stared. ''Joanna,'' she whispered in awe, ''Captain Brainerd will never look at me once he sees you! Look at yourself! I've never seen you look like this in all the years you've lived with us. You're—you're ravishing! Even with that little powder I used, which only covers the sunburn anyway...but if I had those eyes, that finely sculptured face, that hair—''

''For goodness sake,'' Joanna protested again, feeling embarrassed then, ''stop trying to convince me that I'm queen of the ball. That's your department. Anyway, that's my mother's face and hair, except the nose which is my father's, a bit too straight and pointed...''

Marcella laughed, and Joanna, a bit giddy about it all, had to laugh too, something she seldom ever did, her small even teeth flashing a cascade of light that gave her eyes an eruption of stars. And for those few seconds Joanna was startled by her own face, that which she had never really known she had, or else had never taken time to notice.

''That's a nice nose,'' Marcella said, sitting down on the edge of the bed studying the older girl almost with envy. ''I am beginning to feel terrible,'' she said, moaning. ''Why am I bringing out your beauty to dazzle all those officers, especially Captain Brainerd? I bet he will ask you to dance!''

''You are doing none of this for officers,'' Joanna countered bluntly. ''If I am presentable, it is for your father and mother. Anyway, your father frowns on dancing like he does rouge.''

''Mother says it is proper to dance the reels or the waltzes. Besides, it's a matter of protocol when a fort commander honors us.''

''Yes, well, I'm sure your mother knew that when she taught you back home in Northfield when your father was not around...but your father will have the last word. Besides, I don't know how to dance and have no inclination to learn.''

"I can show you! How many times did I offer to teach you in Northfield?"

"Too many. No thanks. I am not at all interested."

Marcella went on arguing about the necessity of knowing, stating emphatically that one day Joanna might be a hostess wife for an army general or a politician and be called on to dance. "I'll stick with your father's suspicion of it," Joanna said. "And I have no intention of being a hostess to an army general or a politician."

Now, walking down alongside that long table in the dining room, she found herself, of all places, sitting to Captain Tom Brainerd's left. He was not yet at the table. She had met him at the formal introductions, but after the confrontation with him earlier in the day she made it quick and brushed by him. Joanna did not relish being parked next to him all through dinner and she pondered whether she should exchange name cards with her cousin Paul, who was at her left. But before she could make the move, Brainerd was beside her, pulling out her chair and giving her a small, polite smile.

"Miss Joanna, now that we have been formally introduced," he said, his voice deep yet quiet, "I am honored to have you next to me."

His dark blue eyes had no lights of amusement in them now, but there was a softness there, tinged perhaps with a little bit of melancholy that seemed out of place in him. His smile was brief but genuine, just a quick turning up of the corners of his mouth. His dark, closely cropped mustache matched the color of his dark hair lying like hay on his head, brushed almost carelessly into place, giving it a windblown effect. He was in his dress blue uniform, the white epaulets of rank on his shoulders, his collar, with the two gold crossed sabres stitched into it, buttoned up tightly to his throat.

"Thank you, captain," she said crisply but politely, and sat down. She was glad when her cousin Andrew sat down to the right of Brainerd. That meant Andrew would keep the captain engaged in conversation about rifles and hunting, leaving her to herself—she hoped.

She glanced down the table, curious as to the seating arrangement that Colonel McDonnel had planned. On his left was Elizabeth; then Jeremiah; an officer named Lieutenant Earl McCoy, the colonel's adjutant, who had large green eyes, big ears, and kept glancing at her with considerable interest; then Timothy Temple, almost fifteen, who was beginning to show broad shoulders and strong arms already like his father and his brothers.

On McDonnel's right was his wife, Alicia, who looked starkly thin, almost emaciated, with blue smudges of fatigue under her large pale eyes. Her once-blonde hair was turning to a white that heightened the paleness of her face. There was something about her that reminded Joanna of a creature having borne too much pain for too long and was afraid someone might inflict more at any moment.

Next to her was Marcella, dazzling the room with her presence. She wore her favorite red silk hoop dress bringing out the rich pink flush of her cheeks, contrasted by dewdrop emerald earrings with a necklace to match. Her deep blue eyes and blonde hair falling down over her shoulders in flowing waves of bright gold, together with that flashing smile, mesmerized the officers as well as Colonel McDonnel, who couldn't keep his eyes off her.

Next to Marcella was Captain Owen Billingsley who commanded two companies of McDonnel's troops. He was a boyish, blonde, tanned young officer and an "academy man," a fact of which he kept reminding Marcella. But he was not right for Marcella, and she knew it, but she was polite to him while her eyes continually darted down the table toward Captain Brainerd.

Next to Billingsley and looking completely out of place was the Negro sergeant, Hansen Bonniface, whom Colonel McDonnel had introduced earlier with some disinterest, if not distaste, as "Captain Brainerd's sergeant major." He had large, dark, friendly eyes, a short mustache and dark curly hair. He was heavyset, short, almost barrel-like, but it was all muscle, stretching tight inside his uniform. Right now he looked as though he knew he was out of place and had the anxious look on his face of one who was going to bolt at any minute.

Joanna sensed McDonnel's discomfort with Bonniface at the table. She had heard him berating Captain Brainerd in his office earlier about what was proper protocol at a fort commander's dinner "and it did not provide for Negras." To which Brainerd said, in his polite but decisive way, "May I in all due respect remind you, sir, that protocol states that a commander of a troop should make certain his top sergeant is at all social functions, regardless of color." There followed a snapping, almost scurrilous, reply by McDonnel which Joanna could not hear clearly.

Between Bonniface and Joanna was her cousin Paul who was big for his sixteen years, with heavy shoulders and torso, already close to a man in stature. He was outgoing, sometimes brash, like his father, but he had his mother's softer looks—smaller nose, mouth and her blue eyes. Joanna remembered boxing Paul's ears when he was twelve for teasing her about being "more boy than girl"; even at that age he was a heavy, stocky kid, but when she lit into him he backed off after that and never brought up that subject again.

As the first course was served, Marcella kept looking down the table toward Captain Brainerd, trying to pay attention to Billingsley at the same time. Joanna knew she would be bemoaning the seating arrangement long after this affair was over. Once Brainerd looked up and caught Marcella's eyes on him; he gave her that quick, small smile, nodding his head in acknowledgement. It was enough to make Marcella suddenly begin fanning herself with the small red fan that she carried to all social functions.

As she ate, Joanna heard Captain Brainerd explaining various types of rifles to Andrew, who, being old for his years, responded with intelligent questions and answers of his own. "The Henry repeater is fine," Brainerd said. "It's a bit old now when you look at the Winchester .44 and the new one that came out last year. The Springfield rifle is best for the long distances. The best repeater for me is the Spencer if I can't get the Winchester."

Joanna did not attempt to enter the conversation, even though she had some quarrel with the reputation of the Spencer rifle's penchant to jam in the breech on rapid fire. Rather, she kept an ear open to what Jeremiah was holding forth to Colonel McDonnel about the 3,000 acres of land he was prospecting in the Panhandle in North Texas.

"Most of the cattle barons are in South or Central Texas," he added as if he had to rationalize his point. "But very few ranches are up north. I hear there is good grass there."

McDonnel nodded, digging into his fruit pie and a side order of cheese "straight from Switzerland." When the dessert was finished, Jeremiah sipped his coffee, cleared his throat and said, "Colonel McDonnel, we noticed on the way over here from Leavenworth that there were miles and miles of buffalo skeletons on the prairie. In fact, it was almost white with bones. Among them were a lot of carcasses, some fresh, stripped of their hides and left to rot—"

"Jeremiah," Elizabeth cut in gently, a note of caution in her voice. "I hardly think the conversation goes with dessert—"

"Quite all right, Mrs. Temple," McDonnel interjected with an assuring note in his voice. He stirred his coffee slowly, taking his time, sensing everyone else in the room had paused to hear his answer. "Well, sir," he said, "it is open season on the buffalo now. Since the price of hides went up to close to five dollars apiece, hunters are turning to new fortunes out of the buffalo."

Joanna felt Captain Brainerd stir in his chair next to her, as if the subject had jabbed a nerve in him.

"But what about the Indians?" Jeremiah countered. "Is that not creating some tension with them, especially in that kind of slaughter?"

"Mr. Temple, there are two ways to bring the Indian to his knees," McDonnel replied with a tone of authority. "Hit him head-on with all the power of our military, which means a lot of expense in money and lives lost. Or we can kill off the source of his food, shelter, and clothing—the buffalo, sir—and force him into our reservations in order to survive. We prefer the latter."

"But...is it working?" Jeremiah pursued, a frown digging between his eyes. "What I hear is that the Indian is becoming more savage and warlike than ever. And I must say I couldn't blame him since his survival is being threatened."

"In time, sir," McDonnel said with a confident smile, "in time they will have no choice but to yield."

"But I read, colonel," Elizabeth ventured then, "that we signed treaties with the Indians to allow them the right to the land, to live off the buffalo and in peace."

"There is no such thing as a peaceful Indian, Mrs. Temple," McDonnel said pontifically. Then he paused. His eyes flicked toward Captain Brainerd. Joanna sensed there was no friendliness in those eyes. It was a measured look, guarded, communicating an animosity that he apparently had had with the captain from some time past. "But we have with us here an officer who spent five years at Fort Abraham Lincoln under circumstances best left to him to divulge, if he so desires. In that time he produced volumes of papers on how to bring peace to the Indians. Perhaps the captain would like to comment."

Joanna felt it was a deliberately leading question by the tone and bluntness of it. Everyone seemed to sense the change in atmosphere then, and they turned their heads to focus on Brainerd, except Marcella who had glued her eyes on him all night.

Joanna looked at Brainerd quickly. His face remained impassive. But his eyes had taken on a certain hardness. The shafts of light came on in them again, but they were chips of smoldering sparks. There definitely was something between these two men that had formed roots of bitterness in both.

"With your permission, colonel," he said. His voice polite and controlled, his eyes shifted directly to Elizabeth. "I have studied the Indians, ma'am, for three years at Fort Lincoln. I felt there was every reason to believe they wanted peace, because they had to know they could not win against the U.S. government's military or civilian expansion westward. But you are right, the U.S. government has made treaties with the Indians and has broken every one of them. The latest was at Medicine Lodge, Kansas, in 1867 when the Indian was guaranteed the right to all land in Kansas south of the Arkansas River without encroachment from the white man. The whites crossed that line in 1872 and later into Texas when the price of buffalo hides in the East went up and the buffalo herds grew scarcer up north. So now we are starving the Indians to death, as Colonel McDonnel stated, to bring them to their knees for their own survival."

"Now what Captain Brainerd is not saying," McDonnel came in quickly in rebuttal, "is that the Indian was raiding and killing years before 1867 and years before any treaties...."

"Only because of the rush of the pioneers, the gold prospectors, and land grabbers, sir," Brainerd countered quickly. "They couldn't understand what was happening and nobody bothered to explain it to them."

"Well, sir," Jeremiah came back, that frown digging deeper, "I always felt, still do, that the white man, after all, is bringing Christianity to the West and the Indians."

"With all due respect, Mr. Temple, they are also bringing whiskey, smallpox, venereal disease, and greed," Brainerd said. "For every peace-abiding Christian, there are hundreds of land grabbers and buffalo hunters who are exploiting the Indian for their own gain."

"The price of civilization comes high," McDonnel argued. "The good and the bad both make their contributions."

"Well, what do your generals think of your ideas, or your papers?" Jeremiah prodded Brainerd.

Captain Brainerd hesitated a few seconds, and McDonnel picked it up immediately with a forced cajoling tone. "Unfortunately, the army of the Missouri, all the way back to Washington in fact, cannot accept idealism of that nature in dealing with Indians. The Indian is a savage, uncivilized and unreasonable. Captain Brainerd lost his case.''

The seconds of silence that followed held an uneasy hush as those around the table became increasingly uncomfortable with the exchange.

Jeremiah cleared his throat as a signal he wanted to get on more neutral ground. ''Well, captain,'' he said optimistically, ''I intend to take my wife and family into North Texas. I intend to lay claim to the land there and run cattle on it. God knows I am not out to kill Indians. I am a God-fearing man, a respecter of life, but I will defend my right to possess free and open land that God has seen fit to give to me.''

Captain Brainerd leaned back in his chair, crossed his legs and folded his arms, presenting a relaxed pose, or at least attempting to. But Joanna noted in her quick glance that there were white patches around his nostrils contrasted by those chips of fire still in his eyes. She noticed also that his hands were shaped into fists and the backs of his knuckles were white.

''I hear you are headed into the Palo Duro Creek area,'' he said to Jeremiah.

''Wolf Creek, this side of the Canadian,'' Jeremiah replied in a voice that sounded as if he had planted his flag there already.

Brainerd nodded. ''It is a good place...sagebrush, pokeweed, Mexican juniper, mesquite, blue stem, bear grass...along with the creek willow, cottonwood, chinaberry and hackberry...all good for timber...''

''Fortunately, Captain Brainerd had a lot of time to read in his years at Fort Lincoln,'' McDonnel added, his voice carrying a slightly sardonic tone that nobody could miss. At that point, Alicia McDonnel began looking ill, and she dabbed frequently at her thin mouth with her crumpled napkin, sending obvious signals to her husband that this line of conversation had to stop.

''So you have not been to North Texas, captain?'' Jeremiah asked.

''No, sir...but my scout, Amos Chapman, just came back from that area. It is all there, Mr. Temple.'' When no one picked up on the statement, Brainerd added, ''But I expect you know too, sir, and Colonel McDonnel undoubtedly informed you, that you are heading into the heart of a growing Indian problem that could explode into a full-scale war at any time. Buffalo hunters have moved over the North Canadian River south into a place called Adobe Walls, which is on the border of Indian treaty lands. Twenty or so hunters left Fort Dodge yesterday for that place. That base will supply them for their hunt into the Panhandle and the Staked Plains. Adobe is a day's ride west of Wolf Creek. The Indians will not tolerate Adobe Walls or the white hunters who are there. Once they start to move, you are going to be in the middle of it."

"Colonel," Jeremiah turned to McDonnel now, "I was not told I was crowding Indian treaty lands. Just what does this Adobe Walls thing mean to us?"

McDonnel gave Brainerd one of those flicking, warning glances. "Mr. Temple," he said with an affected sigh, as if all of this was exaggerated, "we have settlers going into Texas all the time. You are far enough north to be out of the normal forays of Indians. We have no reports of trouble that would endanger you at this time. The captain unfortunately had one disastrous experience with Indians and he tends to overreact about settlers going into Indian territory. If we all listened to the prophets of doom, not a wagon would have moved West."

"I only wish to suggest, sir," Captain Brainerd went on, leaning forward to the table and picking up a fork to turn slowly in his right hand, "that you wait for a larger party to accompany you into that area."

"Larger?" Jeremiah laughed in a jovial way. "Captain, I have three sons and my wife's niece who can shoot a gold coin fifteen feet in the air a dozen times before it hits the ground. My wife is pretty good at it too. And I, sir, have been state rifle champion in Minnesota ten years in a row. In fact, if the Indians have a mind to tussle, and I pray they don't, we might just chase them back to their reservations by ourselves!"

There was polite laughter from McDonnel and his two officers, but Joanna noted that none of the others in the family rose to it, not sure of what to think of Captain Brainerd's concerns. For herself, Joanna was not especially convinced by the captain. She was well prepared to meet any Indians and remaining at Dodge would not fulfill her own need to meet her destiny.

"Well, if it is any comfort to you, Mr. Temple," McDonnel continued to burrow, coating his voice with forced diplomacy but which did not entirely override the tones of the doggerel, "Captain Brainerd will be somewhere in Texas in coming days, even in your area."

"That so?" Jeremiah asked, peering down the table at Brainerd again, that same questioning look on his face. "I heard there were no patrols out much these days. Is yours something special?"

McDonnel picked up the question before Brainerd could answer. "Captain Brainerd is on an experimental foray engineered by some sympathetic officers in Leavenworth—not General Sheridan, mind you, he is in Washington—to show some force in the Panhandle in hopes of bringing peace between the Indians and the buffalo hunters."

"I don't understand," Jeremiah replied, dubiously. "I don't have any ill will toward Indians, but I should think what's needed is the kind of force that will drive Indians into reservations or submission."

"That would demand a troop of highly skilled and experienced Indian fighters, Mr. Temple," McDonnel continued to play all of this out with abnormal tenacity. "And the captain's troop—with apologies to Sergeant Bonniface, of course, as the exception—is a company of Negras who do not own up to those qualifications, to put it mildly."

Bonniface had not spoken during the exchange. Now he sat staring at the wall over Elizabeth's head, his right hand squeezing his napkin into a ball. There was a restless shifting around in the room as everyone began to squirm some in the way that the conversation was going. Captain Brainerd continued to lean forward over his coffee cup, still turning that fork in his right hand, watching McDonnel now with intent eyes.

"Captain Brainerd," Elizabeth interjected then, sensing the tension of the room, "do you think there will be trouble with the Indians where we are going?"

"Mrs. Temple," Brainerd answered quickly before McDonnel could command the answer, "that is the territory where the fiercest Comanche chief does his raiding. His name is Quanah Parker."

"That the half-breed chief I've read about up north?" Jeremiah asked.

"Could be, sir."

"The one who was born of a white woman named Cynthia Parker?"

"Yes, sir...Cynthia Parker was captured by Comanches in 1836. The chief, Nocona, married her and she bore officially three children—Quanah, Pecos, and a daughter named Topsannah.

Legend has it that there was a fourth son named Tanna, that he was born more white than Indian...when he was two years old he wandered out of his tepee across the prairie and was never seen again.

"Buffalo hunters raided the Quahadi camp in the middle of the 1860s and took Cynthia Parker captive, though her sons escaped. She was taken back, along with her daughter, to live among the whites, but she never took to it...she mourned for her sons and the tribe. When her daughter, Topsannah, died of a fever, Cynthia Parker suffered severe shock...she died later from fever as well."

"How sad," Elizabeth said.

Brainerd nodded. "When Quanah heard of her death, he became enraged that the whites had taken his mother to the strange white culture and to her death. He vowed to get even for that...and that's one reason why he is spreading terror among whites now."

There was a moment of silence. Then McDonnel said, "At any rate, Captain Brainerd is now on a mission to protect this savage, Quanah Parker, from the buffalo hunters and the hunters from Quanah."

"That is hardly a command of honor, is it?" Jeremiah inquired.

"The dishonor, sir," Brainerd replied tartly, "is with the U.S. government in allowing the buffalo hunters to breach the Indian treaty lines. In the meantime, I suggest, Mr. Temple, that you remain at Dodge for at least a year before venturing into the Panhandle."

"A *year*?"

"Jeremiah, please," Elizabeth tried again to restrain him.

"Captain, all I have is tied up in this journey into North Texas. To wait a year will be too late! I have to lay claim to that land now before a stampede of land development people begins!"

"Well," McDonnel said with an exaggerated tone of mollification, "at least when you leave in the morning, Mr. Temple, you will have the benefit of Captain Brainerd's troop to escort you for at least a day or so since he is heading for Camp Supply. That should be of some comfort, sir."

The air was thick with innuendo now, and Joanna felt uncomfortable, wishing for the end of all this. Before anyone could say more, the sound of the regimental band in the adjoining reception area struck up with "Rally 'Round the Flag, Boys." It was the cue Joanna had been waiting for. In fact, it seemed that the others in the room sagged in relief with her. The air remained heavy with the exchanges, loaded with knife-cutting tension, vibrating with the subtleties of verbal wrestling the colonel and Captain Brainerd had carried on under the guise of military respect.

"Well, ladies and gentlemen," McDonnel said and smiled pleasantly at them all as if he had done no more than carry out a classroom exercise with them, "the reception is about to begin in your honor. Shall we all adjourn to the next room?"

"Great dinner, colonel!" Jeremiah boomed out and hurried to get next to McDonnel to talk further about what was going on with Captain Brainerd. Elizabeth talked briefly to Alicia McDonnel, who by now looked terribly pained and distraught. Marcella was led out by Billingsley, and she glanced back over her shoulder at Joanna in a desperate signal to get Captain Brainerd to rescue her.

Brainerd still sat in his chair, leaning over his coffee cup, studying the fork in his right hand. But then he rose quickly as Joanna made a move to push her chair back. He helped her up and said, "My apologies, Miss Temple, for this unfortunate display of poor manners."

"My name is Joanna Danforth Temple," she said curtly as she looked up at him. He stood a head or two taller than she. "The Temples took me in when my family was killed by Indians in Kansas eight years ago." She put it to him precisely so that he would know where she stood on the matter of peaceful Indians or peacekeeping among them. "As for the dinner conversation, captain, I would expect you and Colonel McDonnel could settle whatever it is between you out back of the stables."

He sensed the rebuke and gave her a half-nod in acknowledgment. "My regrets for the loss of your family," he said in a tone of genuine commiseration. "We both have lost to the Indians. I lost my wife, Martha, to the Cheyenne at Fort Morrow five years ago."

She hesitated in her move toward the door to the reception area, realizing now why the shadows crossed his eyes. "I'm sorry," and for a moment they both paused, aware of the identity in their separate losses. Then she said, "I should think in light of those circumstances you would recognize the folly of your idealistic position about living in peace with them."

He took a few seconds to weigh the truth of that. Then he replied, "My father was a simple, Bible-believing man, like Mr. Temple. He used to tell me over and over again that the Bible says that a soft answer turns away wrath. When my wife was killed, I was burning with hatred and wanted to kill every Indian I could find. Some of that still hangs on inside me. But at Fort Lincoln I recognized that there had to be another answer to the madness. War took my wife. More war will take more wives, husbands, whole families. Like yours. I don't claim to have the answer, nor that I am even right in what I am trying to do now. It may be a stupid thing to attempt. But I have to at least try to do what I can.''

"Well, captain," she responded, her voice carrying the resentment she had nursed for eight years, "my parents were God-fearing all the way. My father wouldn't bruise an ant if he could help it, nor my mother. But where are they now? Dead at the hands of a renegade band of savages on a land that was well north of any buffalo grounds. My father's soft answers got him an ax in his head from Indians he tried to make peace with in the name of God. Do you wish me to tell you more, captain?''

His eyes studied her face, feeling the intensity of her words, the hardness of them. "I understand," he said.

She turned to go, but he commented, "By the way," and his voice was more congenial, "I'm sorry I roughed you up some today out there on the prairie.''

"I don't rough up easy, captain," she said tartly. Joanna knew she was aloof and icy to him, but a peacekeeping officer did not set well with her right then.

"May I escort you to the reception?''

"No, thank you. Mrs. McDonnel asked me if I would kindly help by serving the punch.''

"May I dance a waltz with you sometime during the evening then?''

"I don't dance, captain," and she began moving away from him. "And my duties at the reception come first ahead of the festivities of the evening.''

She thought she saw a trace of a smile at the corners of his mouth, and those little shafts of light came into his eyes, the inner laughter she had seen there earlier that day. He bowed his head politely to her, and she moved on quickly, brushing by Lieutenant McCoy, who was waiting at the door expecting to escort her into the reception area.

As she took her place at the punch bowl and began filling the cups, she felt a flush in her cheeks but she didn't know why. The band swung into the waltz tune, and Colonel McDonnel did the honors by asking Elizabeth to dance first. Jeremiah, standing beside her, did not object, busy now in conversation with Captain Billingsley who kept looking longingly at Marcella. Despite McDonnel's bulk, he seemed graceful as he whirled Elizabeth around the room. His wife, Alicia, was not present, and had apparently excused herself from the reception.

After McDonnel finished the waltz with Elizabeth, the other officers turned to their partners and filled the dancing area. Colonel McDonnel sought out Marcella who was surrounded by single officers and danced a waltz with her. Marcella smiled dutifully at the colonel, but her eyes constantly shifted to the door, looking for Captain Brainerd.

Joanna saw him come in later with Sergeant Bonniface. He said a few words to Bonniface, who nodded and left. Then he too followed the protocol, dancing with Elizabeth first. His movements were light, graceful, catlike, and Elizabeth looked as though she enjoyed herself with him even more than with the colonel. When there was a pause in the music, the captain sought out Marcella, who quickly brushed by the cluster of officers around her and nearly fell into Brainerd's arms as they began to dance the next waltz. They looked good together, Joanna mused, and the captain looked as much captivated by her as was every other man in the room.

When the dance was over, Captain Brainerd dutifully entertained a few other ladies, then removed himself to stand in the back of the room behind a row of officers. Joanna served two officers punch; when she looked up again he was gone. She felt something of uneasiness within her then. Maybe it was the sharp edge of fear creeping into her heart about North Texas. Still, as strongly as Captain Brainerd had put his case, she felt he had little credibility going for him.

Then, too, the name Quanah Parker intrigued her. Comanche. The same band that killed her family. It was only speculation... nobody could really say. But she remembered after the killings that an officer at Fort Leavenworth had said, "It has all the signs of a Comanche raid." If so, could that Quanah Parker be the *one*? The one who rode that painted pony around her house and killed her dog, then took part in the burning of her family's house? Still, for all she knew, that one was long gone, probably dead.

One thing she was certain about: When she did find him, she didn't want Captain Brainerd around. She wanted no one in her way then.

She had waited too long.

5

Joanna stayed at the reception as long as it was tolerable. By ten o'clock she had filled so many cups with punch that the table was full with no room for more. She became nervous then. The line of single officers, including Lieutenant McCoy and Captain Billingsley, began looking her way. She knew it was only a matter of time before they asked her to dance.

Marcella could not keep up with the requests to dance. But at one point between dances, she came over to Joanna quickly and said, "Where is he, Joanna?" Her cheeks were red from the dancing, her eyes bright blue; she was enjoying being the center of attention, but Brainerd was on her mind.

Joanna shrugged. "He's probably got a lot to do what with going out himself tomorrow."

Marcella, with that same look of despair, went back to her line of waiting officers. Later Jeremiah came over to get a cup of punch. He sipped it, then said, "Those officers are looking at you as if they're going to die if you don't give them a while on the dance floor. Since the rest of the family has taken to dancing, this being one of those special occasions, why not take your turn, girl?"

"Thank you, Mister, but I don't dance. I observed your distaste of it in Minnesota, and I have no reason to take it up now."

"Hmmm," Jeremiah said, frowning into his cup. "Well," and he put on a jaunty air as if to confirm she was right, "you're probably right...but you've been standing here serving punch all night. Won't hurt to talk a little with those officers. Relax a bit, Joanna...do you good."

A few minutes later she looked up and saw the officers now hedging more and more in her direction. She had stacked the table with filled punch cups in an attempt to keep busy. Now she noticed the bowl was empty. It was a perfect opportunity for her to get out of the room on the pretense of looking for more punch materials. She moved quickly out the side door, through the dining room, and out through McDonnel's office beyond. Feeling warm and short of breath, she walked out onto the porch and leaned against a post. The half-moon put a misty glow over the parade ground and the white stucco buildings. The music started again, giving the night another dimension of mellowness.

She felt lonely and leaned her head against the post, folding her arms. She longed to be like Marcella, to plunge into the festivities of the reception. That part of her she knew as distant but insistent begged her to allow herself the moment; but the other, the dominant part, told her she could not. It was always the same war within her. But what bothered her now was that she was resigned to the one part, the part that said she had a destiny out there on the prairies, somewhere in North Texas. There was no room in that to indulge waltzing with lieutenants or captains.

She remembered nights back in Northfield when men would come to pick up Marcella for some big party at the military barracks or the special social occasions that brought out the cream of Northfield's party set. She would lie on her bed in the darkness of her room and listen to Marcella laugh—the animated, anticipating conversation of a man and a woman about to spend exciting hours together. She would listen, then roll over on her pillow...and there would come the stinging tears rolling down her cheeks, the choke in her throat.

Nobody asked her because they knew that the answer would be the same: "No, thanks, I have a lot to do...some other time." But none of them knew that she could not spring open the door within her and allow herself that moment of excitement as Marcella had done over and over again. How could she ever explain to any of them why?

So after a few minutes, her tears would dry, her mind would shift to the practical, to the reason she bothered to live at all...for *the moment* when the door would be finally sprung and she could live again.

"Run out of punch?"

She was startled by the voice and turned her head toward the sound. Captain Brainerd was at the far end of the porch, sitting on a chair tilted back against the wall. His legs were propped up on the porch rail. His hat was on the floor next to him.

"Yes," she said simply. She did not feel tense or on guard with him for some reason. Not like McCoy. Probably only because Brainerd would not ask her to dance out here. Beyond that, though, she had no particular desire to talk to him knowing his position on Indians.

He dropped his chair to the floor with a clunking sound and stood up, walking slowly to her. "It is a bit warm," he said. He looked up at the moon. She stayed leaning against the porch post, debating whether to go back inside or stay there. "But there's something mighty peaceful about a half-moon and a quiet fort in Kansas."

"You're being missed inside, captain," she said, making conversation and hoping he would return to the reception.

He grunted a half-chuckle. "A lot of single officers in there, Miss Joanna...too many to go around for the single ladies. Besides, I've not been much of a party man for some time now."

She presumed he meant since his wife had died. In a way, he was a little like herself...music and festivities and parties had died since the personal loss. There seemed no way to make the connection back again.

"My cousin Marcella has been looking for you since you first danced with her," she said. "She will probably die if you don't show up in there."

"She's a beautiful woman," he admitted after a pause. "There are different types of beautiful women, I suppose. Marcella has the beauty of a baroness—elegance...style...vivacious. Others... others are more quiet in their beauty, like it is hidden and only comes out at certain times and makes a room suddenly go quiet."

"Was your wife like that?"

He hesitated, staring up at the moon as if seeing her there. Then he looked back at the porch steps. "Yes. . .and you're like that, Miss Joanna. If you don't mind my saying it."

She felt a peculiar tremor go through her, and she became afraid. "Well. . .I think it is time I headed back to my quarters," she said, ignoring his compliment.

"No more partying?"

"No more punch," she replied.

"Well," he said, "I am heading to check with the corporal of the guard about the morning. Do you mind if I walk with you in that direction? Your quarters are that way, right?"

She hesitated, not sure she wanted him to walk with her. That little tremor inside continued to hammer around her heart.

"Suit yourself, captain."

They walked slowly. She wished it were faster, but he was in no hurry. He slapped his hat across his leg now and then as if he were venting some frustration. "Good to remember a night like this," he said. "Once you are out on the prairies a moon means you can be seen by every eye, not all of them friendly."

She had a strange impulse to ask him why he had spent so much time at Fort Lincoln, as if somehow in the knowing she might understand him better.

"Is that something you read at Fort Lincoln?" she teased him.

He laughed, and she caught the flash of his white teeth in the moonlight. "Very good, Miss Joanna," he said and chuckled again. "I guess Colonel McDonnel made a good point with that one. But, no, I remember many nights like this up on the Colorado. There's something about the moon and the air here in the West that is totally different from anywhere east of us."

"You grew up here?"

"No. . .all I remember is living along the Colorado River with my folks. My father was a prospector, panning enough gold to keep him and my mother alive, but never anything big. He was a kind man, strong. My mother was a beautiful woman, gentle, intelligent, but feisty. She taught me all the schooling I got. . .and I'd match it with anyone's."

"How many in your family?" she asked, making conversation while eyeing the three Temple wagons ahead parked at their quarters.

"I was the only one...my father was a big man with blonde hair. My mother was blonde too. Swedes, full-blooded..."

"You don't quite fit the image."

He chuckled again. "No...I'm a bit darker compared to them. Neighbors used to kid my folks about where I came from."

"Your parents still living?" she asked.

"My father died about four years ago...lung fever. My mother is still up there in Colorado living at Fort Davis."

They were at the Temple wagons now. "Well," she said, "this is where I get off."

"May I show you something...won't take a minute?" he asked. He stood above her, looking down, and she could see the smooth lines of his cheekbones, the soft eyes with those shafts of light in them, brighter now in the moonlight. She sensed the continual beat of her heart, and it made her anxious to get inside.

He stepped over to the wagon, the last one, closest to them and reached into the back and came out with a rifle. It had a long barrel and a big stock. "I hope you don't mind," he said, hefting the gun. "I mean putting it in your wagon and all. I didn't think your father would appreciate my giving it to him, since he prizes the Henry so. This is a Sharps .50 buffalo gun. It fires a shell with 400 grains of powder in it rather than the 100 in the standard rifle. It is a powerful gun with a range of as much as 1,500 yards. I've had it a while now, hunted buffalo with it some time ago. I want you to take it along."

He extended the gun. It had an octagonal barrel and a large hammer and loading block. She took it and felt the weight that made her arms drop. "Weighs a ton," she protested.

"Eleven pounds...but an Indian will respect the distance and power of that gun. If you fire that to hit in front of an Indian standing at 600 to 1,000 yards, it will make a hole a foot deep in front of him. I know a hunter who killed fifty buffalo in one day with that gun."

"I really can't take this," she protested. "I don't really need—"

"Miss Joanna, I said an Indian respects a gun like that," he persisted. "Sometimes he will consider it to be strong medicine and not take after you. I give it to you to use for that time when you may need it just to make an impression on some band of renegades." She lifted the gun to her shoulder, tried to press her cheek to the stock. It made her arms ache, the barrel waver.

"I've put a box of cartridges in the back of the wagon," he added.

"Well, that's kind of you, captain," she said, but the pulse in her neck was pounding with a suddenly different surge. "But I want to make it perfectly clear that I am not interested in *impressing* an Indian. I don't intend to shoot in front of him but through him! That may contradict your peace-loving balderdash about Indians, but it's best you know!"

She paused then, let the gun drop, walked over and threw it back into the wagon, not sure why, except she didn't feel like standing there any longer.

"One thing more," he continued after the pause, but with an urgent tone in his voice. "I had my scout put an extra barrel of water on your wagons. It's going to be a five- to seven-day trip for you all into Wolf Creek. There's little water out there, much less in a week or so. Your stock will need a drink too. You should have your wagons equipped for a double-trace team, not a single. Two horses are going to find it hard pulling out there. I see one wagon is loaded with lumber, cedar mostly. I expect your father will build his roof with that. I advise you to put sod on top of that cedar. A flaming Indian arrow will catch fast on those combustibles."

He paused then, slapped his hat against his leg as if he sensed she didn't care one way or the other about what he was saying. "I will inform Mr. Temple," Joanna said shortly.

Hesitating, he said, "Then I will say good night, Miss Joanna. It's been a pleasure. I will see you all in the morning."

"Good night, captain." He nodded his head and turned to walk back across the parade toward the corporal of the guard at the gate. His stride was easy, athletic, even light, his feet hardly touching the ground it seemed. She remained by the wagon for a few minutes until he disappeared in the shadow by the gate. That same tremor kept beating around her heart mixed with the flush of temper that had convulsed through her and forced her to berate him. Joanna knew the burden she carried was getting to her now, digging deeper as the time approached.

She swiped at her long dark hair that tickled her cheek. She concluded then that Captain Tom Brainerd was a strange mixture of a man. She could not sort out the feelings she had right then. Colonel McDonnel obviously had no use for him. He had spent five years at Fort Lincoln, but he never did divulge why.

And he was leading a shabby Negro troop out on patrol, something that McDonnel had made snide remarks about. But Tom Brainerd had jarred something out of place in her and she didn't like it. She knew he could not be sympathetic with her journey of vengeance. Yet there was something about him that intrigued her, something of his past maybe, something about his manner.

Joanna turned to walk up the steps to the Temple quarters, not sure how to assess what she felt. She made herself tea and went to bed, shutting out any more thoughts of the captain. But a half-hour after she lay down, she got up and went to the small closet next to the nightstand. Then she took out her Sharps carbine and her Henry repeater along with the cleaning materials. For more than an hour, Joanna oiled and swabbed until the weapons gleamed and the trigger action was as smooth as a wagon wheel turning on a well-greased axle.

She was ready.

* * *

It was near 11:30 when Alicia heard him come in. She remained in bed a few minutes longer, waiting until his boots dropped on the floor below. When she heard the noise, she got up and walked down the narrow stairs into the small but neat living area. As warm as it was, he had stoked up a small fire in the fireplace and sat on the divan staring into the flames. Fire seemed to calm him some as if the bad memories were transferred there to go up in smoke.

Alicia did what she had been doing for the fifteen years they had shared army life together. She put the kettle on to boil on the woodstove, then returned to sit down opposite him, pulling the red cotton robe around her. Despite the warm night, she could not get over the perpetual chill within her.

"You said he wouldn't come back," she began, deciding to get at it, her voice unsteady even yet in the fear which she had carried for so long, now rekindled to near panic with Brainerd's presence there.

"Alicia, I expect you to attend all receptions I arrange in honor of our guests," he reminded her in a grousing tone.

"With him there?" she challenged. "You expect me to dance with Brainerd after all that's happened?"

"I expect you to dance with Quanah Parker if he shows up," he snapped. "Anyway, what difference does it make if Brainerd is back? He's going out to meet Parker's Quahadis tomorrow. He'll never come back from that, not with that bunch of scallywags he calls a troop."

"How did he get orders to lift his house arrest and go into the field?"

McDonnel paused, rubbing his eyes with the heels of both hands. "Colonel Potter's work, who else? Won't matter. When I get to General Sheridan, they'll bust him good."

"Did he ask about Davison?"

"Davison is long gone, probably dead," he replied impatiently. "Last I heard a year ago he was running guns and whiskey to the Indians with the Comancheros. Recently a trapper told McCoy he was killed by Apaches in Arizona territory. Put him out of your mind."

"He's not out of Brainerd's mind..."

"Alicia," and his voice became waspish, "you said you always wanted a big fort and all that goes with it, remember? Nice quarters, lots of social life with the dignitaries, no more of those frontier shacks, too hot in summer, too cold in winter, miles from civilization. Well, you've got it. And I have the command that goes with it. You said whatever it cost, remember? All right, we paid it, and we are still shoveling it out. I cooked Brainerd's goose once, and I am about to cook it good now. He doesn't have a prayer against Quanah in the Panhandle on a peace mission...or trying to keep those hunters grounded at Adobe Walls."

"Maybe you shouldn't have allowed those men to go to Adobe Walls. I mean—"

"Every buffalo they shoot you get to live a little better, remember that too, my dear," he reminded her in a sullen voice, a voice carrying weariness that had been there for the past five years.

"For how long?" she ventured hesitantly, knowing his mood was mean. "Colonel Dodge has been gone for three years now. His time as aide to President Grant is about over. In a year he'll be back...where then?"

McDonnel poured himself a few ounces of whiskey from the side table by his right elbow and gulped it down. "A year from now is not my concern," he said. "The next three to four weeks are. As long as Captain Brainerd is running loose in Texas or anywhere else, each day becomes a year, you know that."

She shivered, then pulled her robe tighter around her. "You picked at him at dinner tonight. I think it embarrassed the Temple family. And Brainerd won't forget it either."

He smiled, but it was only a spasm of his lips. "Indeed," he replied, snidely. "Do you think I would let him build credibility for himself with them? I almost told them about his court-martial and sentence for dereliction of duty. But old Jeremiah Temple heard enough. He's a big man in Minnesota. He could swing a lot of weight against Brainerd if the time comes. The man may be God-fearing, but he's as strong-willed as iron and respects the cut of a man's cloth. He was not the least impressed with Brainerd's case or his abilities as an officer."

"Supposing Brainerd and his troop wind up as the great deliverer of the Temples out there?" she asked. She shivered at that prospect too. Brainerd as a hero would mean Brainerd reconsidered and the whole case reopened again.

He grunted what was supposed to be a chuckle but it sounded guttural instead. "First, he has to get provisioned at Camp Supply," he explained pedantically. "The Indian agent there is just about out of supplies to feed the thousand Kiowas he's got on his reservation. He'll have to contact Colonel McKenzie, head of the army of South Texas, to give Brainerd anything. And McKenzie will want to know what Brainerd is doing in his territory. That will take time to clear up. If long enough, my telegraph message to General Sheridan in Washington will have been answered, meaning I take a patrol out to bring Brainerd back under arrest. He won't even get to leave Camp Supply.

"And if he does, just supposing? He'll run right into that buzz saw Quanah Parker around Palo Duro with that motley bunch of misfits he calls a troop. Do you actually believe the man is going to come out of it?"

She didn't know. Instead she got up, went to the stove, made the tea, came back and put it on the sideboard by his whiskey bottle. "What about the Temple family?" she asked, trying to deal with another jabbing dagger of fear in her heart. "If—if they should get massacred, God forbid, some big people in Minnesota are going to ask why they went without official escort from Dodge. And that will get Sheridan asking—"

"They go on their own risk!" he snapped, his voice cracking like a bullwhip. "I have my orders! I obey them!"

"You told them there was no trouble with Indians around Wolf Creek," she interjected, her heart fluttering in the tension now.

"I have no exact information to contradict that!"

"With Parker already murdering, burning—"

"South at Palo Duro—yes!"

"But with those hunters at Adobe—"

"Alicia!"

She bowed her head under his berating tone and put both hands up to her face, feeling the tears hot on her fingers. In her agony, Alicia heard him pour another drink and gulp it down. He had taken to liquor in copious amounts in the past couple of years. The more he drank, the more distant they had become. As long as Brainerd was alive, neither of them could close the widening gap between them. And even if he were dead, Alicia knew it would never be the same again for them.

"Anyway," he continued, ignoring her tears, "my orders are to button up here at Dodge, let the buffalo hunters take care of the Indians." He gave a smothered chuckle, full of derision. "I can just see General Sheridan or Pope when they hear that Brainerd is loose and leading that command for the cause of peace." He lifted his glass in a mock salute to the fire and said, "To Captain Tom Brainerd, once wonder boy of the army of the Missouri, now riding his last patrol. I just hope he read up on Quanah Parker well. He's going to need it."

Alicia felt no satisfaction in that. She wiped at her tears, sniffed, and took time to look at the fire, to stare into it as he had, as if the memory could be dissolved. Instead, she realized the tightening ring of justice was slowly squeezing the life out of them.

There was nothing more to say. The colonel's wife left him to his tea and whiskey. For her, there would be little or no sleep tonight, just as in the previous five years. She had prayed many times that the truth would emerge and triumph. She desperately needed—craved—peace. Yet she knew if that tranquility came, it would be the demise of her husband and herself, the end of any dreams they once hoped for together.

Yet, as she settled down into bed, staring at the ceiling, hearing the snapping of the flames from the room below, the mocking laughter of whiskey being poured, she felt more than ever that justice would be such a relief.

• • •

It was close to midnight. Company L sat outside, leaning their backs to the stucco walls of the stable. The music floated to them from across the parade, reminding them of a part of the army they would never know, were never entitled to know. Earlier, at nine o'clock, Sergeant Bonniface had come to tell them to remain dressed "until the captain comes."

Corporal Henry Rutledge kept whittling on a piece of pine, a bit troubled now with the shape of events. He had once been a sergeant in the Fourth Cavalry, but a dispute with a black lieutenant over a racial slur had led to "insubordinate conduct." Rutledge was broken to corporal with thirty days in prison added on. But he had put that aside as past. What troubled him now was the strange mixture of the troop here. As he glanced down either side of him, he knew that probably no more than a dozen of them out of the fifty had ever been on a field patrol. All of them had records of disorderly or insubordinate conduct during their time with the Fourth. Though they had become free men nearly ten years previous, the taint of black on them would never go away. Some of them could still remember being part of slave families. Moreover, the adjustment to the army, one of the few occupations open to them, had been hard. Menial tasks were forced on them since they were not considered of genuine soldier caliber, and promotions were rare. So sensitivity to an askew look, a slur of some kind, or a direct insult caused friction and prevented them from holding responsible positions in the army.

All of that made Rutledge feel the ache in his bones even more. He was too old to ride patrols, too old to wet-nurse the far-too-young here who were always looking for a fight with each other more than with the Indians.

"Attention Company L!" a voice broke from the darkness, farther up the horse path, and the slouching soldiers staggered lazily to their feet.

Sergeant Bonniface walked toward them, his short, squat figure rolling in that familiar no-nonsense gait of his. "Ya all get inside and line up each side a' da stalls. Rutledge, see to the stable lamps. The captain is comin' down. I mean on the double now! Or ya'll will rot heah in Dodge!"

They turned and sauntered through the acrid, ammonia smell of the stable, mixed with the pungent sweat of horses. Rutledge assigned three soldiers to light the lamps hanging on the rear of the horse stalls.

"Now face off in two lines facin' each other!" Bonniface ordered.

None of them wanted to challenge Bonniface. He was known throughout the armies of Texas and Arizona as a man who could whip a buffalo bare-handed. Unlike the others, he had never spent time in prison and they all knew he had come through the ranks on his ability to keep men in line. Rumor had it that Colonel Potter in Leavenworth had asked General Crook of Fort Stark to release Bonniface for special assignment to Captain Brainerd's newly-formed company.

"Ya'll look like ya just been throwed out a' saloon!" Bonniface chided them. "Well, dat gonna change 'afore long!"

"Question, suh?" a private named Willie Dunkerton piped up uncertainly. Willie was short and slightly built, looking like he ought to be learning how to tie his shoes rather than soldiering.

"Make it short, soljer!"

"Suh, I ain' evah stood behin' a hohse 'afore," Willie said, his eyes big in apprehension as he stared straight ahead. "I's always been taught never to do it les' I gets kicked through a wall—"

"Stan' still an' dat hohse won' know ya's there!" Bonniface countered. "Anyway, what ya'll need is a good kick in the hind end to get some snap in dem unifoams! Dat yer answer, soljer?"

"Suh," Willie said in a subdued voice.

"Attention, Company L!" Bonniface barked then.

Captain Brainerd stepped inside the door and stopped beside his sergeant. He felt a sag inside as he looked down the two lines. Uniforms baggy, scrubby looking, boots splattered with mud, a certain slouch to all of them despite their attempt to straighten up.

"Well," he began, his voice carrying strong to them, "you were kept beyond taps because I've got something to say to you." He began walking slowly between the two lines, Bonniface behind him, looking up and down each man's uniform. "This isn't exactly the place to talk or bunk up, but there's not much we can do about it. The fort commander does not take a liking to Negroes."

He paused to study Rutledge's face, noting the lines there, the gray showing in the long sideburns and scrubby mustache. "In fact," he went on, "nobody at Dodge has much good to say about Negro soldiers. They say you are good for nothing but to be cooks and horse groomers and don't know one end of a horse from another."

He stared into Willie Dunkerton's eyes.

"The colonel in charge here," Tom went on, "actually called you a bunch of misfits and a poor excuse for a troop. Well, you were given to me as Company L, and I believe you'll prove yourself well when the time comes."

Tom got to the end of the line, turned slowly, waited for Bonniface to get behind him, and started back between them again. "Now, you can get up at reveille and look like scarecrows in a cornfield, like you do now, or you can get those uniforms shaped up, boots scrubbed and sit saddle like soldiers are supposed to. In fact, I am so anxious for the fort commander, and every soldier of the Sixth Cavalry here, who'll be out to see you on parade in the morning, to eat their craw over what they called you, that I promise to leave every man here at Dodge who isn't shaped up when I get here one hour after reveille."

He paused to look at one soldier who was beginning to slouch, shoulders humping, stomach protruding. The captain punched him firmly in the paunch. The soldier took in a quick rush of air and snapped to attention, his eyes coming wide in the shock.

As he approached the stable door, Brainerd turned to face them, Bonniface beside him. "You men were assigned to make up this company for a patrol into North Texas. We are going to put some army presence into the Panhandle and keep Comanches from raiding Adobe Walls where the buffalo hunters are right now. And we are going to try to keep those hunters out of Indian treaty lands over in the Staked Plains. If we do all that, we maybe can stop a war brewing out there between Quanah Parker's Comanches and the whites all through the southern plains. If we don't we'll be lucky to come out with our hair.

"Now I know quite a few of you men have had run-ins with the Fourth," he continued. "Some of you have had time in prison, some yet to serve. I guarantee you, on orders from Leavenworth, that if you do well on this one, your sentences will be commuted, your former ranks restored. If you decide to loaf, give me back talk or refuse to obey an order, you can bet it will be a long ride. If we do our jobs and watch out for each other, we can do what we were sent to do." He paused, waiting. No one moved.

"Sergeant Bonniface, dismiss the troop and be ready for inspection in the morning!"

"Suh!"

•   •   •

Sometime during the night, Joanna woke up feeling restless, uneasy. She had comforted Marcella who kept repeating through her tears that Captain Brainerd had not come back to the party and "How could Colonel McDonnel treat him so shabby at dinner?"

Joanna finally got some warm milk and gave it to her. After a while Marcella, still hiccupping from her emotional outburst, fell asleep. But now Joanna got up quietly and walked to the water pitcher on the nightstand. She took a quick drink and then heard voices coming from downstairs. She recognized Jeremiah's voice, then Elizabeth's. The room flickered with the flames from the fireplace.

"...we should listen to Captain Brainerd," Elizabeth kept urging as Joanna stepped closer to the loft ladder to hear. "We have the children to think of, Jeremiah. We should wait..."

"I can't wait, Elizabeth," Jeremiah said, his voice sounding heavy and very unlike him. "I didn't tell you at the time...but I put up everything we owned to get the money to get to Texas. The land development people wouldn't risk money on it without security. So if I succeed in Texas, I get it all back and a handsome commission. If I fail, I lose it all. I—I'm sorry I didn't tell you, Elizabeth. I just feel God wants us in Texas...God help me if I'm testing Him."

There was a long pause. "Then we are under an even more terrible pressure to make this journey," Elizabeth said, her voice calm and without condemnation of Jeremiah. "We'll...we'll just have to pray harder that God spares us out there with those Indians." Another pause, and then she said, her voice trembling, "Oh, Jeremiah...I—I'm frightened."

"Ah, Elizabeth," Jeremiah soothed, and Joanna heard Elizabeth crying softly then. She had never seen nor heard her cry before. It unnerved her. "Colonel McDonnel said there was no sign of Indians in that area. Don't swallow everything that young upstart captain told you tonight. Anyway, God will go with us, and we are a strong family with heart and skill to face anything that comes..."

Joanna stood frozen there a long time. When Elizabeth Temple broke under any form of pressure, there was cause to ponder. She finally crawled back into bed but didn't sleep right away. If Captain Tom Brainerd was right about Indians being around Wolf

Creek—especially that savage Quanah Parker—it could be a terrifying journey for them all.

As for her, she had expected the worst when she came here. All the years of thinking about it had conditioned her for that. But she had not thought of Elizabeth and her sons...and Marcella. As for herself, life had stopped eight years ago. She had no fear of dying. She had that score to settle. That old part of her that kept the fires of hate and vengeance alive and hot turned her mind away from the dangers—most of it anyway. Joanna knew it was a selfish attitude. But it would not change until she had her moment out there in Kansas, Texas, or wherever.

But the sound of Elizabeth crying had given a different dimension to this. For the first time in years of waiting, she felt the shaft of doubt—about herself, about her intent, even about any of them surviving in Texas.

But Jeremiah Temple was "committed" for reasons beyond the adventure of prospecting land. He had to push out into whatever lay ahead. It did not set well with her, and the night became torn with contrary feelings and second guesses. Finally her mind pushed back the uncertainties and fears. She would not be denied now.

Joanna finally slid into a troubled, fitful kind of dozing. And the scene flashed into her mind again...that young Indian riding around and around the cabin on his painted horse...then that flash of glitter from around his throat as the sun caught it...she stared at him from her protective cover of bramble bushes, the cup half-filled with strawberries tumbled over by her right hand...her eyes wincing against that leering, golden coruscation of light, so that she seemed hypnotized by it...

"Oh!" She sat straight up in bed with a start. Marcella groaned and shifted with the movement. Joanna felt the sweat sticking to her gown. Her throat was thick, her mouth dry. Slowly she moved to the washstand, poured water in the porcelain dish, and scooped water into her face. The snap of it cleared her brain.

She stood there leaning on the stand, trembling, waiting for her heart to stop its wild beating. It was dark and quiet downstairs. She retreated to bed and lay down, her eyes staring up into the dark.

Joanna had not dreamed about that flash of gold in a long time...why now? Why was that segment emerging at this time? What significance did it have?

The young woman felt exhausted, almost weak now, as she turned over and grabbed onto her pillow, something to ease the turmoil inside. She wanted to cry but there were no tears.

Instead she tightened her arms around the pillow, cradled her head on it, and let the creeping shadow of uneasy sleep finally take possession.

6

The Temple household came alive just before reveille at 5:30 the next morning. Jeremiah roused them with a loud, sonorous voice: "Rise up, O men and women of God, and put thine armor on! Come on, all you pioneers up there! Andrew, Paul, Timothy, Marcella, Joanna! 'This is the day the Lord hath made. Let us rejoice and be glad in it!' "

Joanna had been up half an hour before Jeremiah's call, already dressed in tan corded trousers, field boots, and buckskin shirt with her hair jammed up under her trail hat. She put what belongings she carried into one canvas duffel bag. All of them recognized the serious sound of their father's voice, and they made haste to get out of bed and dressed. Marcella, her eyes still puffy from crying the night before, knew that she could not dillydally in front of the mirror today. She pulled on a green cotton dress and a pair of trail boots that came up just over her ankles. They were almost new, still showing the glow of brown gloss on them.

Elizabeth was busy at the woodstove getting ready to fry eggs and bacon while the porridge simmered in the black pot over the fire. Joanna began carrying things out to the wagons while Andrew, Paul, and Timothy went to the stable for the horses. The oldest boy told her he would bring Pointer back with him.

Reveille sounded as they were hitching up the teams. Jeremiah went to Colonel McDonnel's office as ordered, to sign the papers declaring that he was heading out to North Texas "on his own cognizance," which meant, as Joanna figured it, at his own risk.

Then, with the horses hitched and the wagons loaded, Jeremiah gathered them together around the breakfast table. His face showed the inner excitement, his dark brown eyes bright with anticipation of the biblical "promised land" before him. He hooked his thumbs in his red suspenders that stood out in bold relief to the beige cotton shirt and leather vest he wore. Elizabeth at his right showed no signs of the stress she had gone through late the night before. There were the usual fatigue lines under her eyes, but beyond that, her face showed that same quiet serenity and confidence that her faith had given her through the years.

Paul and Timothy kept chattering about wild game "to make any hunter's mouth water" and "They say Wolf Creek has fish as big as hound dogs." Andrew, as usual, remained quiet, smiling now and then at his two brothers. He caught Joanna's eye across the table and gave her a wink as if to say, "They don't have a clue as to what is really out there."

Joanna smiled back, acknowledging his thoughts. It was their way of communicating. Andrew sensed more of her inner turmoil than any of them, apart from Elizabeth. He had protected her in the past eight years from the teasing of both Paul and Timothy, and anyone else who might want to venture it. He was wide-shouldered, strong in the arms and chest, and nobody cared to tangle with him. Whenever Joanna needed someone to be with without having to talk, she would seek him out. They would go hunting and tracking, content to be silent to each other; but in that silence there was genuine friendship and understanding. It kept her from crumbling inside many times.

Next to her, Marcella kept hiccupping, as the tears still crowded up into her throat when she thought about her disappointments of the previous night.

Then Jeremiah, having surveyed his family around the table, put out his left hand and took Paul's in his, his right going to Elizabeth. They all linked hands then, Joanna reaching across the table to take Andrew's. This was the way it had always been in her eight years in the Temple household. But today there was something deeply meaningful, a greater awareness of each other, a locking of their hearts in this common cause.

"Lord God," Jeremiah began, his head bowed over his porridge bowl, his voice strong but trembling in the overpowering sense of the moment, "we thank Thee that Thou hast taken us this far in safety. We trust Thee to take us the rest of the way. We now take Thee as our shield and defender as we go on this journey. May it please Thee to deliver us from the hands of those who would seek to do us harm. As we go in peace, let those whom we confront be subdued by Thy peace within us. May we be strong in heart, quick to courage, slow to anger, but ready in the gallantry of Thy servants of old who did not shrink from the enemy. Accept our praise for all Thou art going to do for us. In the name of Thy Son, Jesus Christ. Amen."

They all responded with the "Amen" in low tones. Then as breakfast began, a festive mood came over them so that Marcella overcame her hiccupping long enough to ask, "Do you think we'll see much of Captain Brainerd today, Pa?"

Jeremiah gave off with a hearty belly laugh. "Marcella," he said, smiling at her, "in all the years of going out with officers, bankers, and politicans, now you pick one who seems to be the biggest loser of them all. Of course, of course, my dear, I don't see how you can avoid him if he's to escort us for today. Now, go on, eat up, all of you! Who knows when we will get a breakfast like this again? Good, hot and plenty of it! And done by the best cook either side of the Mississippi! Do I hear three cheers? Hip-hip!"

"Hooray!" they all shouted three times. Elizabeth smiled in embarrassment, her cheeks flushed with the compliment and the excitement Jeremiah exuded for all of them.

When they had finished, Jeremiah opened his Bible because of the special occasion. "Now I give you a promise to take along," he began, as he put on his round spectacles to peer into the well-worn book. "It says, 'If a man's ways please the Lord, He maketh even his enemies to be at peace with him.' That's Proverbs sixteen, verse seven. Do you all hear that? Do you believe it? Do I hear an 'aye' from all of you then?"

"Aye!" they chorused back. But Joanna did not join in. She knew it was wrong to do so and glanced quickly at Andrew. He gave her a look of understanding. It was not that she disbelieved; it just didn't agree with her own inner intents.

Jeremiah then bowed his head and said, "Lord, into Thy hands we commend ourselves to Thy will. May all our ways please Thee on this journey. Amen."

"Amen," they responded.

"All right," Jeremiah intoned, standing up, looking at them with a certain pride in his eyes, "now let's sing it before we go."

• • •

Captain Tom Brainerd sat on his horse in front of the long blue line of Company L, just twenty feet from the porch where Colonel McDonnel and his two aides stood waiting. Tom was conscious of his troop behind him, holding their horses steady, sitting straight to the saddle. He smiled inwardly. They were so brushed up and polished that President Grant would have had a hard time finding fault.

As he promised, he had inspected them earlier after reveille. He couldn't believe they were the same troopers who had come into Dodge with him the previous day. Walking his horse down the line, he noticed that some of them had puffy lips, others had a few swellings and cuts on their faces. Apparently they had chosen to resist shaping up. Either others in the company had "persuaded" them to get in line or Sergeant Bonniface had done it himself.

"All right," he told them, "you can ride parade this morning with your heads up. You're the best looking Negro troop south of the Colorado. And you'd beat some of the white horse soldiers, you can bet on it! You do me honor, gentlemen, and I thank you!"

Now he prepared to ask permission of Colonel McDonnel to leave the fort. Around the perimeter of the parade and on the walls troopers of the Sixth Cavalry stood and watched. To see a company take to the field out of Dodge was an event these days.

As for Colonel McDonnel, he looked beyond Tom to the long line of Negro horsemen ten yards back. There was nothing to read of pleasure or displeasure in his face, but his aides studied the line with some disbelief, not sure themselves that this was the same outfit that had come in the day before.

Then, as Tom opened his mouth to speak, he paused as the sound of joyful singing came across the quiet fort. He noted that it was coming from the Temple quarters close by. The sound seemed to put an even deeper hush over the fort, mixing the tranquil atmosphere with the red spill of sun washing the white stucco buildings. Tom sensed McDonnel shifting restlessly, his hands behind his back, rocking on his heels with impatience. But the captain held back, deciding to pay his respects to the people who were singing their faith together as a family. The song brought back memories to him and rekindled a longing to return again to a simple life filled with love.

"Let them sing it," he said under his breath to Sergeant Bonniface who was mounted next to him. "God knows, they're going to need it out there."

> Shall we gather at the river,
> Where bright angel feet have trod;
> With its crystal tide forever
> Flowing from the throne of God?
>
> Yes, we'll gather at the river,
> The beautiful, the beautiful river,
> Gather with the saints at the river
> That flows by the throne of God.

They sang all of that familiar hymn, known as the "guardian angel of the pioneers," and then it was quiet. Tom saw the Temple family come out the door and down the walk about a hundred feet to stand there watching.

"Troop!" Tom barked the order. "Attention!"

There was the sound of clanking equipment as the long blue line of men sat straighter in the saddle.

"Colonel, Company L, Fourth Cavalry, prepared to march with your permission, sir!"

McDonnel glanced beyond him to the Negro troopers. He cleared his throat, turned on a small, sardonic smile. "Well, captain," he said, his voice carrying loud enough to be heard by all of his own troopers near him and across the parade, "for a peacekeeping company, not bad." He continued with amusement, "I trust you will find them as smartly capable under fire. My compliments to you and your sergeant major. Good luck!"

For a few seconds their eyes met. Tom noticed the fire of animosity in the colonel's, although they seemed bloodshot and swollen from the lack of sleep. Tom figured McDonnel could see the hard look in his own eyes as well, for both of them nursed their own angry feelings.

"Sir," Tom said and saluted. McDonnel gave him a quick, sloppy wave of his hand to his hat. Tom turned his horse and walked him over to where Jeremiah stood waiting with his family.

"Morning," he said, touching his hat with his right hand.

"Morning, captain," Jeremiah responded readily.

"Mr. Temple, I will proceed with my troop ahead of you and wait across the river. I will then explain our route and check a few details. Are you prepared to move, sir?"

Jeremiah looked around at his family and said, "Ah...well, yes, captain," he said, stammering a bit in the excitement of the moment. "All right, everyone, get to the wagons...Marcella up with Andrew, Timothy with Paul. Joanna to your horse!"

"Mr. Temple," Tom interrupted politely, "you have cattle and horses outside the gate in a corral?"

"Yes, sir. Ten head of cattle and four fresh horses."

"I suggest you appoint one of your family to see to that stock and ride herd on it lest any straggle behind."

Jeremiah looked around. "Timothy, you get down and mount up. Joanna, you help him."

"Sure, Pa," Timothy responded eagerly and jumped down from his wagon seat to mount the black gelding tied to the back of the wagon.

Then Jeremiah led Elizabeth to the first wagon, helped her up and followed himself, taking up the reins of the team. The captain perused the line and smiled at Marcella, who began fanning herself quickly with that red fan of hers. Tom touched a finger to his hat when he looked at Joanna. Then he turned his black-pointed bay and trotted him back to the troop where Colonel McDonnel still waited on the porch as protocol demanded.

"Troop!" his voice bounced off the stucco buildings. "To the right by twos! Yo!"

The line swung to the right, the troops lining up side by side. Tom then galloped to the head of the line, pausing to eye the troopers of the Sixth around the perimeter of the parade.

"Troop!"

"Company L!" Bonniface echoed.

"Forward at a walk! Yo!"

The drums and fifes of the regimental band struck up "Gary Owen," the theme song of General George Armstrong Custer's famous Seventh Cavalry. The troopers on the walls and around the perimeter suddenly lifted their hats and cheered wildly as the Negro troop passed through the gate. Then they cheered again as the Temple family passed by in their wagons.

"Give 'em hell in Texas, Reverend!" somebody yelled from the wall. Jeremiah lifted his hat in response. Elizabeth glanced at him quickly, not appreciating his acknowledgment of that. Jeremiah looked sheepishly back at her as he pulled his hat down firmly on his head. She smiled at him and put her arm through his, realizing that the excitement had put him off guard for the moment.

Coming behind Timothy at the rear of the wagons, Joanna felt the blood running within her in rhythm to the band and the wild cheering of soldiers. It formed a kind of salute of all salutes, a tribute to soldiers and civilians daring to brave the uncertain territories of the south and west.

"You be careful, sonny!" Jake shouted to her as she passed through the gate. She gave him an uncertain smile and a nod of her head, pulled her hat lower over her eyes. Jake smiled knowingly at her.

Timothy had ridden ahead to get the stock out of the corral and was moving them along when she came out of the gate. She put Pointer to a gallop to catch up with him, looking back once to see the fort gate close slowly behind her. There was a strange sense of finality in that. She was glad to be on her way, but at the same time felt terribly vulnerable and lonely.

Joanna chased one of the steers who had begun to wander off, her mind turning to the land ahead and the moment she had prepared for so long.

They crossed the Arkansas River two miles out, at a place where the water was low, hardly up a foot on the wagon wheels. When they arrived at the other side, Captain Brainerd's troop was waiting, standing by their horses, some hunched down taking a breather before the long ride ahead.

Brainerd rode over to meet them, along with Bonniface and a civilian. "Mr. Temple, this is Amos Chapman, my scout," he said to Jeremiah. Joanna studied him, noting his black straight hair falling around his face and the perpetual half-squint of his eyes.

Jeremiah nodded to Chapman. Then Brainerd said, "Mr. Temple, I advise you from here to appoint one of your party to be with Chapman on scouting forays. You will need to learn something about tracking Indian signs if you are going to stay out of their way. You have someone, sir?"

"I can go, Pa," Andrew offered quickly.

Jeremiah frowned. "I need a good man with the horses pulling that wagon loaded with lumber, Andrew. You're the best with a team." He paused, looking at Joanna then. "Well...second best pair of eyes and nose we got is Joanna there."

Brainerd looked at her and nodded as if he agreed with the choice. Joanna sensed Chapman's eyes on her, but his face was expressionless. "Very good, sir," Brainerd answered. "Miss Joanna, when we move out, will you follow Chapman then? He's going to head out a few miles to check for signs."

Joanna nodded, ignoring Chapman's eyes altogether then.

"Captain Brainerd," Jeremiah put in then, "Joanna informed me this morning that you put an extra water barrel on my wagons. I see that. But I was hoping to keep off the weight. I only have a single team to pull..."

"Yes, sir, I understand," Brainerd replied. "But you're going to need the water. It's dry out here and will get dryer as you go south. No sign of rain. Best you have enough if you want to get to Wolf Creek."

Jeremiah saw no point in arguing.

"Sir," Brainerd continued, "we are going to stay a half-mile ahead of you and off to your left some to keep the dust out of your faces. I am ordered to Camp Supply for provisioning, so I may have to travel a bit faster. But you can be sure I will keep you in sight at all times. We will camp just before sundown. Any questions, sir?"

"None," Jeremiah replied.

"Thank you, captain," Elizabeth interjected, "for your kindness in escorting us, even for one day."

"My pleasure, Mrs. Temple," Brainerd replied. He swung his horse around and he and Bonniface galloped back to their troop. Joanna heard his voice commanding the troop to saddle, and then they were moving off in twos to their point a half-mile ahead and to the left.

"Joanna, you be careful out there!" Jeremiah called after her as she fell in behind Chapman's horse. Joanna pulled her hat down tighter on her head. She never did like Jeremiah's doting, and she didn't want Chapman to feel he had to be extra careful with her. But the Indian scout acted as if he had not heard. She followed him beyond a row of undulating dry grassy mounds. Brainerd's troop was far off to the left behind a cloud of dust then, and the Temple wagons were slipping behind the crest of the low mounds that she and Chapman crossed.

The sun was turning to a brassy color now as the heat rolled up from the baked, dusty prairie without a breeze. She kept her eyes on Chapman's back, wondering how anyone could track anything in this kind of terrain—hard, burned out, and not susceptible to tracks.

But Joanna was content to be moving in the direction she knew she had to go. Her right hand kept slipping down to get the feel of the Henry rifle in the scabbard. They were in Indian country. And every small undulation in the prairie could hide a band of renegades.

She only hoped Chapman knew what he was doing.

7

By the sun Joanna figured it was almost noon when Chapman halted his horse and dismounted. They had come at least three miles or so, as she figured, from the Temple wagons and Captain Brainerd's troop. Her throat burned with the dust, but the water from her canteen did little to soothe it. The sun remained a torturous, stabbing glare of heat, blinding her eyes so that the endless horizon danced in crazy double vision. There were few trees, here and there a drooping cottonwood standing a sad and lonely vigil on the forlorn prairie.

Chapman had said nothing to her in the hours they rode. She had kept off to his left a few yards so as not to be eating his dust. He acted as though she were not there at all. Most of the time his head had been straight ahead, but now and then it had turned as he swept the horizon in front of him. At other times his head dropped as his eyes searched the ground.

Now he studied the ground in front of him. Joanna took the opportunity to slide off Pointer to ease the ache in her hips. They were standing in longer, higher grass that looked as brown as the shorter grasses back at Dodge. Chapman crouched down to look at an indentation in the grass. She moved over to take a look.

"What is it?" she asked. After all, she was supposed to learn how to read signs, and he was apparently not paying attention to her.

He said nothing at first, then offered, "Indian ponies here..." as his finger pointed to horse tracks showing on a piece of dry ground where no grass grew. "No horseshoe marks...Indians ride ponies with no shoe..." She studied the tracks, wanting to remember. Then he swung his finger to the left, pointing at an indentation in the long grass. "Indian lie there..."

"Why not a buffalo?" she asked, looking at the shape of the indentation.

He drew his finger along the edges of the sunken shape. "Too short, narrow," he said. "Indian..." He stood up and looked back the way they had come across the long, endless prairie. "He lie here watching..."

"Watching for what?"

"Mebbe buffalo...mebbe for us..."

He led his horse on. Joanna followed. They walked about fifty yards when he stopped again. He crouched down before a mound of horse droppings.

He picked up a dry stick and poked into it, studied it, and stood up again. He shaded his eyes with his right hand as he looked ahead.

"What is it?" she demanded.

He kept looking, ignoring her. "Horse droppings still fresh," he said with some indifference. "Soft and still warm inside...if they be here yesterday, droppings be hard, cold..." He walked on. She followed along behind him, glancing at the mound of droppings, wanting to remember that for future reference.

Then he stopped again, crouching down. He put his hand over a lightly colored sandy spot that looked like ashes. "Ummm," he said.

"What does that mean?"

"Ashes still warm," he said. She crouched down near him and put her hands over the ashes. She felt just a bit of heat. "They camp here," he added, more to himself than to her. "Leave early this morning." He continued to look the ground over around the dead ashes. He picked up something and studied it. Then he stood up. "Kiowa," he said, handing it to her.

She stood up and took the feather. It was almost totally stripped of feathers, except for one short one that had a reddish-blue color in it. "They bad?" she asked. "Kiowa?"

He ignored the question. He glanced toward the horizon again, looked around the camp site once more, then moved over to a shaggy cottonwood and sat down under it.

"Too hot to move now," he said simply. She debated what to do, not particularly wanting to sit here under a tree that gave little shade with a scout who was as spooky as any Indian could possibly be.

"You drink now...slow...then you eat some jerky..."

She got her canteen from the saddle horn and sat under the tree about six feet away. He gave her a piece of dried meat from his leather pouch. It smelled of tobacco, but she bit into it. It was salty, a bit rancid and wild tasting. She took a quick swallow of water to wash it down.

"What is it?" she asked, chewing the leathery texture.

"Buffalo..."

"Of course, what else?" she quipped, glancing around at the white skeletons of dead buffalo that showed up as far as her eyes could see across the prairies. He paid no attention to her. His eyes remained on the horizon. "Those Kiowa mean trouble for us, Chapman?" she asked.

He continued to chew slowly as if he had not heard. "All Indians mean trouble. Kiowa hunting band here mebbe...come this way... mebbe see us, mebbe not. You watch for smoke you know how far they be...they watch your smoke, tell how far you be..."

"So nobody smokes," she tried the banter on him, but he did not rise to it, his eyes staying in that steady squinting appraisal of the rolling prairie ahead. "Chapman," she tested him, "you ever know Quanah Parker?"

His eyes did not waver from their steady scrutiny of the terrain ahead. Then, as he took another bite of the jerky, he turned his eyes toward her.

"I know," he said simply. "When Quanah was a boy, mebbe twelve...I was mebbe fifteen. He hunted buffalo with his father when he was twelve...when fifteen he rode with the warriors...the Quahadi..."

Joanna felt a certain jump within her. "How do you know that?"

"My father...trade with the Quahadi...no guns, no whiskey...just beads to keep peace while he panned the Canadian for gold...no gold there...he told me all about Quanah and Cynthia Parker, his mother..."

"I know she had two sons and a daughter," she added, taking her time, controlling the tremor of excitement, not wanting to crowd him. "But there was another son called Tanna, right?"

"Born two years before Quanah," Chapman said, his eyes going to the horizon again. "More white than Indian...too fair for Quahadis...boy disappears at two, three years..." He paused. She waited.

"You think he's dead?"

"The old chiefs, too old to fight, some blind with the years, smoke the pipe in their lodges and say they see Tanna riding on the clouds. The medicine men see signs of him returning. That's what they say in the lodges."

"How do you move among the Indians? Are you one?"

"My wife is a Cheyenne woman...I share her tepee. I am not a blood brother, but they understand I know their ways. I hear Tanna mentioned many times in the lodges..."

"Chapman," and she decided to get to the core of it, "I lost my own family eight years ago here on the Kansas prairies to Indians. I was told Comanche did it. I hid in the brush and watched them burn my family's soddy to the ground with them in it. I remember one of them...only a boy, not much older than I. He rode a painted horse...but I remember now and then a flashing, glimmering thing coming from around his neck when the sun hit it. I don't know why I remember that. Yet I don't know what it was..."

"Hmmm," Chapman said, taking another drink of water from his canteen, his eyes continuing to squint at the horizon. "Indians wear medicine around their necks, all Indians; sometimes a bear claw, sometimes iron, rattlesnake skin, even gold. I remember Cynthia Parker, as they tell it in the lodges...she made gold chains from nuggets her man Nocona brought back from the Red River. She made them into shape of an eagle and when Tanna was born, her first son, she put it around his neck. She put one around necks of Quanah and Pecos. She said, 'This is a sign that one day my sons will soar like eagles.' All three sons have that charm around their necks. That's what they say in the lodges..."

Joanna watched him, looking for that sign that said he did not believe the story. But there was no change in the stoic face. Now she felt a sense of something closing in, the form of a new revelation; and a strange beat began in her chest. "Then—then that boy riding around my parents' cabin could have been Quanah Parker?" she said it in a half-question, half-demand.

Chapman screwed the cap back onto his canteen and stood up. "We go now," he said and turned to his horse. He acted as if he had said too much. Joanna, still reeling inside about the possibility of who that one Indian was, walked toward Pointer slowly.

"Chapman," she prodded him some as he gave the horizon another 180-degree scan, "did the Comanche raid into Central Kansas back in 1866? A year after the war ended...did they?" Her voice was sharp, insistent, almost too demanding. He caught the sound of it and turned to look at her, his dark eyes the color of black swamp water.

"Comanche, Kiowa, Arapahoe, some Cheyenne, they all raid and kill then," he said. "The white man breaks the treaties, sells whiskey to the Indians to weaken them, shame them. Sure...Comanche, all of them, fight back. Quanah was a warrior at early age. But I don't say it was Quanah, missy. Better you let your family rest in peace. The Kiowa have a saying that a long memory nursed becomes a giant to swallow you..."

He turned away and headed back. Joanna watched him go. It had to be Quanah! That gold chain was enough proof. He was Comanche. He was about the right age then to fit the times. Part of the load she had carried for so long lifted some. At least now she was closer to the one she had been preparing for. No longer was it a total shadow she chased. The fiercest Comanche of them all! Well, it fit! He was all that as a youth when she first saw him on that awful day. Now he would be the whirlwind they all talked about.

"Chapman?" she called to him as he moved to push off.

He turned to look at her through those mysterious dark eyes. "What about Captain Brainerd? What happened to him? Why—why is he leading a company of Negro soldiers? How did he lose his wife at Fort Morrow?"

His eyes remained on her a long time, then he turned his head away. "We go now," he said and put his horse to a gallop, leaving her behind as if she were a bad Indian sign.

"All right," she said through her teeth as she vaulted up onto Pointer. "But I'll be there at Wolf Creek!" She yelled it at Chapman who was already over the mound in the prairie. "A day's ride from Adobe Walls! And Quanah Parker is going there! God, let the judgment begin for him! And let me deliver it!"

She thumped Pointer in the ribs, and the horse took off at a gallop toward the hill and Chapman.

● ● ●

They camped about eight miles out of Dodge in the middle of the open prairie. Captain Brainerd had sent Bonniface to tell Jeremiah of the halt. The sun was dropping over the western lip of the sky giving off a boiling red volcanic glare that turned the prairie to the color of blood.

By then Chapman and Joanna had returned from their scouting foray. Elizabeth and Jeremiah looked relieved. Chapman went to report immediately to Brainerd. When Jeremiah asked her what she had seen, she replied, "Not much...a Kiowa feather...that's about it..."

Bonniface reported to Jeremiah, tipped his hat to Elizabeth and said, "Compliments of Captain Brainerd, Mr. and Mrs. Temple. The captain wishes you to form your wagons in a U-shape, get your stock inside and tie them to the wagon wheels. Cook your supper now while it is still light; if you need a fire later, dig a hole a foot deep and build it. The less light we show the better out here."

"Will you and Captain Brainerd take dinner with us, sergeant?" Elizabeth asked from her place on the wagon seat beside Jeremiah.

"That's mighty kind, ma'am...but Captain Brainerd prefers eating what his troopers eat in the field. Later, he says, he will see you after dark."

"We'll keep the coffee hot then," Elizabeth replied.

"Thank you, ma'am." Bonniface whirled his horse and galloped off to the soldiers' encampment a few hundred yards across the flat line of the prairie.

Elizabeth warmed up the chicken stew that she had made earlier at the fort and made hot biscuits in a portable metal oven she placed on a corner of the fire.

"Pa, will we see the Indians soon?" Timothy asked during the meal.

"I really don't know, Tim," Jeremiah replied. "Probably not this close to the fort."

"Joanna, didn't you see even one Indian?" Paul asked, munching on a biscuit.

"Nope...that scout Chapman saw signs of Kiowa but that was all," she replied.

"Pa, are Kiowas like Comanche?" Timothy asked.

"I guess Indians are kind of like blood relatives," Jeremiah replied, not sure himself how to answer. "They—well, they kind of blend together."

"Was that colonel at Dodge right, do you think, that there aren't any Indians where we are going?" Timothy asked in a tone that said he hoped it wasn't true.

"We'll find out soon enough, won't we, boys?" Jeremiah responded lightly and opened his Bible as a sign the line of conversation was finished. He completed the reading and prayed, "We thank Thee, Lord, for a good first day and may we find the rest of the journey as peaceful."

He had hardly finished when Captain Brainerd, Sergeant Bonniface, and Amos Chapman appeared. They dismounted by the open end of the U-shaped wagon formation. Elizabeth quickly poured coffee into three Irish china cups and handed one to each of them.

"Mighty nice to drink from real cups, ma'am," Tom said. He reached into the cookie tin and took a large butter almond and bit into it. Chapman refused any, but Bonniface helped himself with a smile.

"Well, captain," Jeremiah began, "are we going to have any trouble with Indians?"

"Kiowa hunting party went through earlier today," Tom said. "They are probably a long way west now. But others may be following. Best to tighten down. Set your watch tonight, sir. Four hours on and off until sunup." A coyote bark broke the stillness of the night. Joanna noticed that the three men did not talk—waiting, listening.

"What was that?" Timothy asked.

Captain Brainerd looked at him and smiled. "A coyote, son. If you hear only one, you can close your eyes. If, after you count to ten, you hear another maybe twenty yards either side, then you have

Indian visitors out there looking you over. Remember that. No need to panic, but better to be alert. They'll want your stock mostly; and if they are hungry enough, they'll try for it.''

"Well, captain," Jeremiah went on, handing a map across the low fire to Tom, "this is the route I figure to take to Wolf Creek."

Tom took the map and studied it by the small light of the fire. He showed it to Chapman. "What do you think, Chapman?"

Chapman squinted at the red crayon line. Then he shrugged. "When you cross Cimarron River tomorrow, you push a little more east, stay away from heading into Adobe Walls area. You come to Wolf Creek here, this side of the North Canadian River."

"If the Temples went further south with us toward Camp Supply," Tom said, "then cut directly west, would it be any better?"

"The way the Injuns are gatherin' for the rain dance of Quanah down there in the Panhandle, won't make no difference. Anybody goin' in there now has got to face the problem of Injuns bein' around."

Tom handed the map back to Jeremiah who folded it and put it back into his map case. "So we part in the morning then, captain?" he said with finality.

"Looks that way, sir," and Tom glanced at Marcella across the fire. She had been watching him intently with her large, blue eyes lighting up with the reflection of the fire. He gave her a quick smile of acknowledgment. Joanna thought he seemed preoccupied, a bit troubled. "Mr. Temple, I'd prefer it if you went with us to Camp Supply another three days, maybe less..."

"Captain, that's kind of you," Jeremiah replied quickly, sipping at his coffee, "but I've got to get to Wolf Creek. I've got a house to build and soon. I don't want to get caught by those northerlies that whip in here in the early fall. We'll be all right."

A coyote barked in the dark again. There was another pause among them. "Well," Tom went on, "would you take ten of my men with you? I'll get into your area in about a week and we can join up there."

Jeremiah paused as Elizabeth stared at him, wondering why he hesitated. But Joanna knew that Jeremiah was a proud man. He was not about to shake loose the idea that Brainerd's Negro troopers were no compliment to him, just as Colonel McDonnel had insinuated back at Dodge.

"Captain," he said then, leaning his elbows on his crossed legs, staring into the fire, "I appreciate the offer. Colonel McDonnel assured me there would be no serious Indian activity where we are going. Hunting parties don't worry me. No point in taking any of your command for that."

"It's the stock, sir," Brainerd insisted. "Buffalo are scarce up here now and all along the way you are going. Indians get hungry—"

"Captain, I am sure we can deal with it," Jeremiah concluded.

"Jeremiah," Elizabeth interjected, "we've got the children to think of too—"

"Elizabeth," and his voice carried a tone of irritability. He glanced back at Brainerd. "Captain, will we see you before you go in the morning?"

Brainerd looked into the dying flames that lipped up over the hole in the ground. His eyes carried the orange tongues of light, and there was a frown between his eyes.

"No, sir...we'll be off before sunup." He stood then and handed his empty cup to Elizabeth. Bonniface and Chapman did the same. "Mrs. Temple, that was excellent coffee. I appreciate your kindness."

"Ma'am," Bonniface added, tipping his black peaked trail cap to her.

"Well, have a good trip to Camp Supply then, captain," Jeremiah said, standing up and extending his hand.

Brainerd took it. "And to you—all of you," he said. His eyes swung around to all of them, finally to Joanna off to his right. His eyes lingered on her a few more seconds. "I suggest, Mr. Temple, that you put the best pair of eyes in your family on the last watch around three in the morning, just before dawn. If Indians do come in, they'll try it then. You will need the warning..."

"I'll do that, captain."

"Keep calm, folks," Brainerd said as he put his brown trail hat back on his head, "but keep your weapons handy." Then all three of them were gone, swallowed up in the night, the sound of their horses fading off as they galloped back to their troop a couple of hundred yards away.

"Jeremiah," Elizabeth said then, her voice testy, "I think you and I should have a talk."

"Ah, Elizabeth," Jeremiah protested, extending his palms up in the entreaty.

"To the wagon, please?" she insisted.

Then she walked off briskly to their wagon. Jeremiah followed reluctantly. "I'll take first watch," Paul said.

"Timothy, you take first," Andrew said, countering Paul. "Paul, you are on at ten, I'll take the twelve to three. The last watch goes to the best eyes," and he looked at Joanna and winked. "We better turn in."

The brothers all moved to their wagons and bedrolls. Joanna remained at the fire with Marcella. They could hear Elizabeth's voice rising some in her demanding questions of Jeremiah. And then they heard Jeremiah respond, "Elizabeth, I started out on this journey to get to Wolf Creek on our own. I don't intend to depend on an untrained, misfit Negro army patrol to escort me anywhere—"

"They are still army, Jeremiah, for goodness sake!"

"That uniform don't change a thing, Elizabeth. They probably don't know which end of a gun to point where anyway. I am not going to take on ten limping soldiers that I have to protect in a fight. Never knew a Negro to be capable of soldiering anyway. I don't have any prejudice to the races, mind you—"

"No, not at all, Jeremiah. Thank you for informing me of that. I would never have known!"

Their voices dropped then to a low mumbling sound. Joanna felt uneasy. Jeremiah was being hopelessly stubborn. She felt Marcella shiver next to her. "You cold?" she asked.

"No," Marcella said, her blue eyes still bright in the dimming light of the fire, her voice subdued, almost a whisper. "I guess I'm scared, Joanna. Real scared."

"Sure it's not because of the departure of that captain of yours?" Joanna asked sarcastically.

"Oh. . that too, I guess. I'm scared I'll never see him again. Scared, too, that I don't mean that much to him anyway. But I'm most scared about going on, just us, alone. I felt something in those men here tonight. . .the coyote bark, them listening. . .that Indian scout, Chapman. I think he thinks we're crazy to try it ourselves. What do you think, Joanna?"

"About you and the captain, or what?"

"No," Marcella said impatiently, "about making it alone... us..."

"We're all good shots, Marcella."

"But I never have shot a gun, Joanna...never held one even..."

"Well, I never danced either. I'll shoot for you, Marcella, how's that?" On second thought, Joanna reached back to her saddle on the ground behind her and pulled out the .45 single-action revolver from a pocket. "Here," and she shoved the gun at Marcella, butt first. Marcella recoiled from it as if it were a snake. "Take it...it won't bite."

"I—I wouldn't know what to do with it, Joanna," Marcella protested.

Joanna reached over and took Marcella's soft, finely shaped right hand and stuck the gun butt into it. It hung awkwardly there, Marcella's hand looking far too small and delicate against the menacing gleam of the weapon in the dying light of the fire.

"It's so hard...well, so heavy..."

"Put your thumb on the hammer...put both thumbs on the hammer," Joanna coaxed. "Forefinger around the trigger...there... now pull back on the hammer..."

Marcella's small thumbs tensed and pulled the hammer back slowly. The cylinder turned with it. "It's—so heavy..."

"You got it now," Joanna encouraged. "Aim at the coffee-pot over there beyond the fire...lift the gun, for Pete's sake! Aim! Keep both hands on the gun! Now...pull the trigger...go on!" Marcella closed her eyes as the hammer slammed down with a loud click. "So there you are!" Joanna chirped. "Easier than learning how to dance! If there had been a bullet in the chamber, you would have blown that coffee pot clear over to the wagon there. So now every day you practice with that gun when you're riding that wagon. I'll be around to make sure you are..."

"Joanna, I can't—"

"Yes, you can! It could save your life on the trail. I promise you, you learn to shoot that thing and you can teach me to dance at Wolf Creek. How's that?"

Marcella looked at her, confused, and then she giggled, putting her hand over her mouth as if she didn't want to be heard. It was one of those rare times that she and Joanna laughed together about anything; and Joanna could see Marcella relax because of it, the fear dissolving in her eyes.

When Jeremiah called from the wagon to get to bed, they both obediently made their way to their place under the second wagon. They lay under their blankets looking out at the stars.

"You agree with me about Captain Brainerd?" Marcella asked. "What?"

"That he's handsome...when he gives that small smile...his eyes...well?"

Joanna did not respond but said, "I wonder why he's leading a Negro troop."

"Oh, Joanna," Marcella said with a groan. She rolled over and put her back to Joanna, a sign of disgust. A coyote barked again. Joanna waited, counting to ten, waiting for the sound of another answering. There was none. Her nerves were coming up to the edge in herself. She felt around for her Henry rifle, found it, pulled it closer to her, making sure the safety was on. The cattle and the horses were munching hay around her. It seemed peaceful, almost tranquil. But the quarter-moon did not give enough light. The night seemed dark and foreboding.

She shivered. It would be good to see the sun again.

* * *

Company L had bedded down for the night, the guards were doubled up at the horse picket and all fires had been doused. Only Captain Brainerd kept a small one going as he studied his maps.

"Rutledge?" Willie Dunkerton said, his voice like a child's in the middle of the night. Rutledge turned his head where it lay on his saddle.

"Wha's on yer mind, Willie?"

"Ya see dat cap'n didn' eat wid dem white folks...dem Temples...how's come?"

"He be a tall man, Willie," Rutledge said.

"But I smell dat chicken way ovah heah," Willie insisted. "But he eats hardtack an' bacon like the res' a' us jailbirds." A coyote ripped a ragged tear into the tranquil night with its bark. There was a pause. Then Willie said, "Wha dey say 'bout Injuns an' coyotes? Jackson? Ya hair? Wha' dey say?"

Corporal Rufus Jackson was lying on the other side of Willie. He was the son of slaves in Georgia, but possessed a quickness of mind despite his lack of education.

"Wait for two barks ten seconds or so apart, either side."

"Yeah...das it!" Willie said in awe and kept silent, counting. Satisfied he went on, "Rutledge, how ya figger dem white folks goin' off by demselves tomorrow? No escort, nothin'. Dat blonde one ...dem Injuns see dat hair, dey gonna fight ovah her. She gonna wind up in some chief's lodge..."

"Be three women, Willie," Rutledge said in a lazy tone, sleep coming slowly now.

"I ain' seen but two," Willie countered. "The young blonde one with a smile dat travels miles...and dat be her Mammy...the older one..."

"And one more," Rutledge added softly.

"Which? Dere ain' no other woman—"

"Da one what dresses like a man...ya seen her in da fort dis mawnin'...buckskin shirt...trail hat, brown..."

"Dat ain' no woman, Rutledge!" Willie protested in a hoarse whisper.

Rutledge chuckled. "Big brown eyes dat miss nuthin'...pieces of dark hair come out from her hat...she got long, black hair, I guesses. She don' walk like no man, Willie...she tries...awful hard...but she shows da easy roll of her hips...her shoulders back, nose up. Fine cut of a woman I say...once'n ya get all dem buckskins off...da captain sees her too...under dat buckskin. I judges da captain takes a fancy to her..."

"Golly, Rutledge! Dat be three women goin' on dair own!" Willie exclaimed, his eyes big in the dark. "Two men among dem...da big man and dat son a' his, da older one...dat ain' gonna go, Rutledge! Dey is Injun bait, ya knows it!"

Rutledge yawned. "Wad ya figger to do, Willie? We is headin' fer Camp Supply...den to da Panhandle—"

"Yeah...to do what? We be a bumblebee tryin' to stop two elephants from fightin'—"

"That's very good, Willie," Jackson commented drowsily.

"Well...it be da truth!" Willie snapped. "I mean...I mean da cap'n made us look good dis mawnin' in fron' of dat mean colonel at Dodge—I ain' fergettin'—but now he be leadin' us to nowhere. How ya gonna keep da peace les' ya shoot one er da other a dem...either Quanah Comanche or dem buffalo hunters...and dem poor white folks over dere is in da middle. Not right, Rutledge... dem people should have army wid dem..."

"Willie," Rutledge commented patiently, "ya never had no use fer white folks before...why now?"

"I dunno," and Willie lay back down with a disgruntled sigh. "I jes' hate seein' people—white er black—walkin' into sure death when it be plain stupid!"

Rutledge began to hum the hymn tune he had heard the Temples singing earlier that morning at the fort. He thought back to his slave days in Georgia and his mother singing it softly to him just before bed. The same tune. He kept humming it and then he began to sing:

> On the bosom of the river,
> Where the Savior-king we own,
> We shall meet, and sorrow never,
> 'Neath the glory of the throne.
>
> Yes, we'll gather at the river,
> The beautiful, the beautiful river,
> Gather with the saints at the river
> That flows by the throne of God.

"Amen," Jackson said in the dark.

Willie's only response was a loud, uneven snore. Rutledge smiled and let sleep come. But his final thoughts were the same as Willie's, just how that small family was going to make it on their own. He glanced over toward the captain's station. The man was still sitting by the low fire, studying that map, chatting with Amos Chapman and Bonniface. Rutledge figured that Captain Brainerd was not feeling very good about the Temples going off by themselves either.

But the man who ought to be sweating, Rutledge mused, was that colonel back at Dodge. If anything happened to the Temples, that colonel was going to have a lot of answering to do. But right now Rutledge wondered what Captain Brainerd was thinking. He was all the army North Texas had right now...and all the protection the Temples could ever hope for. But the miles were going to separate them starting in the morning.

Rutledge felt uneasy, but at the same time helpless. He listened to the coyote bark, waited subconsciously for any answer. There was none. He let sleep come.

8

The next couple of days were hotter than Joanna could remember. Jeremiah set the pace in his lead wagon, keeping the horses walking briskly but slowing them now and then so that they would not wear out. Joanna spent her mornings helping Timothy keep the stock together as they followed the wagons. The dust was thick, and Joanna had to wear a yellow kerchief around her nose and mouth most of the time. She insisted on Timothy doing the same.

The routine on the trail was set by Jeremiah. At noon they stopped for a drink of water and beef sandwiches. When Joanna finished, she would leave on a scouting foray ahead. She promised Jeremiah to stay within range of the wagons; and she did—most of the time. But when she got on to a jackrabbit, she found herself a couple of miles beyond them. Still, when she brought back the scrawny thing for the food cupboard, Jeremiah said nothing.

She saw some Indian signs the first day. A few mounds of horse droppings that proved by Chapman's stick test to be cold and hard. She noticed some ashes from old campfires, but the sign of fresh unshod Indian ponies was what stood out the most. She reported it to Jeremiah, who said, "Well, girl, we just got to keep our eyes open from now on."

They camped just before sundown, forming the wagons into the familiar U-shape. The horses had suffered from the heat and the heavy pull. Their mouths were thick with foam, their backs lathered white from the sweat. The brothers rubbed them down with damp cloths, gave them a drink, and let them forage in the long buffalo grass until dark. The small cooking fire was started as Elizabeth and Marcella prepared the hot meal. Joanna searched for buffalo chips for fuel, there being only a few scrubs of cottonwood trees that provided little or no wood.

They ate mostly in silence. Their own bodies had been drained of fluids that the sun had hungrily sucked out of them during the day. Jeremiah kept studying the map, measuring the distance to the Cimarron River over and over again, then from there to Wolf Creek. He kept mumbling that they were "right on schedule." But it couldn't last. All of them knew that the horses were pulling hard and could not keep up the pace for long. When the sun went down and dusk enveloped them, shutting them inside the open-ended wagon formation, they built a smaller fire in a hole in the ground. Jeremiah read from the Bible and prayed. Then he ordered Timothy to bring the stock in and hitch them to the wagon wheels. Paul went on guard duty. The long night had begun. A night of listening to coyotes, their nerves on edge, trying to find sleep in the uncertain night.

The next day they came to the Cimarron River, just after noon. Jeremiah figured they could replenish their water barrels there. But the river was almost dry. Here and there a few stagnant pools allowed the stock to get some kind of drink. But the river bed, about fifty to 100 yards at this crossing, was mostly muddy silt. The wagons bogged down in the mud up to the axles. The horses strained to pull the weight, but it was too deep. Finally Jeremiah ordered them all to put their shoulders to the wheels.

"Joanna, you stay there with Timothy and watch the stock," he ordered. "I don't want any Indians coming up behind us when we're working through this mud."

They pushed, strained, pulled to get one wagon over at a time. The heat was killing on all of them, including the horses. After two hours of exhausting work, they got the last wagon over. They were all covered with mud as they sank down by the wagons, totally exhausted. Joanna and Timothy got the stock across with no problems. It was then about three in the afternoon.

"We'll rest here a half hour and be on our way," Jeremiah told them.

"Can't we camp now?" Marcella asked. "I have to get this mud off. It's in my hair, everywhere..."

Jeremiah grunted a laugh. "Marcella, that's the best I've seen you look since you made mud pies back in Northfield!"

"Oh, Pa," Marcella groaned. "All we got is mud, heat, dust, bugs and now—now no water. No water to drink, no water to clean up with. Why don't we go on back home, Pa?"

"Home?" Jeremiah responded. "Girl, we're only a few days from home! Wolf Creek! Look at you now! You all got Texas mud on you! That's what they call pay dirt in this country!" He laughed again, but none of them lifted their heads to join him in his chortling sounds of optimism. They were too numb with fatigue to care. It was Elizabeth who told him they would camp right there for the night. Jeremiah protested, but Elizabeth was not to be cowed. Joanna wished they would push on. She felt uneasy for some reason. Being on the move made her feel less vulnerable. But looking at them— the mud, their faces strained with exhaustion—she knew Elizabeth was right.

On the afternoon of the third day and roughly three days from Wolf Creek, as Jeremiah had told them that morning, she rode out on a scouting foray. The prairie was changing in contour now as more hills broke up the flat line of the horizon. The ground seemed harder and there were more rocks in the brown buffalo grass. She noticed horse droppings as she walked Pointer along. She checked them by Chapman's test. They were fresh. She noticed marks of unshod Indian ponies and a few mounds of white ashes that still held some heat as she stretched her palms over them.

Warily she mounted Pointer again and moved forward, her eyes on a small upgrade of a hill ahead of her. There were some cottonwoods on top, bunches here and there. She removed her Henry from the scabbard, checked the breech, and rested the stock on her thigh as she kept moving. As she came closer to the small hump she felt warning vibrations shooting through her like the rattling of rain on a sheet-iron roof. Her eyes studied the cottonwoods above her. There was no sign of movement. She lifted herself up in the stirrups and looked back. The Temple wagons were about a half-mile or more behind her.

The warnings within her said to wait. Instead, as if drawn by an overpowering curiosity, she pushed on up the hill, came to the top and stopped. Her eyes swept the scene below. From her position, about twenty yards up the hill, she was startled by the sight of two wrecked, burned wagons. Flies buzzed around the scene in a black cloud, the sound of them a kind of drone in the dead hot air hanging over the land. Whatever had happened here had not been long ago.

Joanna moved Pointer slowly down the hill, her eyes sweeping around in Chapman's 180-degree check of the horizon. Then she saw the rustic wooden cross off to her left. Dismounting slowly, she leveled her rifle, glancing back up the hill, then around the scene of destruction. She knelt and felt the mound of earth that covered the grave. It was still moist. The name on the crosspiece of the wooden maker—ANDERSONS, June 17, 1874.

What was today? June 18. The grave was one day old. Someone of the Anderson party had escaped the massacre, dug the grave, and pushed on. The taste of danger was on her lips, the sweat hot as it rolled down her back. Pushing against the jump of her heart, she walked slowly through the debris—furniture, tools, a plow, clothing. She caught sight of an Indian feather near an old trunk and picked it up. It was not Kiowa. This one had many colors in it—red, yellow, blue, white. The painted feathers ran completely down the shaft of the quill, with only a half inch clear at the end. Comanche? She wasn't sure.

The flies swarmed around her. There was a smell now that made her stomach jerk in spasms, her throat constrict against the bile. It was the smell of death she remembered from a long time ago still fresh in her mind. She turned then, vaulted up on Pointer, and whirled him around as if the memory had suddenly stabbed her to reality. She pushed the horse to a gallop, catching sight of the Temple wagons approaching the hill below.

Jeremiah saw her coming pell-mell down the hill and pulled up his team. "What is it, girl?" he yelled at her.

"Over the hill!" she exclaimed, feeling the nausea rolling over her in waves. "Two wagons...burned out...only a grave...fresh!"

"Any sign of Indians?"

"Indians did it all right...but I don't think they are around here right now!"

"All right, let's take a look." He stood up and yelled back at Andrew. "We stop at the top of the hill, Andrew! Keep your eyes peeled! Tell Paul and Timothy!"

When they came to the top of the hill, Jeremiah pulled his team to a halt. Andrew moved his wagon alongside, followed by Paul. "Timothy!" Jeremiah called back to him. "You keep the stock down there! And you fire a shot if you see Indians, you hear?"

"Okay, Pa!" Timothy shouted back.

"God have mercy," Elizabeth said as she looked down on the charred wagons.

"Better have a look," Jeremiah said and helped her down from the wagon. "Give me my rifle there on the seat. Andrew and Paul, you both better come on down too. Marcella, you stay on the wagon seat and make sure Timothy's all right back there."

They walked down the hill slowly, brushing at the flies that rose in a cloud around them. They paused to look at the grave and the marker. "Can't be more than a couple or maybe three in that grave," Jeremiah commented solemnly. "Can't figure why such a small party was allowed to come out here alone."

"We're only a couple more, Pa," Andrew said solemnly.

Jeremiah glanced at him, then nodded. "You're right..." He walked on to explore the wagons, then the debris strewn around them. He came back where they stood by the grave and said, his voice heavy, "I expect we better commit these poor folks to the Lord now..." He paused, took off his broad-brimmed trail hat and bowed his head. Andrew and Paul did likewise. "O death, where is thy sting?" he intoned. "O grave, where is thy victory?..."

As Joanna listened, her heart turned cold. Death *had* its victory here! Couldn't he see that? Her eyes kept scanning the hill behind her and then the line of trees a hundred yards off to the left. Her nerves pulsed with the torment of anger within her. Whatever Captain Brainerd had in mind about peace with savagery like this...well, he should be here now!

"Lord, we commit Thine own here unto Thyself," Jeremiah went on in prayer, his voice trembling. "We don't know them, but, Lord, Thou dost know them like us. We don't know why they should die this way, so far from home, but Thou dost know. Forgive those who so brutally took these lives for they surely do not know what they do."

They know! Joanna almost screamed it at him.

"Now to these departed, we give them to Thee and Thy peace...in the name of the Father, Son and Holy Spirit...Amen."

"Amen," Elizabeth, Andrew, and Paul responded. Joanna held her tongue that felt swollen from thirst and the thickness of nausea.

"Whoever made that sign was one of the family or someone who happened through here ahead of us," Jeremiah added, pulling his hat back onto his head. "He can't be far ahead, if he's going on. Let's keep our eyes open."

With that, Joanna turned on her heel and strode back up the hill to the wagons. Marcella, still sitting on the wagon seat, said, "Joanna?" her voice carrying childlike fear.

"They're dead and buried," Joanna replied impatiently.

"But—why? Who?"

"Who? This is Indian country, don't you know that yet?" Joanna saw Marcella's face turn whiter as if she had only now come to realize the fact. Her sunburned lips began to come to a firm line as she held back the tears. Joanna climbed up on the seat beside her and put her arm around her, even though she did not have the right attitude for comforting anyone right then.

Timothy came up to them from behind the wagon and asked, "Can I go down and see now?"

"No," Joanna replied emphatically. "They're buried now... nothing to see. You wanted Indians, Timothy, take a good look at those wagons down there," she added as Marcella began to shake with the sobs that boiled over despite her attempt to hold them back. "That's what Indians do to you, do you understand? They're not the same ones you saw in those stupid horse shows in the circuses back in Northfield! Do you hear me?"

"Yes, ma'am," Timothy replied, his face turning white under his trail hat, the spray of freckles, like cinnamon, standing out across his nose and cheeks in bold relief.

"Better get back to the stock, Tim," Joanna added, modifying her snapping tone. "Keep a sharp eye. They could be still hanging around here. This happened only yesterday or so.''

Timothy turned obediently and went back down the hill, leveling his rifle in readiness. In a few minutes, the others came back up the hill. ''Suppose those people were heading to the same place we are, Pa?'' Paul said as they paused at the wagons.

Jeremiah hesitated, glancing back at the grave again. ''Don't know, son . . . but best we now get moving out of here and on our way. Won't be long to camp.''

Joanna mounted Pointer and rode back down to join Timothy tending the stock. Jeremiah started the wagons out again, skirting the scene of death and cutting back over the hill, keeping a good distance from the tree line. They kept moving for an hour or more. When the sun dropped to the familiar molten ball of red on the horizon, he called a halt for camp. It was an open place on the prairie near a shallow gully that had a few cottonwoods and some mesquite off to the right. Not enough to hide many Indians.

They prepared camp and saw to their duties without saying much to each other. The shock still hung on them, together with the weight of the possibilities that awaited them here. They ate little. Jeremiah read from the Bible later by the light of the small fire and then asked that they double the guard, one of them on each side of the wagon U.

None of them slept much. Joanna kept walking around the wagons, rifle at the ready. Finally, not wanting to call attention to her nervousness, she crawled under one of the wagons and fell into a restless doze. She was awakened by Andrew for the final watch before dawn. The half-moon was going to three-quarters now, hanging low in the sky and flooding the prairie and the low distant hills with stark illumination. Andrew took a station on the left side of the wagon camp, she the right. She noticed a light in Jeremiah's wagon. Not much sleep there either. She heard Elizabeth talking in low tones. Again it sounded as if she was pleading with Jeremiah to go back.

But Joanna knew that this far out, going back was just as dangerous as going ahead. Whoever had attacked the Andersons had to be watching the Temples as well.

All she could hope for them all was that they would make it to Wolf Creek, although there seemed no good reason to look to that place as any kind of haven. Still, that would put them within a day's ride of Adobe Walls where there would be help. But there was little comfort in that really—a day's ride was a long way.

She finally got up from her place and walked around the wagons until she found Andrew lying on his stomach facing out toward the moon-washed shallow gully in front of him. She dropped down prone beside him.

"How close do you figure we are to Wolf Creek, Andrew?" she asked, her eyes watching the gully.

He took a deep breath as if he had been thinking of that for some time. "Well, we're across the Cimarron," he replied meditatively, his voice low. "I expect we'll cross the North Canadian River tomorrow the way Pa is pushing the horses. Then we're a day and a half maybe from Wolf Creek if everything holds as is."

She paused, not wanting to broach the subject he must be thinking about. "You think we'll get hit by the same bunch that raided the Andersons?"

Andrew did not reply immediately. Then, "Well, one thing is sure: We could use good old Captain Tom Brainerd about now...even those ten troopers he offered would truly be a comfort. I wonder where Brainerd is now?"

Joanna listened to a coyote bark and waited. No reply. "I suppose at Camp Supply," she replied indifferently. "A good two days' ride from us, at least by the map."

Andrew grunted. "I've a feeling he knows what we are into here. If there's any hope—and even then it's a slim one his being so far off—it has to be in what he can do to get here...and in a hurry."

"I don't put that much stock in Indian lovers," she replied in a low, carping tone. "Certainly not after what we saw today...what I saw a long time ago..."

She felt his gaze on her, but she kept her eyes ahead. The sun was beginning to smear the horizon with dabs of pink. "Army blue would look pretty good about now anyway, Indian lover or not," he said, shifting his body around to get more comfortable. "Anyway, I think you are a bit hard on Brainerd. He's trying to do what he thinks is right..."

Before she could respond, she heard the coyote again. They waited. Then the second bark sounded to the left. She felt him stiffen beside her. Her own heart took a skip and she shoved her Henry out in front of her, releasing the safety.

"Hear that?" she asked, her eyes peering intently through the moonlight that was gradually giving way to the growing pink glow on the horizon.

"Ah-huh," Andrew replied, studying the gully more closely.

The coyote sounded again from the center of the gully where there was tall buffalo grass at the bottom. It was answered by another to the right, up out of the gully toward a small clump of mesquite.

"Three," Andrew said, the tone of his voice tighter. She nodded to confirm it, her mouth going dry. They continued to wait, wanting to be sure. Then the coyote bark sounded dead center in the gully about thirty yards in front of them; it was answered from the left on the rim of the gully from the direction of a low scrub of cottonwoods, then picked up again on the right from the mesquite trees.

"Where's Pa?" Andrew asked, his low voice steady but a bit strained now. "How can he sleep through that?"

She turned to go back for Jeremiah, but he was already moving toward them in a low crouch, his red suspenders loosely flopping down around his brown cord trousers. He had no shirt on. The light played on his white undershirt top showing some of the sweat lines around the neck. His bushy hair stood up in clumps like bramble, and his dark brown eyes seemed large in the light of the rising sun. He held his Henry rifle loosely, as if it were extra baggage.

"Stay steady now," he said to them softly, going down on one knee to study the terrain in front of them. Then Paul and Timothy moved up from behind, rifles ready, their eyes big with fear and wonder. "Get back to the wagon there," Jeremiah said to them in a low, commanding voice. "Make sure the stock don't pull loose. Get your mother and Marcella under that wagon too. Paul, you and Tim get those boxes of tools in Paul's wagon and stack them under the wagon...we may need that cover if we have to fall back."

"Sure, Pa," Paul said and the two of them obediently crawled back to the wagon.

"Nobody shoots until I say so...understand?" Jeremiah called softly after them. Paul looked back and nodded.

Now the sun poked its red hat brim over the eastern horizon, flooding the gully and the grassy terrain on either side. They waited.

Joanna felt the pound in her throat thinking that the Andersons had probably gone through this same scenario before death hit them with a fury.

"There," Andrew said suddenly, and the Indian on horseback appeared in front of them out of the gully so quickly that it was as though he were a ghost. Another appeared to the left from the cottonwoods, the third moved in from the clump of mesquite to the right. The three of them converged and stood silently side by side watching the wagons.

"Steady," Jeremiah said again to Andrew and Joanna, his voice a bit hoarse with the tension.

The three Indians moved their horses forward slowly and stopped about thirty feet away. All three had streaks of war paint slashing their faces—yellow, black, and red. The Indian on the center pony lifted his hand and said something. Jeremiah stood and lifted his hand back. Joanna noticed that all three carried repeating rifles cradled in their arms. The Indian spoke again, pointing behind him, using sign language.

"I don't know what he's trying to say," Jeremiah said, frustrated.

The Indian lifted his hand to his mouth several times then and spoke in his language again. "I think they're hungry, Pa," Andrew said.

Jeremiah waited, not sure if Andrew was right. The Indian continued to talk in his own tongue, moving his hand repeatedly up to his mouth. Joanna wondered where the rest of the Indian band was; she was sure these three would not approach them alone without a force of their own prepared to back them up. And if Jeremiah did not act soon in response to what the Indian kept trying to convey, the rest of them would be on them in a hurry.

"Paul?" Jeremiah called out, his eyes staying steady on the three Indians.

"Yes, Pa?" Paul answered from behind the barricaded wagon directly behind Jeremiah.

"Cut out one of the steers and bring him out here."

"Sure, Pa..."

The three Indians watched silently now. Then, as the time dragged, they began to talk to each other, their voices becoming more agitated. The one in the center seemed to be disagreeing with the other two. Joanna's hands were feeling more sweaty as she gripped her rifle tighter, her finger sliding to the trigger.

Jeremiah turned as Paul came up with the black steer named Walt. He was a beautiful animal, heavy in the flanks and chest. "You can't take Walt!" Timothy yelled from behind the wagon, running out to pull at Paul who was leading the animal by a rope around its neck.

"Timothy!" Jeremiah's voice was sharp, almost explosive in the stillness.

"Pa?" Timothy appealed, and there were tears in his eyes now. "I raised Walt from a calf! You can't give him to those Indians!"

The Indian who had done all the talking lifted his voice, one hand raised, pointing to the steer. "Too late, Pa," Andrew said. "He wants Walt all right..."

"No!" and Timothy lifted his rifle to take quick aim at the Indian. The three Indians pulled their horses back quickly, bringing their rifles to the ready.

"Timothy Temple, you put that gun down right now!" Jeremiah commanded. "You want to kill us all here?" Timothy, tears streaming down his cheeks, slowly lowered his rifle and ran back to the wagon, disappearing inside the camp site.

With a frown digging between his eyes, Jeremiah took the rope that Paul extended to him and led Walt out to the Indians. Joanna felt Andrew shift beside her, pulling his rifle up a notch to get ready. Jeremiah stopped a few feet in front of the Indians and dropped the rope.

"You can have him," he said, nodding at Walt. "If that's what you want..."

The Indians looked at him but remained silent. Then the Indian in the center lifted his hand again, palm up. He turned his head and shouted across the gully in a string of words in his own language. From behind the line of Mexican juniper and cottonwoods across the gully, about 200 yards off, the rest of the Indian band moved forward. Joanna watched them carefully. There were about twenty mounted Indians carrying repeating rifles. Some of the ponies, however, were pulling travois—two long tree limbs, one end of each lashed to the horses' backs, the other dragging on the ground. Blankets were spread between the poles and fastened down. On the blankets were Indians, old or sick. The women followed behind with the children, carrying what little of their belongings they had.

They came across the shallow gully and moved up over the rim, passing the three Indians in front of Jeremiah. The Indian in the center spoke to Jeremiah again, and there was a sign of pleasure on his face as he received Walt.

"Hee-ha!" he shouted and the three of them turned and moved off to follow the others, pulling Walt along with them.

Jeremiah continued to stand there a long time until the entire band had disappeared beyond a tree line over a low hill to the west. Then he turned and walked back toward Joanna and Andrew. Elizabeth moved out from behind the wagon barricade, along with Marcella.

"You were right, Andrew," Jeremiah said, slapping him on the shoulder. "Never saw a more starving looking bunch of Indians. But they were surely ready to take us on if we didn't produce a head of beef."

"Surprises me they didn't try to take it all," Andrew commented.

"They know we've got more," Joanna reminded Jeremiah. "They've got Walt, but that won't feed them very long. With buffalo so scarce around here, they'll be back for more."

"Ah, that's no fighting band as I see it," Jeremiah countered. "They're sick, carrying their old people and children with them...hardly the bunch that hit the Andersons..."

"Their warriors are well-armed, Mister," Joanna insisted, standing up now, Andrew following her.

"Well," Jeremiah replied, his voice lifting in that tone of optimism, "I quoted Proverbs to you all when we left the fort back there, remember? About when a man's ways please the Lord He makes even his enemies to be at peace? Well, you've seen the first proof of that promise. And we have no reason not to expect more of the same. Now I think we best get to breakfast, thank God and be on our way."

"You better have a talk with Timothy," Elizabeth cautioned him. "He's pretty upset over Walt..."

"Of course," Jeremiah replied. He turned to walk back to the wagons, then paused as he glanced at Paul. His head was down as he made circles with his foot in a sandy spot in the hard brown grassy ground. "Paul, you did right, son," Jeremiah said and went over to put his arm around the boy's shoulders. "If you had offered one of the scrawny steers, those Indians might have taken it...but I think maybe they would have demanded more..."

"I—I loved Walt too, Pa," Paul appealed. "I know how Tim loved him. I did too...but...well, I just didn't think right, I guess..."

"You and Timothy may have saved us a fight here, son," Jeremiah assured him. "Sometimes we have to sacrifice the best we have to keep the peace. Come on, let's go talk to Tim." Reluctantly Paul turned with Jeremiah and walked beside him toward the wagons. "God will make up for our losses," Jeremiah continued. "Remember that, Paul..."

"I hope Tim goes along with that," Paul responded in a despondent tone.

"He will," Jeremiah said with confidence. "Elizabeth, Marcella, come on along...we need to get to breakfast."

Elizabeth glanced at Joanna, then at Andrew, as if she wanted to add something. But, deciding against it, she walked on, Marcella following her.

Joanna remained with Andrew, looking in the direction the Indians had gone. "You see what that Indian who did all the talking had around his neck?" she asked him.

"You mean the gold watch and chain?" he replied. "I saw it..."

"You think it was taken off the Andersons?"

Andrew shrugged. "Could be..."

"And the Indian on the left?" Joanna commented.

Andrew pulled his tan hat lower against the sun that stabbed a mean shaft of heat into his eyes. "Yup...the strap over the shoulder tied to that brown leather pouch with the big 'A' burned into it?"

Joanna nodded and then removed the Indian feather from her belt. He took it and studied it for a long minute. "I found it at the Anderson camp," Joanna explained.

He sighed. "Well, I guess it's the same bunch all right...at least it seems..."

"You think your father saw the watch or the pouch?"

He shrugged again. "Pa's not good on secondary details. If he did, he's keeping it to himself. But he knows you and I have the sharpest eyes here. I doubt he noticed..."

"Why should they or would they be dragging their old and sick and children with them?" she asked.

"Probably broke camp after the Anderson attack," he offered. "Maybe they're heading for the Panhandle and Parker's rain dance. I dunno for sure..."

"You think they'll leave us alone now? Really?"

He rubbed the back of his neck with one hand, pondering it. "Well, I expect they came in here to look us over...see what we had, how many guns. They were probably arguing about whether to take us...the middle one, probably the chief, talked them out of it. But I guess the fact that they didn't attack has to be charged to God Himself. They could see we weren't a large company. I trust God will see fit to smile on us the rest of the way. Coffee smells good...how about it?"

Joanna knew he felt uneasy, even as she did. She was not ready to write off the incident as the final one with that renegade band. Andrew knew it too. He touched her arm gently and added, "Some things you leave alone as being beyond the figuring," he said. "There's enough good in what happened here with them to allow us reason to hope for more. Let's enjoy what we can, Joanna."

She gave him a reluctant smile and walked with him to the wagons. Glancing back, a shiver passed through her, born of an intuition built over the years. Her mouth felt cottony dry again and her heart still flip-flopped with the intensity of the encounter. God could not assuage the deeply imbedded need she had for one solitary act of justice against those savages. She wanted Him to do that. But only in the act itself could the boil inside her be lanced and free her of the poison that engulfed her soul.

God help me, she thought, not to endanger these good people for the satisfaction of my own vendetta!

9

Captain Tom Brainerd waited as General James Brook, commander of Camp Supply, looked over his orders. Brook was a graying man, rather thin and wiry and showing the demeanor of a man who should be teaching school rather than commanding a fort. But Tom knew from the past that the troopers who rode with him considered him the toughest, most disciplined officer in the field, but also the fairest.

"Well, captain," he said with a resigned note. "I respect Colonel Potter and General McClelland who signed these orders. But you must know that I cannot release supplies to you, even if I had them, for a patrol into the Panhandle without Colonel McKenzie's clearance. I have more than a thousand Kiowas and Arapahoes on this reservation, living off government beef. They come first or I've got trouble."

"I understand, general," Tom replied, feeling the hard shaft of disappointment. "But time is of the essence, sir. I have to get to Adobe Walls right away if I intend to do anything about keeping those hunters out of the Panhandle and Quanah Parker off their backs."

"That should be the province of Colonel McDonnel of Fort Dodge, captain," Brook replied, his blue eyes measuring Tom carefully. "That's a big assignment even for a regiment, let alone a company. At any rate, it will take three days for a courier to get to Colonel McKenzie at Fort Clark and another three back. I suggest you wait it out, captain."

Tom weighed that carefully, uneasily. He thought of the Temple family, probably about two days out of Wolf Creek, just north of the Canadian River—if they had made it that far. He pictured the golden-haired beauty, Marcella, taken captive by Kiowa or Comanche. Or the quiet, serene loveliness of Elizabeth Temple suffering the indignity and savagery of captivity with Indians who treated older women like dogs.

Yet Joanna's face stayed the longest in his mind. She would give the Indians all they could handle for a while. But having lost her family to Indians, she would find captivity among them the cruelest torture of all.

Something about her had fascinated him from the first day he had met her out on the prairie at Dodge. Maybe it was in those brown eyes that carried sparks of anger at one moment or the deeper subdued colors of melancholy the next. He could see the tumble of her dark waves of hair, the soft pout of her lips enhanced by the hesitant, guarded smile which gave her face a certain radiance like the flash of a dove's wing in the sun. She was a no-nonsense girl on one side, fighting the emergence of her beauty with a certain pain on the other.

"Captain?"

He was startled out of his musing by General Brook's impatient tone of voice and came to attention. "Sorry, sir," he said. "Well, sir, my troop can't stay long in the field without provisioning. I need at least a month's worth."

"Captain, you should have re-provisioned at Dodge," Brook insisted.

"Well, sir, I tried . . . Colonel McDonnel said he could not do so without further confirmation of my orders from General Sheridan."

"He may be right, captain," Brook responded hesitantly.

"Sir, my orders say to try..."

Brook's steel-blue eyes stayed steady on Tom's face a long time, as if he could not believe the conviction behind the statement. He sighed then, glanced down at the orders again. "I have no choice but to make you wait, captain. I am sorry."

Tom took his orders back and nodded. "Thank you anyway, sir," he said, saluted and walked out.

When he stepped out the door, he saw Sergeant Bonniface and Chapman waiting for him on the porch.

"Suh," Bonniface said urgently, "a settluh just came in lookin' like he be about done in. Man's name is Anduhson. Says he lost his family while headin' fer Chicken Creek."

Tom stared at him. "The Temples were heading into the same area. Where is he?" he asked.

"Over ta infirmary..."

"Let's go."

When they got to the fort infirmary, the surgeon grudgingly allowed them a few minutes with Anderson. He was lying on a bunk, his face red and peeling from the sun, lips cracked from thirst. He had a graying, unkempt beard. He was going on fifty or so, Tom figured.

"Mr. Anderson, my name is Captain Brainerd," Tom began slowly. "I'm sorry about your family..."

Anderson swallowed hard, the grief still holding him in a tight fist. "I should never gone scoutin' fer water," he began, his tongue darting out over his blistered lips. "We come over Crooked Creek...but it was about bone dry...earlier the Cimarron not much better...figured we was about ten to fifteen miles from the North Canadian. I had one youngster, Ted, burnin' with fever...the stock was dyin'...so I told my wife, Jenny, I was goin' to scout around and see what I could find, mebbe a spring. I put my oldest, Ray, who's twenty...or was..." and Anderson's lips trembled then. "I—I put him in charge...good shot ...and my other son, Leon, was good at shootin' too. I told my wife, Jenny, I'd only be gone awhile, maybe a couple a' miles out..."

Anderson reached a shaky hand to the tin cup of water on the stand next to his bed. Tom helped him, holding the cup to his cracked lips. "Thank ya kindly, sir...anyway...I seen sign of Injuns most a' the day, mostly pony tracks an' such. I figgered with it being close to sundown and all no Indian would attack at that time a' day. I been gone no more'n half-hour...I heard the shootin' a long way off. I—I knew I'd gone too far out then...'' He swallowed again, his eyes turning cloudy with the memory. "The wagons was burnin' when I got there...nobody left. They took the two milch cows we had, one spare horse...and what belongin's they took fancy to. I—I buried the four a' them in one grave...''

Tom nodded, taking it slowly. "Mr. Anderson, where did you start from?''

Anderson sniffed. "Fort Dodge...that colonel told me to go at my own risk...all that...and I did it, I guess. I got nothin' to show fer it now...all we wanted to do was start over...piece a' land fer ourselves...Jenny and me and the boys.''

"Okay, you better try to get some rest,'' Tom said to him quietly.

Anderson's small gray eyes focused on him again. "I tell ya...I think they was Kiowa...maybe Comanche. But one a' them's got my watch with a gold chain...was a gift...was a gift from Jenny to me when we was married twenty-five years ago...'' His eyes blinked back the tears.

"Thanks, Mr. Anderson,'' Tom said, patted him on the shoulder, and turned to walk out.

Outside he paused on the steps of the infirmary. The sun was almost down now, casting a fiery blush over the tormented land. "Sergeant Bonniface,'' Tom said then, taking his trail hat off and slapping it against his leg a couple of times, "I want you to mount up the troop. The moon is on to three-quarters full. We'll be able to see like it was near daylight out there.''

"Wolf Creek area, captain?'' Bonniface asked with anticipation.

Tom glanced at him. He had an eagerness in his large dark eyes. "Our final destination, sergeant, is Adobe Walls...for the record,'' he replied. "But we can catch up with the Temples in a couple of days if we ride hard tonight, then push it again tomorrow. I want every man to load up with two canteens of water. How's the supply of hardtack and bacon?''

"I guess each man has a few days' rations, suh...''

"It will have to do until we make Adobe Walls. Muster out a pack pony and load him up with two 20-gallon barrels of water and two 50-pound sacks of grain for the horses...every man to carry thirty rounds for revolvers, fifty for rifles. You see to that, and I'll sign out with General Brook.''

"Suh!" Bonniface chirped, and Tom glanced at him. "I's sure glad, captain, we's goin' after dem Temples. They's the nicest folks..."

"So were the Andersons undoubtedly," Tom said flatly. "Question is are the same renegades that attacked them ready to do the same with the Temples?"

"Yes, suh," Bonniface said solemnly.

"Chapman, give me the quickest way to Wolf Creek," Tom went on, turning to his scout. "I need a lot of flat-line terrain, no hills so we can make better time. I want you to figure just about where the Temples will be by tomorrow evening and how close we should be to them given we push ourselves all the way." Chapman nodded with no change in expression. Tom slapped his hat against his leg one more time, then put it on his head, jerking it down firmly. "All right, let's go!"

*   *   *

The horses gave in first. It was the middle of the afternoon, the sun blazing its fury from a backdrop of a blue, mirrorlike sky, turning every living thing to a choking, withering death.

Andrew's team staggered in the pull while climbing up a low-grade hill. One of the horses went down onto its knees. "Whoa!" Andrew called out. Joanna saw the horse go down from her position behind the wagons where she was helping Timothy with the stock. She rode up quickly and dismounted.

"Paul!" she yelled toward the rear wagon. "You get back there and stay with Timothy!" She watched him hop off his wagon seat quickly and mount up.

Jeremiah had halted his wagon and returned with Elizabeth. "Unhitch him, Andrew," Jeremiah ordered. The horse was still down, trying to get on legs that wouldn't work for him. As he struggled in the harness, the other horse staggered trying to keep balance. Joanna noticed the downed horse's mouth thick with foam, eyes wild as the thirst and exhaustion drummed a signal of death within him. "Better unhitch them both," Jeremiah added, working the harness off the horse still standing while Andrew worked over the other. "Pulling all that lumber did them in," he added, as if looking for an excuse. "Joanna, go get some water in your hat from one of the barrels."

She ran back to Andrew's wagon, reached into the barrel hanging on the side. The water line was almost to the bottom. She managed to get only about a quart into her hat and went back.

Andrew and Jeremiah got the horse standing again, free of the harness, but its head still drooped. Jeremiah held the hat with the water under the horse's mouth. It drank greedily. Then Jeremiah gave some to the other horse in the team.

"Water's awfully low, Mister," Joanna said. He nodded as if he knew that but said nothing, his frown working up between his eyes.

"Can't be far from the North Canadian," he said with some hope in his voice. "Maybe by tomorrow noon...maybe sooner...bigger river, more feeds from the hills." He handed the hat back to Joanna. "Get a fresh team up."

"They've all pulled their load once today already," Andrew advised. "They're beat, Pa...without water and all..."

"Don't redefine the problem, son," Jeremiah cut him short, the first sign that he was beginning to get frayed by the strain.

"Yes, sir," Andrew said politely.

Joanna looked around at the horizon again. This was no place to be standing still, here in the open, wagons strung out, Indians probably watching. She studied the low-back hills to the left, the clumps of mesquite and Mexican juniper big enough to hide a band of renegades.

She walked back to Timothy and Paul and cut out two fresh horses and led them back to Andrew's wagon. They hitched them up quickly.

"All right," Jeremiah said, surveying the land around them, his voice trying to communicate confidence. "We'll keep moving until the horses just can't go another foot. Joanna, take a look ahead and see if there is water of any kind, maybe some spill-offs from the Canadian. Need to find a good open place in those hills to get through too, but don't go far, you hear? I want you in sight all the time."

"Pa, I think I ought to go with her," Andrew spoke up then. "Paul can take my wagon..."

"I told you that handling a team with that load—"

"Paul can handle them for a while," Andrew insisted.

"And who takes Paul's wagon?" Jeremiah demanded.

"I will." Marcella had been standing a few feet away, unnoticed.

Jeremiah looked at her, a trace of a smile coming to his face. "Now, girl," he soothed, "no cause to get head up over this. . . ."

"You showed me how to handle a team when I was fifteen years old, remember?"

"That was a long time ago, girl—"

"I still know how," she insisted. "Anyway, I'm tired of just riding—and cooking. I want to do something, Pa, something useful."

Jeremiah frowned at the dry clumps of buffalo grass under his feet. "Let her do it, Jeremiah," Elizabeth called to him from the wagon seat. "I don't want Joanna out there scouting by herself anymore. . .it's too dangerous."

Jeremiah hesitated, then pulled his hat lower over his eyes and said, "You got yourself a team, girl! Just let 'em out easy. . .don't let them pull too hard—"

"Pa!" Marcella countered impatiently, and she turned quickly and walked back to the third wagon without further word.

"Pa," Andrew put in, "I wonder if we could tie some of the stock to the back of the wagons. I mean, we could spread out more, move the wagons side by side. . .if we could tie up the horses to the backs and a few of the cattle, it would take the strain off Tim. He's been back there since we left Dodge. . .easier watching out for a few than many. Anyway he's not been looking so good since he lost old Walt."

Jeremiah nodded. "Why not?" he answered Andrew. "Time we gave Timothy a little breather anyway. Let's get to it then. Paul? Marcella? You keep your wagons up close alongside me in case we have to circle in a hurry."

Andrew mounted his big roan horse and followed Joanna out. She was glad for the company, especially his. He was a good tracker, better than she. They trotted their horses a few hundred yards and slowed to a walk as they headed toward the mound of hills ahead. As was their custom, nothing was said as they tracked together. But in the back of Joanna's mind was that picture of the gold watch and chain around the Indian's neck. She hoped that band of renegades was halfway to the Panhandle by now.

She swung off to the left, dismounted, and examined a mound

of horse droppings. Andrew pulled up and watched her. "They're fresh," she said. "A few hours at the most maybe..."

"Tracks through the grass there," he said, pointing ahead into the higher buffalo grass. She walked a bit, leading Pointer, pausing to look at an indentation in the grass.

"Someone was lying down here," Joanna stated, pointing to the spot where the grass was bent about five or more feet long and maybe a few feet wide. "That scout, Chapman, showed me what it looks like."

She turned and mounted Pointer again. They progressed forward to the hills in front of them. As they approached, she noticed that the hills started out in gradual lumps, then jumped rather steeply.

"Horses won't pull up those," Andrew advised glumly. They walked their horses into the grove of mesquite and cottonwoods, their eyes on the hills and the thickening trees in front of them.

"There's a narrow opening down there," she pointed with her finger. It was about fifty feet clear of trees, but it was rocky.

"Good for an ambush," he commented uneasily.

Joanna agreed, but as she looked around at the steep crop of hills again she knew the narrow pass would be the only way. Then, as her eyes made a quick sweep, she saw the Indian. He was sitting on his horse on a ledge not more than thirty or forty feet above her, half-hidden in a crop of mesquite. She felt the warning beat pick up in her chest, triggering a skipping tattoo through her brain.

"Don't look now," she said tightly to Andrew. Joanna pulled up Pointer. Andrew stopped also, looking at her. "There's an Indian right above us. He's got war paint on—same colors as that bunch this morning."

Andrew let out a long sigh, keeping his eyes on her face. "Angle to the left slowly," he cautioned her. "If there's one, probably there are more of them close by. When we get turned we beat it out of this bush in a hurry back to the wagons...okay?"

Joanna urged Pointer to the left, dodging the low-hanging branches of mesquite and juniper. Her eyes darted here and there for sign of more Indians as the sweat rolled from under her hat and down her left cheek. She reached out to touch the stock of her Henry in the scabbard, itching to yank it out and get ready.

They were half-turned to face back out of the grove and Andrew yelled, "Now! Yee-ah!" Joanna hit Pointer in the ribs with her heels. The horse took the prodding and jumped in a long leap forward. The branches slapped into her face, cutting, scraping. She ignored them. The choking grip of fear held strong within her. She and Andrew were out of the grove, letting out their horses to the full gallop. Joanna glanced back once. The Indian was gone from the ledge, but she saw one coming on his horse with a companion, then two more behind him. She led out Pointer to his full stride, going like the wind across the buffalo grass. Andrew stayed right beside her.

They pulled up a few hundred yards from the wagons and looked back. The Indians had not come out of the grove.

"What's wrong?" Jeremiah called as he pulled in his team. Joanna and Andrew walked their blowing mounts back to the wagons. "You see something out there?"

"Couple of Indians, Pa," Andrew explained, wiping at the sweat on his forehead under his trail hat. "From the same bunch who visited us this morning. Two or three of them took out after us, but we got the jump on them."

"Jeremiah?" Elizabeth questioned, half-demanding to know what he was going to do. Paul and Marcella came up from their wagons. Timothy followed on his black gelding.

"Well," Jeremiah said calmly, "they didn't hurt us this morning." He looked beyond to the grove 600 yards away.

"Mister, there's no way through those hills except through a small pass about fifty feet wide," Joanna said. "They're waiting for us to go through. There isn't a ghost of a chance to get by them."

Jeremiah's eyes swung across the hump of hills ahead. "Well," he concluded, "we trust God and go. We can't backtrack, not with the water so low and the horses done in." He scowled at the poor options facing him. Then he reached under his seat and took out an old single-barreled field glass and held it up to his right eye, studying the small hilly hump just off to the left where Joanna and Andrew had been. "Yes," he said meditatively, his eye to the glass. "I see him all right...sitting on his horse on top of that small hump. Can you see him?"

Joanna turned and looked. She didn't need the glass to catch the form on top of the mound, his body silhouetted against the dying sun, his rifle held across his lap.

"What are you going to do, Jeremiah?" Elizabeth asked, her voice shaky.

"Can I look, Pa?" Timothy asked. Jeremiah handed him the glass.

"He does look like the same one who talked to us this morning, all right," Jeremiah commented. "The one who did all the talking. Maybe we can buy him out with another steer."

"I don't think so, Pa," Andrew responded quickly. "If they chased us, they're probably ready to take all we got. They're just waiting for the right time. Maybe we better camp and make a stand of it here, don't you think?"

Jeremiah paused, taking the field glass back from Timothy and looking again, then putting it down and scratching his whiskered chin, trying to come to a decision. He had to know too that they could not fight twenty armed warriors with repeating rifles.

Joanna dismounted then and walked back to the last wagon, off to the left of Jeremiah's. She went to the rear, reached inside among the sacks of flour and pulled out the heavy .50 Sharps buffalo gun. The weight of the weapon pulled on her arms. She took three cartridges from the box inside the wagon, then walked back to the others.

"What are you doing, girl?" Jeremiah demanded, and he jumped down from his wagon seat, staring at the big gun. "What have you got there?"

"Mister, it's a Sharps .50 buffalo gun," she replied factually.

"I will not fire the first shot here, Joanna—"

"Mister, I've waited a long time to fire the first shot at an Indian," she replied impatiently. She inserted a long cartridge into the chamber and slammed the bolt home. "Our Captain Tom Brainerd gave me this rifle back at Dodge. He said it could be used to 'impress' Indians. . . strong medicine, he said. If you want to take the captain's word on it, Mister. . ."

"Just what do you intend to do?" Jeremiah asked doubtfully.

"If we could roll the wagons another hundred yards ahead, it would give me a better edge," she said. "Then swing your wagon right and give me the tailgate for resting this rifle on. I'll try to 'impress' that Indian. It's worth a try, Mister."

"Do what she says, Jeremiah," Elizabeth implored.

Jeremiah's face worked up lines of storm. "You may be asking for trouble that isn't here now," he argued. But when no one supported him, he lifted his hands in resignation and climbed back up on the wagon seat. "The rest of you follow on with me—stay close."

He moved his team and wagon forward the distance Joanna had requested, then swung the wagon to the right. The other wagons closed in, forming the rough U-shape. Joanna dropped the rear gate of Jeremiah's wagon and rested the gun on it. The tailgate was too low to aim properly, however.

"I need something higher to rest it on," she said to Andrew. He brought a flat-lidded toolbox to her.

"That's 500 yards," he warned her. "You ever gone out that far before?"

She did not answer, squinting down the sights of the long barrel. Jeremiah tied the reins of his team to the wagon wheel to hold them in check and got down with Elizabeth to watch. Paul, Timothy, and Marcella crowded in with him.

"The glass, please, Mister?" Joanna asked.

He handed her the field glass with reluctance, his face a glum editorial on the prospects of what she was about to attempt. She peered through the glass with one hand, holding the rifle on the toolbox with the other. She caught the Indian in the lens and saw his form amplified much more now. The branch of the mesquite tree was a bit to the right, the end of it hanging just in front of the Indian pony. Joanna put the field glass down, shifted the barrel of the gun to get it more in line. She caught the Indian down the sights, but hesitated. The urge to take him with one shot was strong, and her hand turned sweaty on the stock of the rifle as her nerves pulsed within her. She bit down hard on her lower lip, resisting the impulse, knowing that Jeremiah was trusting her not to start the fight from this end. She shifted the barrel slowly then to get it more in line with the tree.

"I'm going for that mesquite tree," she said to Jeremiah, who glanced quickly toward the small hump and the tree, his eyes widening some in the impossibility of it.

"You're only going to antagonize him," Jeremiah warned. "Then he'll have them all on us."

"Pa, they'll come at us anyway," Andrew advised. "We can at least give it a chance."

Joanna shifted some, glancing at the buffalo grass ahead of her, judging how much wind was bending the thin reeds. Hardly any at all. She leaned her shoulder tighter into the stock of the gun, feeling the smooth walnut of it against her cheek. The Indian continued to sit his horse in the same spot, not moving, his head turning toward them. He was frozen still as if he were no more than a painting. She now felt for the trigger slowly, her eyes fixed down the sights, the tree limb seeming to move farther and farther away.

The boom of the gun going off was like the sound of a cannon. The kick threw Joanna back flat on the ground, the gun flying six feet away. The shot echoed off the surrounding hills and rattled across the prairie in undulating waves of sound. It made the cattle bawl, the horses dance and snort nervously.

Andrew helped her up, brushing the dirt off her buckskin shirt. A column of blue smoke still hung in the air from the spent powder. "By Jove!" Jeremiah crowed looking through the field glass. "Joanna! That's the greatest shot I've ever seen made, the greatest you've ever made!"

"Let me see, Pa!" Timothy demanded. Jeremiah handed him the glass.

"What about the Indian, Pa?" Andrew demanded impatiently.

"Well," and Jeremiah laughed in delight, "that tree limb had to be all of six inches thick as I figure. It dropped right in front of him as if it fell out of the sky! He hightailed it like he'd been stung by a swarm of bees!" He laughed again, the belly laugh of pure delight. "Girl," and he turned to give Joanna a bear hug that embarrassed her, "I don't know if that 'impressed' that Indian or not, but I kind of think he's going to be thinking long and hard about it. Let me handle that gun for a minute..." He took the heavy rifle from Andrew, examined the breech, lifted it to aim. "Five hundred yards!" he bellowed like it was nothing more than a shooting match. "At least that!"

"Buffalo hunters have been known to kill buffalo at 1,500 yards with that thing," Joanna reminded him.

Jeremiah handed the big gun back to Andrew, then looked back toward the low hill where the Indian had been. Joanna rubbed her aching shoulder, hoping only that Brainerd was right about that being "strong medicine" to Indians.

"What now, Jeremiah?" Elizabeth questioned. "Do we go or stay?"

"Well, maybe we ought to try for that pass through the hills,"

Jeremiah replied, stroking his chin with his right hand. "While that Indian ponders it . . ."

"Pa, I think we better let him talk it over with the rest of his band," Andrew suggested. "He has to tell them what he saw . . . if we go now he'll have to try to take us because he has to save his own pride. Anyway, our horses can't pull any longer today. We're all spent. We'd be in better shape for them in the morning, don't you think?"

Jeremiah continued to ponder it. "I think that's the best idea of the day," Elizabeth said with finality.

"Well," Jeremiah concluded, "maybe you're right, Andrew. I hope you're right for all of us. We better tighten up tonight and get some barricades under the wagons. Just in case they come at dawn. By Jove, Elizabeth, this calls for a special dinner tonight," he added, beaming at her. "A kind of celebration of the best shot this side of the Mississippi, maybe the other side too! What say, Elizabeth?" He turned toward her, smiling warmly, but Elizabeth's face under her blue bonnet had turned a deeper shade of pink beyond the sunburn. "We got those cans of stewed lamb yet, browned potatoes, vegetables, strawberry jam, biscuits—" he reminded his wife.

"Hurray!" Timothy shouted.

"Let's do it, Ma!" Paul echoed eagerly.

"Anything's better than rabbit," Marcella added emphatically, looking at the palms of her delicate hands already showing abrasions from handling the reins of the team.

"We are not at Wolf Creek yet," Elizabeth replied tartly, a note of warning in her voice. "I don't think celebrating the frightening of one Indian or a record shot, as much as I'm impressed by Joanna's marksmanship, is any reason for festivity. We will eat the leftover rabbit stew and ask God to spare us in the morning."

"Oh, Mother!" Marcella sighed with disappointment.

"Ah, Elizabeth," Jeremiah entreated. But she turned and walked back to her wagon in short purposeful strides, her back stiff, informing him that she was not compromising.

Jeremiah looked abashed and confused. Then he put on that smile as if to say, "She's right," and grinned at Joanna. "Well, girl, we'll have to settle with a cup of coffee, how's that?" Joanna nodded and gave him a half-smile. "All right now, all you valiant brothers, get started on building barricades under the wagons. Except Timothy...get the stock inside, Tim, and give them all a little drink and some feed. But not much, we've got to conserve. Marcella, go help your mother...Joanna, gather buffalo chips and get the fire going. No big fires, you remember...tomorrow we cross the North Canadian, we get water there! And best of all we are almost home— Wolf Creek!''

Joanna walked Pointer outside the wagons trying to rise to Jeremiah's optimism. Her shoulder still ached from the buffalo gun. She glanced once toward the small hump across the prairie where the Indian had sat his horse. Just what was he telling his warriors right now? Was he really "impressed" as Tom Brainerd had tried to assure her he would be? Or was he even more intent on killing them all?

She picked up the buffalo chips and tossed them into a small bucket she carried in one hand. Her thoughts suddenly turned to Captain Tom Brainerd. She stopped, wondering why he, of all people, should step to the front of her mind. She had not given him a modicum of thought since the day he left for Camp Supply with his troop. Was it because of the buffalo gun? Her mind shifted to the night at Dodge when he had explained the gun to her. Maybe that was it.

She paused now, and out of habit glanced at the tree line for any sign of Indians. Then she walked on again, leading Pointer, searching in the grass for the buffalo chips. She remembered Brainerd again, wondering why he led a Negro troop, wondering what had happened to him at Fort Morrow. There was something about the man that formed misty shadows intriguing her. There was that quietness about him combined with a quickness and lightness in his step; his smile came more from his eyes than his face, and in those eyes was an intentness that carefully studied everything and everyone.

Who was Captain Brainerd? She stopped again, not knowing why she should allow the question to linger in her mind now. She filled the bucket with chips, swung back up on Pointer and headed back to the wagons. An apprehensive chill ran up her spine at the thought of what the morning might bring. At the same time, a mounting urgency grabbed her around the heart. Adobe Walls kept hanging out for her. She inwardly sensed that her final destiny—the moment of reckoning with Quanah Parker—was at Adobe Walls. Until then, all that would happen would be more of an aside.

Shooting any Indian would not do; she had proved that when she had one in the sights of her buffalo gun. No...it had to be that *one* from so long ago whom she remembered as if it were yesterday.

Joanna dismissed Captain Tom Brainerd from her mind as the larger picture of her thoughts commanded her. She dismounted within the U-shape of the wagons and set about to build the fire. The sun was sliding beyond the small range of hills to the southwest, turning on its farewell of red fire, a mocking promise that it would be back tomorrow with the same deadly heat.

Tomorrow...it could all change for them with the first smear of that sun on the horizon. The fear of it turned her throat tight, her mouth dry. Only the gratification of taking enough of them with her faithful Henry rifle offered any sense of balance, and it was weak at best.

There would be no easy way to die.

10

Again there was little, if any, sleep for them that night. Jeremiah took to walking around the wagons, listening to the night sounds, the chortle of a whippoorwill, the bark of the coyote. He paused to exchange light banter with Paul and Timothy, using a tone of optimism and good cheer with them. The moon was a bit more than three-fourths full now, pouring a luminosity over the prairie and the distant hill and tree line that was close to a sunrise glow. A jackrabbit couldn't jump out of its hole fifty yards away without them seeing it, Joanna mused.

She and Marcella were lying on their bedrolls under Andrew's wagon. Joanna gazed out into the tranquil night scene and hoped to get some sleep before her watch. Her body ached from too much time in the saddle, and her shoulder still throbbed from the kick of the buffalo gun. She heard Jeremiah talking in low tones to Andrew a few feet away. "We've got to make the North Canadian tomorrow or the stock won't hold out. Been a long dry spell out here it seems. Just pray the North Canadian is running full...or at least enough to resupply."

"They say it can be a rough river," Andrew responded. "Really wide, tricky with rapids sometimes."

"Well, we're moving toward the upper bend where it swings east and south to join the Canadian," Jeremiah added. "Should be narrows, easier to cross. All we got to get by is that band of renegades out there."

Joanna heard them mumble some more, and then Jeremiah bent down over her, peering at her face. "Ought to sleep, both of you," he said quietly, his voice carrying a lilting sound. "Remember, you can't change what's coming by worrying about it...let the Lord do the worrying and the changing. Everything's going to be all right."

"Good night, Pa," Marcella said sleepily, but Joanna knew that, as for herself, she was far from sleep. Jeremiah walked on. Joanna continued staring out into the moon wash, pushing thoughts of the morning further back into her mind. Then she heard the loud clicking sound next to her and turned to see Marcella holding the .45 Colt in her two hands, pulling back the hammer with her thumbs.

"Better load that thing pretty soon, Marcella," Joanna advised her. "If you intend to use it..."

"It is loaded," Marcella replied calmly.

Joanna turned full around to face her then. "Well, don't start shooting out the bottom of the wagon," she warned. "Let that hammer down easy now...easy..."

Marcella giggled at the sound of concern in Joanna's voice. She let the hammer down and put the gun back under the pillow.

"You taught me, Joanna," she said with a sarcastic tone of voice.

Joanna did not respond. She wondered at the way Marcella had changed in less than a week on the trail. The delicate, fussy beauty who had been concerned only for her coiffure and dress had emerged into a gun-toting, mule-skinning pioneer lassie. Joanna was sure Elizabeth was not happy with the change. But in a way Joanna felt that it was a much-needed transition. Survival out here was dependent on shooting to defend oneself and hunting successfully for game. Yet Joanna, having become so used to Marcella's fragile beauty and careful grooming, felt a bit uneasy nevertheless.

Still, the summer so far had altered all of them in some way. The heat, dust, and sweat had chewed at the very fiber of their true selves, chafing and blistering, cruelly cutting at their naivete about pioneer life. The careful politeness of Minnesota life and their roles there had disappeared to be replaced by short tempers, quick, sharp exchanges with each other, impatient demands. Joanna noticed it as much in Elizabeth who, despite her maintained gentility and dignity, had become more assertive in her exchanges with Jeremiah and with Paul and Timothy.

They had all become the anvil upon which the hammer of the sun and the fear of Indian attack pounded continually. They had managed to remain civil at meals and during the bouncing, bone-shaking ride on the wagons or in the saddle. But their faces now showed the drain of it all, the growing lines of fatigue around the eyes and mouth.

A bath would help, Joanna concluded. Jeremiah insisted that what water they had would be used for drinking—and that sparingly. Joanna had a touch of water once back at the Cimarron when she dashed a handful of the muddy stuff in her face to ease the heat. That was it. In the meantime, in the days since, they all had taken on the smell of dust, horse dung, leather, sweat, and the smoke of cook fires. They had not changed their clothes since leaving Dodge, and the rubbing filth caused itchy blisters that made them turn restlessly in their bedrolls at night.

The tough summer was either going to break them or make something of them that they had never contemplated in Minnesota. Right now Joanna wasn't sure which way it was going to go. Perhaps the morning would decide it.

• • •

She awoke with a start. Instinctively, sensing danger, she swung her rifle around, levered the action and looked up. The sun was already well up above the eastern horizon, burning a hot stream down on her. She caught the shadow above her and saw Andrew smiling down at her.

"Take it easy," he said calmly. She smelled coffee and frying bacon. "You fell asleep . . . sometime during the night. Dead to the world."

"What?" and she rolled out of her blankets and stood up. She took a few seconds to shake off the heavy webs of sleep on her brain. "No...no Indians?"

"Nope...no sign. I don't think we're gonna see them. I think you did the job with that buffalo gun yesterday. I've ridden out for signs...none."

" 'This is the day the Lord hath made!' " she heard Jeremiah booming from somewhere around the cook fire. "Let's eat and get the horses hitched! Today we make Wolf Creek!"

"You think they're gone?" Joanna asked Andrew. "I mean, completely?"

"Well, I don't know about that...could be they may be still waiting over there for us to go through that pass. But it's strange they didn't attack at dawn; I thought that was their usual style. We'll just have to chance it now."

Joanna nodded. "You should have wakened me," she said, feeling embarrassed that she had slept through her watch.

"You looked so tired last night," he replied. "Anyway, it was a quiet night. Let's get some breakfast and be on our way."

It took them less than a half-hour to finish up with breakfast and hitch the horses. Jeremiah told them the line of march. "I'll take the lead...then Paul, Andrew last. Marcella up with Andrew, Joanna ride with Timothy bringing up the rear. Now if we get attacked in there, you keep running your teams full out. If we stop, we are dead. Keep going! Understood?" They all murmured their assent. Jeremiah looked at each of them with a smile that said they couldn't lose. "Remember the prayer of the psalmist," he said. " 'Deliver me, O Lord, from mine enemies: I flee unto thee to hide me. Teach me to do thy will; for thou art my God: thy Spirit is good; lead me into the land of uprightness.' Well? Is He our Shield and Defender or not?"

"Aye!" they chorused, though it sounded more muted now than at Fort Dodge.

"So, let's go!" Jeremiah shouted.

They moved out in a single line toward the low hump on which the Indian had sat on his pony the day before. When they came to that spot, Jeremiah pulled up to look at the tree limb that Joanna had shot down with her buffalo gun. "I told you it was all of six inches thick!" he yelled back at the rest of them. "It's more like eight inches! That is some gun, Joanna! Some shot!

You get up there now and check that pass for us!''

Joanna galloped Pointer out front and studied the narrow pass carefully. It was a thirty-foot-wide opening between two hills thick with cottonwoods and Mexican juniper. She saw nothing there, but it was almost impossible to detect anything behind that wall of brush.

She rode back to Jeremiah. He was already pushing his team toward the pass opening that sloped downward. "Nobody I can see," Joanna told him. He waved his hand in acknowledgment, not wanting to waste a minute in his determination to get through.

Joanna rode back to be with Timothy. She held her Henry rifle in one hand as did Tim. Most of the stock was tied to the rear of the wagons, bawling now in the heat that had come with the climbing sun in the brassy blue of the sky. The dust was not as thick here where there were more trees, but the wagons and the stock nevertheless stirred up a thin cloud of it that burned Joanna's throat. She finally called to Timothy to follow her as she rode around the rear wagon and up along the slope line. They pulled up halfway into the pass and watched the wagons move on through it, bouncing over the rocks and dead tree limbs. Jeremiah set a fast pace, urging his team on. Joanna kept her eyes on the slopes above, watching for any movement.

It had to be a good quarter-mile through that pass, but Joanna could not tell for sure. As she and Timothy caught up to the last wagon that Paul drove, pushing the stock ahead of them, she heard Jeremiah yelp from further down and knew then that they had gotten through. Jeremiah was standing up on his wagon seat waiting for them, a broad smile on his face.

" 'The Lord is my strength and salvation! Whom shall I fear?' " he shouted at them. "Do I hear it?"

"Aye!" they all yelled back at him.

"All right! Joanna, you and Andrew get out there and scout for the Canadian! Marcella, you take Andrew's team! Let's go!"

"Joanna?" Timothy pleaded. "Please, can I go with you? I've been riding dust all the way from Fort Dodge! Let me go with you, please?"

Joanna rode forward to where Jeremiah was getting ready to move his team again. "Mister, okay if we take Timothy along? He needs a breather. We'll watch out for him."

Jeremiah looked doubtful, glancing ahead to the open prairie.

"Let him go, Jeremiah," Elizabeth encouraged him. "It will get his mind off old Walt."

Jeremiah wiped the sweat off his face with his sleeve, pondering it. Then he nodded. "Timothy, you watch out for yourself, hear?" he called.

"I sure will, Pa!" Timothy responded with a big smile.

The three of them galloped off across the prairie toward terrain that was more hilly, some jutting up into whale backs that were covered with trees. Joanna noticed, as they rode farther on, that there were thick groves of cottonwoods, poplars, and juniper...and much greener. That had to be a sign of water.

The sun was climbing higher to midmorning, pouring out choking heat again when they broke out of the thick tree line and saw it.

"The North Canadian!" Timothy yelled jubilantly.

Joanna pulled up alongside Andrew and looked down the gradual forty-foot slope. There was more water running here, but it was wider which would not make it easy to get the wagons over. But just seeing the water flowing around rocks and catching the sound of its merriment was a sight worth seeing.

"We better look for some narrows to cross," Andrew said. "Too wide here."

They rode east along the bank for a half-mile, but the river seemed to get wider as they went. They reversed course and went west a bit. As the river rounded a bend to begin its course down to the main Canadian River, they discovered the narrows they wanted. It was not more than 100 yards across there. "That should do it," Andrew said, studying the river carefully in that frowning kind of concentration that was so much like his father's.

Joanna moved Pointer down the bank and into the water. The horse walked out twenty yards or so, the water coming halfway up his legs. The bottom seemed firm enough. She went out a bit farther, watching the ripples of current. Pointer kept his footing all the way. Satisfied, she turned him around and headed back to shore. There she dismounted and belly flopped into the water, unable to resist it any longer. Timothy jumped in after her, delighted. Andrew watched, smiling at both of them. Joanna let out a high yelping hoot of delight, so that Pointer turned his head to look at her. She let the water seep through to her skin, then stuck her head into it, pulling off her hat to let it get to her hair.

Andrew finally rode his roan into the water too, dismounted and sat down in the water. It came up to his chest. They both splashed at each other, yelping in the pleasure of the cool water cutting away the heat and the dust.

Finally Joanna stood, wiping at the water on her face, coughing on the gulps she had swallowed greedily to cut her thirst. When she looked at Andrew, he was studying her with considerable interest and surprise. The water had plastered her buckskin shirt tight to her chest and tumbled her black hair down into wet black streams. Her brown corded trousers felt like a tightened leather band. It was as if she had nothing on. Feeling the flush in her cheeks, she stumbled out of the river and leaped into the saddle, sending Pointer into a gallop up the bank. She didn't look back. As she rode to tell Jeremiah, she pulled the buckskin shirt out, trying to squeeze some of the water from it so she wouldn't reveal any more of herself. Still, Andrew was her cousin and stepbrother! *Kinfolk*. It wasn't as if he was—well, like *Captain Tom Brainerd*. She felt the sting in her cheeks again as she approached Jeremiah's wagon. No man had ever seen her like that, cousin or no cousin!

Jeremiah stood up from his wagon seat as she approached. He pulled his team to a halt. "The North Canadian, Mister!" she shouted at him.

"May God be praised!" Jeremiah shouted. "Hear that, Elizabeth? We got water! Marcella! Paul! Water straight ahead!"

"Joanna, it seems you've already had a good taste of it, my dear," Elizabeth said then. There was no indictment in her voice, but it had a note of specific reminder.

Jeremiah looked at Joanna again, and he smiled, then he laughed. "Well, girl, you look wonderful! Absolutely wonderful!"

"Jeremiah," Elizabeth chided him gently. "I think it might do you a lot of good to get to that river and jump in yourself. A moose could not possibly smell as bad as you do right now."

"So be it!" Jeremiah bellowed. "Off to the Canadian and a bath then!" And he let go with another of those belly laughs that had the sound of pure joy.

When they approached the river, Jeremiah took one look at it and immediately moved his team down to the river's edge. He let them drink. The rest of the stock had been let loose by Paul, and they ran to the water and drank eagerly. Marcella and Paul moved their teams down to the water as well, as they all sat waiting for Jeremiah to decide the best approach.

"All right," he finally said, "we'll all take our baths when we get to the other side. Let's move them on over. I'll go first. Andrew, take Marcella's wagon. Paul, back up to yours. Joanna, you and Timothy see to the stock. Wait until we are over before you push them."

Jeremiah took his time, allowing the horses to feel their way. The water was up to the axles, but it did not move swiftly there. The horses found firm enough footing it seemed. Now and then a ripple of current tugged at them and they snorted nervously.

They were past the middle and heading to the far shore when Jeremiah's wagon plunged down suddenly, the water coming up over the wheels. The horses snorted, whinnied, and jumped in their harness. "Go around me," Jeremiah shouted at Andrew and Paul. "I hit a sinkhole! Keep going! Joanna! Get Elizabeth off this wagon!" he called back. Joanna pushed the stock into the river, shouting at Timothy to keep them moving across. She rode out to Jeremiah and came alongside the seat. Elizabeth reached out and grabbed Joanna's shoulders as she awkwardly straddled Pointer, her arms going around Joanna to keep from falling.

Jeremiah jumped down into the water and it came up to his waist. Andrew had arrived at the far shore, then mounted his roan and rode back out to help. Timothy rode by, pushing the stock, and Jeremiah called to him: "Tim, you stay over there with Marcella and your mother! You see anything fire a shot!"

Then it was Andrew, Jeremiah, and Joanna down into the water putting their shoulders to the back wheels. Jeremiah was yelling, "Yah! Yah!" at the team, urging them on. He finally moved back from the right rear wheel to the back of the wagon, pushing with all his weight. Suddenly he disappeared under the rear axle.

"Pa!" Andrew yelled in alarm.

Joanna didn't wait. She threw her hat aside and slid under the water, looking around for Jeremiah. He was being sucked into the sinkhole, fighting current as well. She shoved her head back up for air. "Andrew! Help me!" she yelled.

Andrew went under with her then, grabbing his father by the shirt. Joanna managed to get him by the waist. By this time Jeremiah's eyes were bulging as he fought for air. He still wouldn't budge.

Joanna grabbed him by the belt, then tugged with all the strength she had. Andrew had Jeremiah around the shoulders; then with one hand he reached up for the axle for leverage and strained. Joanna felt the suction from the sinkhole give and the water bubble in a big cloud around them.

They broke to the surface only a few feet above, coughing and gagging. Jeremiah was vomiting water now, and Andrew was squeezing his chest in and out to help him empty his lungs.

After a few long minutes, Jeremiah was breathing normally but the purple color on his lips remained. Finally Jeremiah looked at them both and grinned, though it was weak.

"Well, the good Lord never said this would be easy," he said, shaking his head, wiping the water and mud from his face. "I'm beholden to the two of you. I—I don't think I would have made it without you. God bless you both." He coughed again, took a deep breath and laughed. "You know...Elizabeth said I needed a bath. Ha! Would you say I had one, you two?" Joanna leaned against the rear of the wagon, still breathing heavily from the effort. "Well," Jeremiah continued, "we still got to get this wagon out. That Captain Brainerd was right...should have had a double-trace outfit...four horses in harness, 'stead of two."

It took an hour, but only after they hooked up two more horses with spare harness and tied extra lines to the wagon wheels. When they finally made the far shore it was early afternoon. Elizabeth looked pale as Andrew recounted what had happened.

"It will kill us all in the end," she commented dolefully. "Indians, water, mud..."

"Ah, Elizabeth," Jeremiah countered in entreaty. "We're almost home now. Look, Andrew and Joanna, I hate to ask you—you've been worked to death already—we can't be far from Wolf Creek. If you think you can get the strength, take a look-see a mile or two ahead. I think we can move the wagons while you are looking...if we keep going till sundown, well, we might be in sight of Wolf Creek. What say?"

Nobody responded. They were all sobered over his near brush with death. Even though the fresh water of the North Canadian had revived them, the fatigue of days on the trail still hung heavy.

"Jeremiah, we need a bath, all of us," Elizabeth reminded him. "We need the rest. Wolf Creek will be there in the morning or whenever. I'm not moving."

Joanna knew why she stood firm on that. She was worried about him. Even as he talked now, Jeremiah coughed a lot, and the water still rattled in his lungs.

Jeremiah looked up at her, surprised. She had never asserted herself so vehemently before. Then he laughed. "My Elizabeth's getting spunky! You know...all these years, darling, you never so much as argued a decision of mine? Ha! By Jove! I kinda' like you snapping off at me! And I think you're right. I don't say you'll always be right, my sweet, but I'm coming to know that tone of voice...so ...let's park right here then, have our bath, water the stock, fill our water barrels, have a decent meal, and look to the morning! What say you all?"

"Hurray!" Timothy cheered and ran for the water, Paul following him. Jeremiah, taking the spirit of the moment, ran after them and jumped in behind them.

"Oh, Mother," Marcella said in a weary tone. "You'd think he would have had enough of that river..."

Elizabeth took off her blue bonnet slowly and glanced at them playing in the water. Joanna saw a trace of tears in her eyes.

"It's okay, Ma," Andrew said soothingly. He put his arms around her, and she put her face to his chest. "It was close...but I think Pa's got God going with him regular..."

Joanna looked across the river again from where they had come toward a hill that jutted up sharply, higher than the others. She saw the four puffs of blue-black smoke climb lazily into the windless air. Then it was repeated again. She looked down the river on this side, to a range of whale-back hills downstream. She saw the puffs of smoke come up there too, undoubtedly in answer to those across the river. That meant whoever was behind them had told those ahead on this side that they were here.

She decided not to say anything to any of them about it. This was a time to free up their minds of the dangers. They had lived with it too long already. But later on she would have to tell Andrew. It was certainly not the time to drop their guard.

• • •

Captain Tom Brainerd leaned over the map and studied it in the dim light of the small fire. Chapman's finger was on the spot where the Anderson wagons were hit.

"We are a mile south of that," he said. "The Temples would be here...on the North Canadian...mebbe...if they didn't get jumped by the same bunch that took the Anderson family."

"What's on the other side of the Canadian?" Tom asked.

Chapman paused. "At Camp Supply, Kiowa there say Quanah is making the war dance down on Palo Duro Creek. Here." His finger moved over from Wolf Creek, west, which would be about a half-day's hard ride away."

"What tribe hit the Andersons?"

Chapman paused. "Kotsoteka Comanche...looks like." He pulled out part of an arrow, the head still intact. "Kotsoteka make heads out of stone." He tossed the arrow into the fire with a flip of his hand as if he did not wish to be contaminated by it.

"You find any sign that they might be following the Temples?"

"Plenty. I saw wagon wheels a few miles west of the Anderson massacre. Plenty of Indian pony sign out there too. But Kotsotekas don't like to tangle with Parker's Quahadi over in Palo Duro. Mebbe they would follow the Temples if they are hungry enough...or mebbe they wait until the Temples get into Wolf Creek or just across the Canadian. Mebbe they hit them already before they cross the Canadian." Chapman shrugged.

Tom sighed. "All right...when can we get to Wolf Creek? Let's get on that same trail the Temples took as far as you could scout them. If they didn't make it, we'll come across them. If they did, we maybe can get there in time. How much time the long way, following them?"

"Mebbe a day...if we ride hard."

"Sergeant Bonniface?" Tom said, peering down at his map using the light of the fire.

"Suh," Bonniface replied, leaning forward from just behind Tom.

"Pass the word among the men...we ride before sunup. Double the guard on the picket lines."

"Beggin' ya pahdon, captain," Bonniface put in hesitantly. "Well, suh, da troop is ready to ride now if ya give da order."

Tom looked at him. "What's got into this troop? They didn't look too eager to ride last night...why tonight?"

"Suh...dey's kinda feelin' fer dem Temples...out dere alone ...dey know what happened to dem Anderson people."

Tom paused, weighing the possibilities of a night ride. The moon was almost full, splashing the prairies and tree lines with the glow of early morning daylight sun. It was plenty to see what was ahead in case Indians hid waiting in ambush. Time weighed heavier on him now too. The Temples were crossing deeper into dangerous territory.

"Are you sure you speak for the troop or just a few of you?" he asked Bonniface, folding the map.

Bonniface hesitated. "Well, suh...I admits dat Corporal Rutledge, Private Dunkerton and Private Rufus Jackson is da main talkers...but I ain't hearin' no quarrel from da rest a' da troop."

"Well, my thanks to those three," Tom concluded. "But I think we better bed down for a few hours anyway. Tell every man to get some sleep. When the moon climbs to past midnight, we'll saddle up. Better relieve the guard every two hours so they all get some shut-eye."

"Suh," Bonniface responded and stood up to walk down the line of the troopers who were lying around carrying on small talk.

Tom stood and tucked the map inside his buckskin shirt.

"Amos," he asked his scout standing next to him. "You got any idea when Quanah will attack Adobe Walls?"

Chapman paused, taking his time, weighing his answer, wanting as always to be sure. "Kiowa and Arapahoe at Camp Supply say that Quanah will strike at the full moon. They got the word from some old men of the Quahadi who came into the reservation too sick to fight. They been dancing big medicine down at Palo Duro. They will strike then in two moons."

"Hmmm," Tom responded, taking off his hat and slapping it against his right leg. "That is too close...we will have to ride tonight and tomorrow. We have to be sure the Temples are safe. Then we'll get to Adobe Walls. Maybe we can still talk the hunters out of there. Billy Dixon is there, and he always listened to sense in the past." He paused. "Amos, I need to know where the Temples are and what's between us and them. Get a couple of hours' sleep and get on out into that general area. I'll mount my troop in five hours and follow the route we planned, so you will know where to find us. Good luck, Amos."

Chapman lifted his right hand, three fingers extended as a sign he understood. Tom watched him walk away toward his saddle that lay on the ground twenty feet away. Then he sat by the fading fire, staring into it. He thought of the Temples again, each of them...

remembering that man Anderson, eyes clouded with grief, wide with the images of how his family died. And his mind came back to Joanna. Those soft brown eyes that flashed warning lights as her anger stoked quickly and the rose-kissed line of her lips. She tried hard to hide her womanhood in those buckskins, but he had seen the beauty there the night of the dinner at Colonel McDonnel's.

Brainerd worried, though, at her snapping tone of voice when she referred to her dead parents, her intensity in the handling of weapons, her fixation about evening the score with the Indians. He also worried now that she might be short on the trigger out there and provoke a fight that perhaps was not necessary. He knew one thing for sure: She had to complete her vendetta some way, even if it meant death for her. The thought of that brought a tightening in his chest, a chill around his heart.

The weary captain sighed and pushed a small mound of dirt over the fire. Then he rolled into his blankets, lying back on his saddle to stare up at the moon now almost full, the stars hanging like overripe fruit in the cloudless sky. He thought of his dead wife Martha again, the loneliness jabbing at him.

Above the night air he heard the same Negro voice among the troopers begin to sing that same familiar hymn tune again. The song drifted off into the moon-misted night and left him with those same memories and longing for his parents. And then Martha again.

Finally by the discipline of the years, he shut off his mind and let sleep come, strangely now seeing only the image of the long waves of raven hair tumbling over the shoulders of a woman who fought contrary winds in her heart and soul: Joanna Danforth Temple.

11

Joanna was out ahead of the wagons by herself the next day just before noon. She had informed Andrew about the smoke signals of the previous day. Because of the danger, he had especially wanted to ride out with her, but Marcella's hands had developed painful blisters from handling the team. He had to take over.

"Go slowly out there and stay in sight," he told her bluntly.

She nodded. And she had kept the wagons in view most of the morning. But as the terrain changed again to undulating prairie hills, she lost sight of them in the troughs. Joanna kept going anyway, knowing how important it was now to find Wolf Creek. They were all too tired to drag it out much longer. Jeremiah was coughing more after a fitful night, and his breathing still rattled of water. Elizabeth was afraid he might be coming down with pneumonia. He needed rest. Besides that, the stock were getting skinnier, the forage here still being scarce. They had to get to water where there would be green shoots of grass to feed on.

She calculated as best she could where Wolf Creek would be and how far. But as the sun climbed higher and turned on its blast furnace, the young woman was wary of going too far alone. When Joanna looked back once after coming out of a dip between the hills, she could not see the wagons. She debated whether or not to go on, but finally decided to go it another mile anyway. Though the hills were perfect places for ambushes with clumps of cottonwoods here and there, she was driven more by finding Wolf Creek than for her own safety.

She had no idea how far she had gone, but upon reaching the summit of another long rise of hill, she pulled up. Joanna looked down a gradual slope covered with buffalo grass. There were some trees at the top near her but not enough to hide behind. As she studied the two- to three-hundred yards of the slope ahead of her, she saw the tree line farther down. It looked especially green and thick. That had to mean water.

Looking back, there were still no wagons. She was aware then of how alone she really was. Her eyes swept the hills around her, looking for any sign of movement. It was very still, yet Joanna felt the compulsion to look beyond that tree line below her. To go back now to the wagons with no sign would be discouraging to the rest of them.

Pulling her Henry from the scabbard, she urged Pointer down the slope at a walk, keeping her eyes fixed on the trees ahead. She flipped the safety off the trigger guard of her rifle, taking a firmer grip on Pointer's reins.

Approaching the tree line, Joanna noticed the usual Mexican juniper and mesquite, but there was also a lot of what she figured was hackberry and chinaberry. She remembered Captain Brainerd saying that Wolf Creek had a lot of that. There was excitement in the prospect of this being it as she angled off to the left a bit where there seemed to be a break in the thick brush. Joanna paused and looked down into it, standing in her stirrups to see better.

She saw the creek bed first. It was sunbeaten sand mostly—and very dry-looking. Her heart sank. Pointer moved slowly down into the break. That's when she saw the two pools of water directly in front of her, about twenty yards further down the path. This break must have been a watering hole used by buffalo at one time, she thought.

Springs! She looked around carefully, then dismounted and walked across the muddy bank to one pool. Scooping up some of the water in both hands, Joanna drank it. It was sweet and cool! Her heart jumped with excitement. With that kind of water supply the Temples could find this a perfect spot to build and settle in. Anxious to get back to the Temples with the good news, she turned and walked back, her eyes studying the ground. There were fresh pony tracks. Her mind sounded the warning: It was too quiet. The young scout swung up on Pointer and moved back up the break quickly, pausing briefly there to look around before moving out into the open buffalo grass and up the slope.

Satisfied, Joanna put Pointer to a gallop and kept him moving over the hills, anxious to find the wagons. She rode hard over three or four of the prairie hills, looking back now and then to make sure she was not being pursued. Only once did she sense something moving on one of the crests of a hill behind her. But she wasn't sure.

Finally, coming over a rise, Joanna saw the wagons below her, perhaps a half-mile away. Jeremiah pulled up his team as he saw her coming.

"Wolf Creek!" she shouted at him. "No more than three to four miles ahead!"

"You were not to go out that far, girl!" Jeremiah scolded.

"I—I'm sorry, Mister! But I had to be sure!"

Jeremiah frowned his disapproval, but then asked, "Any water there?"

"The creek isn't running much, but there are two big springs with water—pure, clean, and running over!"

"Hear that, Elizabeth?" he crowed then, though his voice sounded hoarse. "You hear that, Andrew? Marcella? Timothy? Paul? We're on to Wolf Creek! By Jove, we're going to have our dinner tonight, Elizabeth! We're home!"

For all of the booming sound of victory in his voice, his face looked drawn, the fatigue peeling off the lines of his smiles.

"Jeremiah, don't strain your lungs so much," Elizabeth cautioned.

"Strain?" he countered, trying a smile that slid off in the muddiness of his face. "We're home, I said! Let God be praised!"

Joanna rode back to talk to Andrew. She told him about the Indian signs at the creek. "Probably their water hole, too," he commented. "I don't think they'll like us horning in on it."

"I think we should tell Jeremiah," she said.

He nodded. "Go ahead. I have to check the harness on the team."

She rode back to Jeremiah as he got his team moving again. She told him about the Indian signs at the creek and the smoke signals the day before. He nodded. "I saw the smoke too, girl," he replied. "We'll worry about the Indians when we have to, Joanna. Right now I'm more concerned that these horses hold out long enough to get us there. Keep your eyes sharp."

"Yes, Mister."

In an hour they were moving over the hilly mounds of prairie grass. It was tough-going on the horses, and Jeremiah stopped at every rise to let them blow. Late in the afternoon, they moved down the gradual slope to the tree line by the creek where their wagons formed into the usual U-shape.

The entire family walked down to test the pools, except Andrew who chose to stay with the wagons. Elizabeth walked through the soft mud to the first pool and cupped a mouthful of water and drank. "Oh, that is lovely," she said, and her pale, tired face seemed to light up some. Jeremiah tried some, and he immediately lifted his hat from his head, and staring up at the turquoise sky, said in a loud voice, "Lord, we thank Thee for leading us to these springs of pure water...to our new home. May we know a long and happy life in this place!"

"Amen," they said.

Jeremiah coughed harshly, and his face turned pale. "Well, let's fill the barrels with this water and settle in," he told them, his voice seeming to get stronger at the thought of it. "Then we'll have our banquet, a good sleep, and tomorrow we can plan our house. How's that, Elizabeth?"

She smiled weakly at him, but there was relief showing in her eyes now too. "You rest right away," she admonished him. "You are still barking and you sound as if you have a death rattle in that chest."

"Ah, Elizabeth," he pleaded with her, his hands reaching out to her. "This is a time I've dreamed about for too long! We got to get a fire going and start cooking! How's that, everyone?"

"Aye!" they said as one.

"I can't believe it," Marcella said as she splashed water from the pool into her face.

"Believing is what brought us here, girl!" Jeremiah said with victory in his voice.

"Through all that dust, mud, Indians," Marcella commented wearily. "I just hope, Pa, that what we got here is the paradise you told us about in Northfield."

"Ha!" Jeremiah laughed as Elizabeth led him back up the path to the wagons. "Look around you, girl! You got everything here...trees for lumber to build...good water...ground to turn over if we have to...lots of rangeland for cattle."

Joanna watched them head back to the wagons, then looked down at the mud at her feet again. Andrew came down the path and looked at the prints in the mud. "Yeah, well, it's their watering hole all right," he said, crouching to study the tracks more closely. He stood again, squinting across the river bed, then up and down the shore. "Best I guess just to forget it for tonight. Pa needs his moment to celebrate and dream. We'll know soon enough what all this means." She nodded, and they walked back to the wagons.

They ate their "celebration" meal and their mood was light. When the sun went down, a fire was built in a hole to keep down the light. Andrew rose twice in a half-hour to circle the wagons with his rifle. Joanna looked up when he came back, but his look said he wasn't sure what was out there.

After coffee and applesauce and stale chocolate cake, Jeremiah opened his Bible and read to them.

" 'Blessed is the man whose strength is in thee; in whose heart are the ways of them. Who passing through the valley of Baca make it a well; the rain also filleth the pools.' " He paused, moved by the words and the significance of them to where they were now. He wound up, his voice trembling in the immensity of the reading, " 'For the Lord God is a sun and shield: the Lord will give grace and glory: no good thing will he withhold from them that walk uprightly. O Lord of hosts, blessed is the man that trusteth in thee.' "

He closed the Book slowly, as if his mind were still with the words. "Well, do I hear it from you?" he asked as always.

"Aye!" they chorused back.

Then he invited them to sing the last verse of "Old One Hundredth."

> Praise God from whom all blessings flow;
> Praise Him, all creatures here below;
> Praise Him above, ye heav'nly hosts;
> Praise Father, Son, and Holy Ghost. Amen.

"All right, then," he went on, and his dark eyes glowed as the joy of the moment continued to flood through him. "Now we can sleep. We put the guard on tonight as usual. Keep a sharp eye."

"Pa?" Timothy interjected. "Aren't you going to play your violin? You said you wouldn't play it until you got to Wolf Creek, remember?"

Jeremiah looked questioningly at him, then his face broadened in that smile again. "By Jove, Timothy, I plumb forgot. Let me have my fiddle out of the wagon, Elizabeth!"

"You should go to bed," Elizabeth urged him again, but she went to get the case and brought it to him. He took out the instrument carefully, coughed a few times, then put it under his chin and stroked it with the bow.

He played a couple of hymns, then wound up with "The Girl I Left Behind Me." He stamped his foot to the music of that tune, and the others clapped their hands with the rhythm. Joanna felt the lift in all of them, and it seemed like an omen of good things. Elizabeth soon called a halt to anymore celebrating, however, when she doused the fire as a sign that the festivities were finished.

Joanna got up and walked outside the wagons, looking around at the tree line. The moon was full, turning the night to a hue of near daylight. There was a softness in the warm air, fireflies flitting around the trees, snapping their flashing signals in salute to the moon. She felt Andrew beside her. They stood a long time saying nothing to each other—watching, listening as their trained ears were bound to do.

"Something strange going on," Andrew said then, his voice subdued almost to a whisper as if in awe. "I've been hearing those hoot owls a long time...all over the place...but mostly up there on the slope."

Joanna had heard them earlier as well, coming in regularly-spaced intervals. "Must be a hundred of them up there," she commented.

Then Jeremiah was there.

"Pa," Andrew began.

"I know," Jeremiah said quickly, peering around toward the sounds. "I heard them all through dinner. More out there now, I think, than that bunch we ran into a few days ago. We better get barricades under our wagons again tonight."

"Pa, sounds like more'n we can handle out there," Andrew reminded him.

"Well," Jeremiah said with a sigh, "we've come this far by the grace of God. I don't think He will let us be run over now. We face it when the time comes. We best start barricading. I'll get the boys on it."

It was long afterward as the night wore on with its peaceful glow of full moon and the puncturing dialogue of hoot owls up on the slope that Joanna stuffed her saddlebags. She put in a few pieces of dry beef and filled both canteens from the water barrels. Then she placed her saddle near Pointer at the far end of the wagon.

The young woman did not sleep as she lay in her bedroll next to Marcella under the wagon. She dared to entertain thoughts of surviving what was coming in the morning in order to get to Adobe Walls. She had studied the map. Quanah Parker was in the Palo Duro area, according to what she had heard at Dodge. Adobe Walls would be his target. That was less than a day's ride away. She could not believe that she had come this far to be denied what she had come to do.

"Joanna?" Marcella whispered softly from next to her.

"What?"

"Sounds like the whole Indian nation is out there."

"What are you talking about?"

"I know when coyotes or birds or whatever keep talking back and forth like that...well, that Indians are out there."

"Owls...all you hear is owls," Joanna replied.

"Joanna?"

"Yes?"

"What...what do Indians do to white women?"

Joanna paused. She needed Amos Chapman for that one. She thought carefully as to how to respond.

"I really don't know, Marcella..."

"I heard they torture and rape and make slaves of them...of us," Marcella continued, her voice shaky.

"You can't believe everything you hear. You got that revolver on you?"

Marcella turned toward her and lifted the gun from under the pillow. It gleamed menacingly in the moonlight. "I never shot anyone, Joanna," and her voice was pleading now. "I—I don't think I can kill a living thing...not even an Indian."

"Don't worry about it. You do what you have to do when the time comes. Anyway, maybe we won't have to shoot anybody. All you hear is owls, remember? Now, get some sleep."

"Will this ever end?" Marcella went on after a pause. "It seems our whole life has been spent lying under a wagon waiting for Indians to attack at sunup. Is this all there is?"

Joanna sighed. "Some days, yes...some days, no. It balances out in the end. Just take it a day at a time."

"Joanna?"

"Yes?"

There was a pause. "I love you."

Joanna felt her breath stop for a few seconds. Marcella had never expressed that to her before. Joanna finally turned her head and reached over to touch Marcella's blonde hair that was scraggly from the journey. She looked into the blue eyes clouded with fatigue and wide with the fear that had dogged them all for days. Then Marcella's mouth fixed into a tight line and the tears spilled down her cheeks. Joanna reached over and pulled her head gently down to her shoulder.

"Thank you for that, Marcella," she said, not quite sure how to handle her confession. "I love you too."

Marcella continued to shed tears, choking in those hiccupping sounds as she did so. "I—I wish Captain Tom Brainerd were here," she said then, sniffing loudly against her tears. "I never did get to say good-bye to him." Joanna did not respond. Then Marcella added, "You do believe he's handsome, don't you, Joanna?"

Joanna remained silent, unwilling to acknowledge that. She remembered Brainerd's eyes again as they were in the moonlight back at Dodge. Yet over him had hung that continual shroud of something from his past, something not yet settled in his mind, very much like her own.

"He's your kind of man," Joanna managed then, because Marcella wanted assurance that her judgment was right. But sensing her answer was inadequate, Joanna added, "Yes...of course...handsome."

"I knew you saw it in him," Marcella exclaimed, her tears drying quickly as if that was all that mattered here. "But—but I like Captain Billingsley too. I dreamed of him last night. Do you remember him?"

Death might be a few hours away, but for Marcella there was still time to weigh the choices of men in her life.

"Of course, Billingsley is right handsome," she assured Marcella. "And he looked at you with considerable interest."

"You think so?"

"He was hanging all over you at the reception at Dodge. He never took his eyes off you."

"Do you know he's up for major in three months?" Marcella went on eagerly. The owls kept hooting in the background, a constant reminder that all of this was a bit absurd. "He'd have his own command, a fort probably, or even a post in Washington with the adjutant general."

"You would do well to pay attention to him then," Joanna replied. "Not many officers have a future like Captain Billingsley."

"No...poor Captain Brainerd seems to be stuck with a rather shabby command, if that is a command."

"Well, then, choose wisely, Marcella," Joanna reminded her. "Now, get some sleep. The sun will soon be up."

It was quiet then. After a few minutes Joanna glanced at Marcella whose head was still on her shoulder. Joanna eased her slowly over to her pillow. For a moment she studied the face awash in the gold of the moonlight, turning her hair to the sheen of a halo. Maybe it was Marcella's naivete about this kind of life that made Joanna feel protective toward her.

Whatever it was, looking at her now, Joanna felt a certain sadness that it had to come down to this: Marcella fighting for her life under a wagon on some strange dry creek bed in a territory she had never heard of before they started out from Minnesota. And even if not to be killed, then to go through the torture as an Indian captive.

Joanna reached over once more and gently pushed a small golden curl back from Marcella's forehead. It was her first gesture of tenderness toward her cousin that she could remember, but it seemed appropriate now. Then she turned and stared out into the night again, catching the first hint of dawn over the hills. The hooting owls turned to mourning dove songs repeated back and forth.

She checked her rifle again, slung a belt of bullets over her shoulder, and crawled out from under the wagon to walk toward Jeremiah's wagon. He and Elizabeth were lying prone under it, their rifles resting on the barricade of toolboxes. Andrew was beyond them at the head of the wagon over a barricade of grain bags. The stock was tied to the other wagon that formed the base of the U-shape.

Elizabeth looked strange lying behind the barricade, her repeater pointed toward the rising slope in front of her. Something of the dignity and quiet sophistication that so characterized her was gone, but her smile at Joanna was the same one as always.

"You two girls all right over there?" Jeremiah asked softly.

"Yes, Mister," Joanna replied and moved on to drop down by Andrew. "See anything?"

"Take a look," he answered and handed her the single-barrel field glass. She looked through it toward the upper end of the slope where Indians were milling around on their horses. She couldn't count them all.

"Maybe we should try the buffalo gun again," she suggested. "There's one big Indian moving around up there who looks as if he might be the chief."

"Pa's got the gun," Andrew replied. "When they line up to move, he intends to drop a shot in front of them...maybe it will work. Lightning never strikes twice the same way. But who knows? Only the Lord..."

The predawn bird-calling was suddenly replaced by the sound of Indian drums beating a rapid, thudding tattoo, mixing with the war chant. It turned the warm, misty atmosphere to one of chilling foreboding. Joanna waited with Andrew, listening, feeling a shiver up her back. She looked at her cousin as he continued to study the slope ahead, wanting to say something to him for the years they had experienced together. But there didn't seem to be time for good-byes. So she simply punched him lightly on the arm, her way of saying, "I love you." Then she returned to Marcella.

It was about time for something to happen.

● ● ●

Captain Tom Brainerd halted his troop in a trough between two small prairie hills. He could hear the drumming and chanting. He glanced at Amos Chapman on his horse beside him. The scout had been out a night and a day tracking the Temples. He had only an hour ago intercepted Company L's line of march and led them to this point. The troopers bunched up in the gully, trying to keep their horses and equipment quiet. They were bone-weary from two nights and days of hard riding.

"What tribe is up there, Amos?" Tom asked, glancing at the eastern horizon to see how soon the sun would break.

"Kotsoteka Comanche," Amos replied. "Mebbe close to a hundred, maybe a little less. All dog soldiers wanting a fight...and the stock the Temples got."

"The Temples?"

"Down by the creek behind the wagons...two hundred yards down a grassy slope."

Tom moved his horse to the top of the hill in front of him, Amos following, Bonniface behind him. Amos pointed out the steeper crest of the hill beyond where the Indians were gathering. "Sergeant Bonniface?" Tom asked.

"Suh?"

"Form the charge. Send up my bugler and my guide and form up behind me up here. Do it as quietly as you can."

"Suh!"

In a few minutes the troop of Company L was lined up behind him side by side, revolvers in hand. Tom studied the hill in the light of the fading moon, noticing the Indians jockeying around for position on their mounts. He knew that when the drums stopped they would be on their charge against the Temples.

He swung his horse around and faced the long line of troopers. "All right, you horse soldiers," he said in a crisp voice that carried down the line on both sides of him. "This is what you were born for! This is what you rode all night and day for! We're going to charge right through a hundred Comanche up there on that hill and head for the Temple wagons on the other side! Then we're going to turn around and charge right back up the hill and chase them all the way to the North Canadian if we have to!"

He paused, all eyes on him now. Then he reached down and drew his sabre, lifting the blade straight up, even with his shoulder, the steel glimmering in the fading moonlight and the coming of the sun. "Nobody fires unless fired upon! We may be able to spook them off when we charge without firing a shot!"

Suddenly there was a booming sound that rolled a thundering bellow above the sound of the Indian drums and chanting. "That was a buffalo gun," the captain said. "All right! Bugler, sound the charge!"

Tom swung his big black horse around, pulled his hat down lower over his eyes, and pointed his sabre straight out in front of him. The bugler let out the blast.

"Ch-a-r-g-e!" Tom yelled and gave spurs to his horse. The troop let out a yell that rattled across the hills in a jagged mixture of sound that tore out the slowly rising curtain of dawn. Tom felt the excitement rush through him as he went to the gallop, the long blue line charging on his heels. The horses beat a ground-shaking rumble as they galloped over the one hill and then under the prodding of their riders made the rush up the other where the Indians were.

Tom saw the confusion among the Indians as the troopers thundered toward them, their yells enough to make any man's skin crawl. They tried to swing around to get into a new formation to meet the charge. But by then the troopers slammed through them, knocking Indian ponies and riders to one side. Shots rang out from the Indians. The troopers answered. They galloped down the slope, leaving the Indians on the hill in disarray, trying to form up again.

"Troop halt!" Tom yelled as they came up to the Temple wagons.

Tom's eyes darted around to see if everyone was accounted for there. Jeremiah and Elizabeth Temple were out front of their wagon, Jeremiah waving his hat, a big smile on his face. He saw Marcella come out from under a wagon, then the three boys. Where was Joanna?

Tom swung his horse around, facing the slope again. "Ready for the charge!" he yelled at his troopers. The troop urged their horses around to form the line. "Bugler, sound the charge!" Tom yelled.

The snapping sound of the bugle tore another huge chunk out of the dawn as the lava-colored sun peeked one eye over the eastern horizon. The red hues spilled over horses, gun metal, and wild-eyed troopers. Tom pointed his sabre forward again and yelled, "Ch-a-r-g-e!"

They thundered up the slope again at full gallop with the same piercing yells. The Indians at the top were still trying to organize. Now they saw the line coming at them again, soldiers with weapons in hand, mouths wide with their screams. It was too much. The chief tried to hold his band together, but the younger braves, apparently unaccustomed to the heat of battle, turned and fled down the other side of the hill. Finally it was turned into a total retreat.

Tom kept his troop on the heels of the Indians at a steady gallop. He drew his pistol and fired into the air. The troop galloping behind him did likewise. The explosive cracks of the firing added to the bedlam, and the Indians scattered in all directions in front of them, ignoring the discipline to always stay with their leader. Tom kept on them for more than a mile and then lifted his right hand and yelled, "Troop...halt!"

They came to a sliding stop, the dust kissed red by the sun boiling around them. Horses whinnied and snorted, still eager for the run, as tired as they were from the long march, the smell of battle fresh in their nostrils. The troopers kept yelling excitedly, shouting insults at the departing Indians, then laughing over their victory, congratulating each other. Tom knew they probably had never been in a charge like this. So now he let them savor it, for it would be an action they would remember a long time.

Captain Brainerd continued to sit his horse, waiting until the last of the Indians disappeared over the hills a long way off. He let the dust settle around them, then turned his horse and said to them, "You have again done me proud, gentlemen! And I thank you! But we have just begun. Adobe Walls is a half-day ride from here! We water up at the creek and be on our way. Column by twos!"

They swung around to double up behind him. "Forward—yo!"

After walking their horses back to the Temple wagons, Tom ordered Sergeant Bonniface to dismount the troop, then see to the watering of the horses. By now there was the fragrant odor of coffee through the morning air.

"Captain, please ask your men to help themselves to coffee," Elizabeth Temple told him. "There's a big urn over the fire, plenty for all of you...please!"

Tom turned toward his troopers who had dismounted now under Bonniface's order. Their tongues were hanging out, eyes eager for the coffee. They had not eaten or drunk much of anything for a day or more.

"Sergeant Bonniface, check for any wounded among the men," Tom said. "Then ten men at a time get some coffee."

"Yes, suh!" Bonniface said with a big smile that flashed in the sun. And he turned to count off the troopers who moved quickly to the big coffee urn by the fire, tin cups at the ready.

Jeremiah still stood by his wagon with Elizabeth.

"Captain," Jeremiah said to him, his voice cracking a bit with emotion, "that has to be the most thrilling thing I've ever seen— yes, sir! And I might add, you saved our lives, but I expect you know that."

"Not bad for a Negro troop, I'd say, sir," Tom replied with a slow smile.

Jeremiah looked a bit embarrassed, but Elizabeth seemed to revel in it as if a point had been made.

"I'm sorry, captain, for what I said back there—"

"Mr. Temple, I probably would have felt the same. But every man has to have his chance to prove himself."

"Hear, hear," Jeremiah agreed.

"By the way, where is Miss Joanna?" Tom asked, taking off his hat to slap it against his right leg, getting the dust out of it.

Jeremiah turned around and glanced inside the wagon formation. He then looked over at Elizabeth with a question in his eyes.

"Joanna!" he called. When there was no answer, he and Elizabeth walked inside the wagon compound, concerned now.

"When did you see her last?" the captain asked in a calm voice.

"Well..." Jeremiah scratched his beard, trying to recall. "She was under that wagon with Marcella last I saw..."

"She's gone," Andrew spoke up then from where he stood a few feet away.

"Gone where, son?" Jeremiah demanded.

"I dunno, Pa," Andrew replied. "I saw her mount Pointer and head that way across the creek...about the time the troopers made their first charge down the slope."

"Why didn't you stop her?" the older man said impatiently.

Andrew shrugged. "I figure Joanna knows what she's after, Pa." Jeremiah looked confused by his answer.

Tom glanced toward the creek, his mind trying to splice what pieces he could fit from what he knew about Joanna. "Did she know anything about Adobe Walls?"

"No more'n what you said back at Dodge, captain," Jeremiah replied. "About those hunters and that Quanah Parker maybe going after them..."

"That might be it," Tom said, and he turned to move for his horse.

"Captain?" Jeremiah asked, holding him. "You got real reason to believe she's heading for Adobe?"

"Mr. Temple," Tom replied, mounting his horse, "Joanna showed real interest in Quanah Parker when she spent some time with my scout the first day out. She asked a lot of questions about Parker...Chapman answered some. But she got excited about some of those answers, and she's sure Parker was in that Comanche band that killed her parents some time back. She heard Quanah is going to hit Adobe, so she's probably going to try to get to him there."

"Oh, Jeremiah," Elizabeth said with a mourning sound.

"Sergeant Bonniface?" Tom called to his sergeant who was standing by the line of soldiers waiting for their coffee.

"Suh!"

"Assign fifteen men to stay here with the Temples. Choose your best corporal to stay with them. You take the rest of the troop in ten minutes and get to Adobe Walls on the double. You know the way?"

"Yes, suh!"

"Chapman, I will need you!" Tom added. Chapman vaulted his painted sorrel in one quick move as if anxious to get going.

"Captain?" Jeremiah asked again, almost pleading now. "Why would Joanna go to Adobe Walls...why Parker? What can she do by herself?"

Tom looked down at him. "She's trying to settle something in her mind, something she's been carrying a long time," the officer replied.

"Captain," Jeremiah said quickly, reaching his hands out in a pleading way. "I'd be obliged if you bring her back safe," and his face looked gray as he coughed harshly.

"I'll do my best, sir," Tom said. Then he moved his horse out quickly to the creek and across it with Chapman following.

12

Joanna kept Pointer at an even canter over the hills and prairies, following the south shore of Wolf Creek and leaning toward the southwest where she figured Adobe Walls should be. Now and then she stopped to give Pointer a breather, trying to conserve his strength in case she had to outrun any Indians. At those times, Joanna took out Jeremiah's map and studied it carefully. She would have to make it by dead reckoning but figured she was only a few hours away if she could keep up the pace.

The sun was just halfway up over the rim of the eastern horizon now. She saw Indian signs all along the trail but did not stop to check them. Her one intent was to keep moving, staying away from the Indians if she could. She knew her chances were not all that good of making it through without a fight—or making it at all. Still, Joanna's mind was honed to it: She had to get to Adobe Walls. People there would know where Parker was or maybe Parker would attack Adobe. In that case, she would have her day.

Figuring she had about an hour's start on anyone attempting to pursue her, Joanna expected Tom Brainerd to be right behind her with his troopers. But his troopers and horses had been on the move for days. They would not be able to keep up a steady pace.

She kept Pointer moving, picking her way through protective gullies, using the tree lines for cover when she could. At times she let Pointer out to a gallop on open prairies. At one point Joanna, ducking into a clump of cottonwoods and mesquite, watched Indians moving away from her in the distance. In three more hours she caught sight again of a band of Indians moving a half-mile to her left, heading in the same direction she was. Were they part of a major gathering of Indians further ahead—perhaps to join Quanah in his move on Adobe?

Suddenly Joanna heard the sound of gunfire. She reined in and listened, then nudged Pointer straight ahead in the ribs. She charged through a line of cottonwoods and mesquite, up a sharp rocky slope, ran the rim of it and came to a small tree line. The firing was coming from her left and below the rim. She pushed Pointer up higher and dismounted.

Henry in hand, Joanna crawled under a sandy hummock, shifting her belt of ammunition around over her shoulder and under one arm. She peered through a low scrub of weeds and buffalo grass to the buildings below that had to be Adobe Walls. There were three separate buildings, rectangular soddies, sitting squat in the beating sun. There was a corral to the left of the building to her extreme left and there were a couple of covered wagons out front.

The Indians were dashing in on the buildings on horseback, firing point-blank, then falling back. The rushes continued, but the gunfire from the buildings seemed heavy and very accurate. There were some Indians lying still in the sun-baked, sandy yard out front.

She continued to watch from her thin cover above them, fascinated by the horsemanship of the Indians. She had a strong sense that they were Comanche—and Quanah Parker's tribe. They rode their ponies recklessly across the raking fire from the buildings, leaning way down under their horses' necks to shoot back. She watched one Indian back his horse into the door of one of the low-roofed soddies and urge it to kick its hind legs against it. The door held. A shot from inside hit the Indian, and he went down.

But Joanna's eyes were now fixed on one Indian, the colored feathers of his warbonnet standing out from the others, his dark hair hanging long around his face. Her heart skipped some, and she pulled her rifle up closer. She waited, wanting to be sure, yet feeling certain with every passing second. Joanna realized she was in a tight spot overlooking the fighting just below her, not more than thirty feet away. Once she was spotted by the Indians, they would be on her in a minute. The fighting went on, the Indians making the charge again and again, being beaten back, then taking up positions behind a watering trough or the wagons to continue firing. There were loud thundering cannonades now and then which meant that buffalo guns were being used by the hunters.

Still she waited, watching, her eyes continually following that one Indian who kept urging his braves on, sometimes charging the buildings himself, oblivious to the heavy fire. It was when he turned toward her that the sun was full on him, and she saw the flash of gold from around his neck. Her heart took a quick jump. He rode off in another direction, turned and came back again—once more in the full glare of the sun...and once more the brilliant coruscation of gold.

The young woman took a deep, agonizing breath. "Oh, God, forgive me," she said softly as she lifted her rifle slowly to rest on the sandy lip of the mound she hid behind. "But this is the day You have made for me!" She had him in her sights. "Quanah Parker, remember it well if you can," she whispered, the sweat sliding down her chin, greasing her hand on the stock of the rifle. But as she squeezed the trigger, the Indian's horse jumped. The bullet caught the animal, and he went down, dust boiling around him. She saw Quanah crawl to the protection of a wagon. There was no second chance for another shot. The horse rose slowly, apparently only grazed by the bullet, and limped away.

Joanna felt the stab of disappointment run through her. She watched as a few Indians ran over to Parker. One of them was pointing up toward her own position. She had been seen! She got up quickly, vaulted onto Pointer's back, and charged down the slope straight for the back door of one of the buildings closest to her. Dismounting and pounding her rifle butt on the door, she shouted, "Let me in! Let me in!"

• • •

Tom Brainerd and Amos Chapman rode at a fast gallop most of the way, finding it rather easy to pick up the tracks of Joanna's shod pony. They stopped now and then to examine the Indian pony tracks as well, giving their horses time to blow. Then they were off again. Tom figured they had closed the time gap lost back at the Temple camp. The sun was rising higher over them. Adobe Walls had to be close now.

Then they heard the gunfire ahead. It was too late, Tom knew then. The Comanches had already attacked. Any hope he had of bringing peace was about gone. But his concern now was for Joanna. He pushed his horse at a gallop, staying with the signs of Joanna's horse, Chapman by his side. They rode up the rimrock incline and dismounted, crawling to the sandy hump to look down over the yard of Adobe. The firing was more sporadic now. There were Indian bodies on the ground, and he recognized the war paint of the Comanche on them.

Amos nudged him and pointed to tracks in the sand. They were of a shod horse, moving over the sand and down the slope to the back of the building directly below.

"Chapman, find cover up here," Tom said. "I'm going down." Chapman nodded.

Tom mounted his horse again, took out his revolver and charged down the slope to the nearest building on the east side. He saw a window with barricades of grain sacks behind it.

"Hey, inside!" he shouted. "Captain Tom Brainerd of the Fourth! Let me in before I get skinned alive out here!"

A head showed uncertainly above the barricades of grain sacks and then a long rifle barrel poked out. A pair of steady blue eyes leveled down at him over the sights.

"That you, Billy?" Tom called out. "Billy Dixon? It's me, Tom Brainerd! You gonna let me stand out here all day?"

The rifle lowered. "Tom Brainerd?" Billy called back, still not sure.

"Billy, let's argue about it inside!" Tom urged, turning to look for Indians.

"Okay...hurry up!" Billy finally yelled back.

Tom hoisted himself over the sill and up the grain sacks, falling down over the parapet to the floor. He picked himself up and turned to Billy Dixon. Tom hadn't seen Billy since their early days together in Wyoming when they were both too young for Indian chasing.

"Now, Tom," Billy said, bewildered, "how come you ride in here? I thought you was in Fort Abraham Lincoln waitin' for the noose!"

"I was...but they lifted the house arrest and sent me out here to get you buffalo hunters out of here so Quanah will stop killing every white face between here and Dodge."

"Aw, shucks, Tom, a buffalo hide gets lots a' money, you know that. Anyway, don't look like we're gonna stay here much longer. Indians don't take much likin' to us right now, that's fer sure!"

"Billy," Tom pressed him then, "I'm looking for someone who might have ridden in here a couple of hours ago maybe...a white...riding a tan gelding..."

Billy glanced out the window, then said, "Yeah...a guy named Joe somethin' or other...over at the general store next to us. Came poundin' on the back door...almost didn't get in. Indians been poundin' our doors all day..."

"Billy," Tom interrupted, anxious now to know where Joanna was. Just then he heard the sound of a bugle in the distance. A bugle out here? the captain wondered. His own troop was at least a couple of hours behind him, so it couldn't be them. "Billy, I hear a bugle out there," he said, still not quite sure, but his mind fastening on the fact with some amazement.

"That's fer sure," Billy said and turned toward him. "Been blowin' all day since they jumped us after dawn..."

"What's an Indian doing blowing a bugle?" Tom prodded, feeling his mind lay hold of it like the closing of a fist.

"Ain't no Indian," Billy replied laconically. "Probably some soldier taken up with a squaw in Quanah's outfit or the Cheyenne. Don't blow very good, mind you, but he knows all the calls, all right..."

Tom continued to savor that statement for a long minute, then he came back with, "Billy, about this—this Joe?"

"Oh, yeah, well, Quanah got his horse shot out from under him, then I seen his braves haul him off. Fight's been gone from them for a while now. I think most a' them are headin' back to Palo Duro...only a few Comanche left out there takin' potshots at us..."

"What about Joe, Billy?" Tom interjected. "Remember?"

"Sure...well, that feller, soon's Quanah retreated off the field, his warriors with him, he ups and tears out the general store and takes off after them Comanche. Craziest thing..."

"How long ago?"

Billy paused, frowning, glancing out the window into the yard again. "About an hour maybe. No way he's gonna get near Parker. They'll be watchin' their back trail on the retreat. I sure wouldn't want to land in Quanah's lap after the lickin' he took..."

Tom looked out the window for his horse. He was still standing there, waiting. Tom climbed up over the sacks to the window, paused and looked down at Billy. "Billy, there's a company of horse soldiers right behind me. They're here to see to it that you hunters clear out. I don't want any trouble here. Understand?"

"Aw, Tom," Billy pleaded. "I got a stack a' hides out there in the wagon to deliver to Dodge—"

"Then take your hides and skedaddle!" Tom yelled back as he jumped to the ground and hopped up on his horse. He glanced once out to the front yard, then spurred his horse up the hill. Chapman moved out of his cover to meet him.

"Palo Duro!" Tom yelled at him. "She's chasing Quanah's Comanches!"

Then they both urged their mounts into a gallop over the rim, heading north. There wasn't much time, Tom knew. Joanna would ride straight into that Quahadi bunch to get Quanah. He was sure of that. The thought of her doing that—and the slow death she would surely face—made him push his horse even harder.

● ● ●

They tracked the Quahadis for more than an hour when Chapman lifted his hand to halt. They were on a high slope of trees and rock descending from a tall butte. The sun was going to late afternoon, beginning to cast long shadows here and there. Then Tom heard the drums in the distance below them. He looked at Chapman, whose face remained impassive, his eyes studying the valley below.

"They stop," he said. "Means they take time to dance." Tom knew that they wouldn't stop to dance unless it was for something special. Could it be Joanna? Had they taken her?

They moved on forward through the tall Texas pines, keeping their eyes sharp for sign of Indians. They paused, dismounted, and crouched to look through the brush at the encampment.

There were a few tepees and a big fire burning in the center of the circle. The braves were dancing and circling the fire. Amos tapped Tom on the arm and pointed to the right of the fire.

Tom's breathing shallowed, his heart quickened. Joanna was tied to a post, hands behind her, as the squaws circled, jabbing her with sticks. She stood proudly tall against the post, defying them, and ignoring their taunts. Her dark hair streamed down over her shoulders, and occasionally a squaw would pull on it.

To the left a few braves were running their horses in practice sprints, indicating that Quanah might let them compete for Joanna, if he decided not to take her himself.

"What's the worst?" Brainerd asked Chapman.

Chapman paused. "Mebbe she go with one of the braves who wins the race. Mebbe they hang her over the fire for a while..."

Tom took off his hat and wiped the sweat forming on his forehead. "Okay...I'm going down there." He took his rifle from the saddle, then his sabre and revolver, handing them all to Chapman.

Chapman took them hesitantly, his dark eyes warning Tom not to enter the camp unarmed. "They roast you with her," he said bluntly.

"Well, so be it," Tom replied, mounting. "It's what I have to do. You stay put. If you see us both going over the fire, head back to Adobe and report to Sergeant Bonniface. May the sun set well on you, Amos."

"God go with you, Tom Brainerd," Chapman said softly, lifting his right hand with three fingers raised in a familiar salute.

• • •

Joanna felt the pain again as the sticks jabbed her ribs, then her stomach, and then down around her legs. She felt the heat of the fire a few feet away. The drums were louder and faster, picking up the tempo for the finale—whatever it was. The yelling of the Indians was becoming a screeching sound. A squaw flashed a toothless grin at her and then spit in her face, laughing fiendishly. Joanna glanced to the larger tepee where Quanah sat on a blanket, legs crossed, watching the dance, turning his head slowly now and then to look at her. The medicine man had put some kind of poultice on his back where a bullet had apparently nicked him.

When Quanah looked at her, Joanna saw only an expressionless face, but the intense stare from those blue-black eyes promised only death. She had followed the Indians for more than an hour before running into the ambush Quanah had left behind on his back trail. It had been careless to trail them directly. And now she would pay for that indiscretion, as all white people in this territory did. The pitch of the drums and dancing rose, and the squaws beat harder on her until she had to bite her lip to keep back the screams.

Then suddenly everything stopped. The silence was eerie. Only the loud crackling of the fire and a barking dog sounded behind her. She closed her eyes. It was surely time for that final gruesome act of torture.

Nothing happened. Nobody moved. Slowly she opened her eyes. The squaws were all turned to the right, looking across the open area away from Quanah's tepee. The braves had halted their frenzied dancing so suddenly that they still stood frozen in their various poses.

Then she saw the horse and rider coming slowly from the far end of the camp, across the sandy clearing. She saw a yellow bandanna showing brightly through the open neck of a buckskin shirt. But Joanna couldn't be mistaken about the tall figure in the saddle, the way he rode in that relaxed bent of his, his body leaning a bit to the right.

She opened her mouth to yell to him to forget it, that there was nothing here that he could do for her, that he was only asking for the same kind of torture and death. But her tongue wouldn't loosen, her throat constricted, caught in the pain she felt and the rush of something else that was like a sob.

"Tom Brainerd, you are a fool," she said hoarsely, mostly to herself.

She looked up at him as he pulled his horse in front of the warriors clustering together between him and Quanah. Then his voice carried sharply to Quanah, "I come in peace, Quanah! I carry no weapons."

The silence hung over the camp. Nobody moved. Then Joanna saw Quanah rise slowly, folding his arms across his chest and looking long and hard at Brainerd.

Noting the bright stripe down the officer's pants, he replied in halting English, "Does yellow legs find life so cheap that he would ride unarmed among his enemies?" Then he repeated the line in Comanche, and the hundred or so braves and squaws let out piercing, defiant yells, lifting their rifles and hatchets at Brainerd. Joanna noted, though, that he did not flinch or move, keeping his eyes on Quanah.

"Is the great Quanah a barking dog in torturing that white woman?" he called back.

Quanah turned his head and looked at Joanna. "Maybe yellow legs wishes the white woman for himself?" he asked, challenging Brainerd. He said something to one of his warriors nearby, and the Indian marched over to Joanna, pulled his knife and cut the ropes that held her to the post. Then he took her roughly by the arm and pulled her along, finally flinging her down in the dirt in front of Tom Brainerd's horse. She stayed there and slowly looked up at Brainerd. "You didn't have to come," she said.

"I know that," he replied quietly, his eyes glancing at her and turning back to Quanah.

Joanna saw Quanah approach in long, purposeful strides. He stopped ten feet from Brainerd, looking up at him on his horse. "If yellow legs wishes the white woman, then he must fight to the death for her. That is the Quahadi warrior's honor!" He repeated it in a loud voice in Comanche, and the warriors let out another whooping scream.

Tom waited, savoring it, then he dismounted slowly. An Indian moved up and led his horse away. Tom took off his hat and slapped it once against his right leg, then tossed it to the ground. "I seek no death here," he said to Quanah. The drums began to beat a rapid tempo pounding out the death signal. A squaw grabbed Joanna by the buckskin shirt and dragged her roughly aside.

Quanah ignored Brainerd's appeal and slowly took off his warrior's breastplate of beads and feathers. He was bare to the waist, the strong muscles of his shoulders and arms standing out like ropes in the light of the sinking sun. Tom unbuckled his sabre belt and tossed it aside. Quanah pulled an eight-inch knife and threw it to the ground at Tom's feet. It landed, the blade penetrating the ground. Then he took the same-sized knife from one of his warriors and stood ready in a half crouch.

Tom unbuttoned his buckskin trail shirt, moving to put his back to Joanna to better see Quanah in the sun that had been hitting his eyes. He folded the shirt carefully and laid it a few feet away, as if he were sure he would be wearing it again. He was tanned brown by the sun, his back and shoulders showing tight-knotted muscles.

As Brainerd backed to the right again, Joanna gasped. The sun's rays caught the flashing gold around his neck. Feeling the shock shatter her with the force of a club, she glanced at Quanah. He had the same necklace! They both wore the same golden eagle!

A vibrating tremor rattled through her now as Quanah noticed the chain around Brainerd's neck. His eyes widened as he stared at it. She glanced back at Brainerd. He was in a low crouch, the knife held loosely in his right hand, his eyes fastened on Quanah's necklace. Then Quanah let out a screaming yell and charged Brainerd. The Indians yelled for the victory they expected. Brainerd was not prepared for the assault as Quanah caught him below the waist. Brainerd went down on his back with a loud grunt. Quanah straddled him across the chest, his left hand holding Tom's knife hand to the ground, the other pushing the blade of his own knife to touch the gold chain around Tom's neck.

"Where did you get this!" Quanah snarled, his voice filled with hate and outrage.

"I don't know," Tom responded, not fighting Quanah at all now. "I had it...I had it for a long time...as long as I can remember...as a child..."

"You lie, yellow legs!" Quanah countered, his knife moving up against Tom's throat. "Who did you steal chain from?" he demanded. Suddenly he reached across Tom's body with his left hand and twisted Tom's left arm around to look at it. He stared a long time. Then slowly he stood up, sheathing his knife, backing up a few steps to stare long and hard at the captain. A low murmur of wonder began among the Indians like the sound of approaching locusts, and then it went very still among them.

"You!" Quanah's voice cut the air, a note of awe in it, maybe even some fear. "You...you are Tanna! My long-lost brother!" The sound of the name "Tanna" triggered another low hum among the Indians. Then Quanah lifted his head and hands to the pink hews of the sun against the cluster of white clouds overhead, and his voice rose almost in a singsong prayer: "This yellow legs has the sign of my father, Nocona, on his arm, the mark of fire given to all firstborn males born into Nocona's family! He has the sign of my mother, Cynthia Parker, in the gold eagle around his neck! This is Tanna, my long-lost brother. He has returned as the medicine said he would!"

He paused and looked down at Brainerd who still lay on the ground. The captain was leaning on his left elbow, his face expressing the wonder and shock of Quanah's revelation. When the Indian leader repeated the same words in Comanche, the silence held for a long time. It was broken by the sound of a rising chant among them, and they all fell prostrate to the ground, facing Brainerd.

For Joanna, it was a moment of terror and confusion.

"Rise, my brother," Quanah said then in his broken English. "You will eat and drink with me, your brother Quanah, in my tepee."

Then Quanah shouted, in English, apparently for Tom's sake: "Let the drums tell the message far to the mountains in the north and west, to the deserts in the south, to the wind that blows from the east! May every chief's lodge know that Tanna, son of Nocona and Cynthia Parker, has returned from his journey to the stars!" Then he repeated it in Comanche.

The camp broke into a flurry of celebration, the mood of terror and wonder changing quickly. The cooking fires were started as women scurried to prepare the feast. The drums beat out a new tattoo, and wild, frenzied dancing began again around the huge council fire.

Tom slowly stood up. Quanah walked over to him and put his two hands on his shoulders. "My brother shall join me now," he said. Tom put his hands on Quanah's shoulders in return, an expression of their common blood.

Quanah dropped his hands and turned to walk back to his tepee. When Tom hesitated, Quanah turned to him in question.

"I wish the woman to join us," Tom said. Quanah looked both astonished and mystified at the request, glancing at Joanna still sitting on the ground. Then, with some reluctance, he nodded his approval.

Tom retrieved his discarded buckskin shirt, put it on, and retied the yellow bandanna around his neck. After he put on his hat, he reached down, extending his hand to Joanna.

She hesitated. "I can't believe any of this," she gritted her teeth and refused his hand. "So maybe it was *you* riding around my parents' soddy. You both wear that same chain..."

He stood over her, still bending toward her, his hand extended. "Joanna, I was fishing up on the Colorado with my father during that time—my adopted father, I guess. I didn't even have a horse until I was fifteen...and he was half-mule. If you think I can figure this all out, you are wrong. But there is no question that I am Tanna, Quanah's lost brother."

She hesitantly gave him her hand, and he pulled her up. "If you think I'm going to sit down and break bread with that savage, you are mistaken," she snapped at him, pulling her hand away.

"Then the squaws will have you again," he replied. "If that's what you want..."

Joanna looked at the Indian women watching her even as they started preparations for cooking. She didn't relish the looks on their faces. When she glanced back at Tom again there was that trace of smile on his mouth, the same shafts of light coming from those blue eyes. But there was a light of sudden awareness in them now, a realization of his heritage.

"So come on," he said softly to her and turned toward the tepee where Quanah had already disappeared. "I need someone to witness this." He took her hand in his. His hand was strong and firm. It seemed natural and easy for him to lead her, but she didn't know why. Yet, beyond that strange feeling, the storms continued to swirl in her brain. Quanah Parker was still her enemy! He still had to account for what he had done to her family. And as she moved into Quanah's tepee, Joanna immediately felt repelled by the thought of sitting down to eat food with him.

Quanah had his council of seven warriors next to him. She and Brainerd sat, with Tom next to Quanah, and she next to Tom. Outside, the celebration continued with the drums pounding feverishly, the shouts of the warriors mingling with the sound of the drums. Quanah began by recalling, in English and then in Comanche, the day Tanna was lost from the tribe, disappearing in the night.

"I only remember my home on the Colorado," Tom explained. "I do remember walking a long way in grass, but nothing else . . . except the two people who raised me from a child."

So it went for an hour, Brainerd and Quanah exchanging in English, then Quanah interpreting to the council. Joanna ate her rabbit stew, but the food stuck in her throat. Her mind still could not abide sitting there, eating with that *one* Indian she had kept in her mind for eight years.

Suddenly the flap of the tepee opened and a figure in tattered buckskins fell inside. Joanna stared at him. Underneath the layers of dark wood smoke on his face and the deep tan from the sun, she realized that he was white.

The warrior who stepped in behind him explained in Comanche to Quanah. The man in buckskins stood slowly.

"Well," Brainerd said in a tone of rising interest, "I do believe I am seeing Corporal Jack Davison!"

"You know this man?" Quanah asked.

Joanna looked at the man, at his scruffy blonde beard and watery blue-gray eyes. A bugle hung on a strap from his left shoulder. "I believe he knows me well," Brainerd went on, his voice a short, clipping sound of accusation.

"This man has Quahadi squaw for wife," Quanah explained. "He try to steal food and buffalo robes and leave camp . . ."

"Yes," Brainerd responded, as if he had expected that. "He probably saw me here earlier. Well, Davison, I trust your memory still works well. You do remember Fort Morrow, your message to me that day five long years ago? The message that resulted in twenty troopers killed and my wife with them?"

Davison blinked at him. "Sir," he offered, "I don't recall—"

"Corporal Davison out of Fort Lyon five years ago, with a message from Major Mark McDonnel, officer in charge! To me, Major Tom Brainerd then. I looked into your face then, Davison, and you are the same man right now."

"Sir," Davison said, his eyes going wide now in the realization of being caught. "It wasn't me, sir..."

"Your face has stayed in my brain a long time, Davison—"

"Sir, I mean it was me, sir," Davison stammered. "But Major McDonnel offered me twenty gold eagles, tells me to deliver the message to you, and then get lost in the Indian nations or be hung for desertion if I showed up at any army post—"

"For twenty gold eagles you let me rot in Fort Lincoln with a death sentence hanging over me for dereliction of duty and the memory of my dead wife?"

Davison's mouth began to quiver in the awful truth. He bowed his head in defeat. "Sir, I didn't know..."

"Quanah, my brother," Tom said, turning to Parker then, "I wish this man bound over to me for lying, desertion from duty, and causing the death of my woman five years ago. I wish to return him to Fort Leavenworth for punishment."

Quanah looked at Davison, hesitated, then finally shrugged. "Quahadi have no time for crooked tongue," he said shortly. He ordered the warrior to take Davison out.

Joanna looked at Brainerd in amazement. His face was set in hard lines, but his eyes had grown softer. She now knew something of the secret he had locked inside for so long, the reason for his tension with Colonel McDonnel at Dodge. She had learned enough to understand the melancholy in his eyes at times. And she sensed right then a certain sudden quietness in him beyond what he had ever shown before.

The captain said no more to her or to Quanah about Davison. He turned instead to the conversation with Quanah again. So the evening bore on. But for Joanna the pressure continued to mount in her until finally she whispered tersely, "Ask him about killing my parents in Kansas."

The council was smoking the pipe now, and Tom took it, puffed once, offered it to her. She shook her head. He handed the pipe back to Quanah, then looked at her again, reticent about broaching that subject with Parker.

"I really don't think he would remember," he cautioned her.

"Ask him," she insisted. "I want to know. Either you ask him, or I will!"

Quanah had turned toward them, catching the urgency in her voice. Tom cleared his throat and turned to the chief. "This woman claims you were in a war party when you were twelve years old or so...up in Kansas near the Arkansas River. You and other Comanche braves killed her parents. She says you burned her home..."

Quanah's eyes turned and fixed on her intently. There was something now in those eyes that said he was either trying to recall or that he knew even now.

"How she know it be me?" he asked Tom.

"The eagle necklace around your neck, like his," Joanna cut in quickly, nodding at Tom, feeling the tension pick up within her again. "I remember it...you wore it then as you do now."

Quanah kept studying her intently. Then he said something to the warrior on his immediate right. The Indian rose and went out, returning with an aging Indian woman. Quanah spoke to her in Comanche. When she hesitated, he snapped at her again, and she exited slowly. A few minutes later the woman reappeared, carrying something wrapped in a blanket. Quanah motioned to her to put it down in front of Joanna.

"Look!" Quanah commanded Joanna.

Joanna reached out, hesitated, then pulled the blanket off. There lay a small dark mahogany box, a bit scarred and scratched from too much travel, but still intact. Her memory suddenly saw that box on a table beneath the lamplight in a Kansas settler's soddy. Joanna gasped as she lifted the cover to reveal the tintype of her mother and father still pasted on the inside cover. It was her mother's sewing box. The sewing things were still in it, even the half-finished doily, the one her mother was working on the night before the awful massacre.

"It is yours?" Quanah asked then, demand in his voice.

"Yes," Joanna choked it out.

"I was there," Quanah said then. "At thirteen years...it is the way of the Comanche boy who must prove his manhood to enter the tribe. To kill. It was not the wish of my mother nor my father, Nocona. But I do it as the Comanche teach. I take box...to give to my mother...to show I did not like killing white people who are not warriors..." He paused. "I knew you be there."

Joanna looked up through the mist in her eyes. "Wh—what?"

"I see you in the grass. I do not tell other braves...but I take box from house. I take to my mother. She say to me one day I give box to you, tell you I did not have a proud heart that day. I did not feel like a warrior or Comanche or...a man."

Joanna lowered the lid on the box, the tears streaming down her cheeks despite her attempts to check them. There was nothing more to say. All the years of waiting, the hate, the vengeance building inside her, poisoning her soul, destroying her sense of self and life. Now it had all spilled out here with her tears that fell on the box she was clutching to her chest.

"Why," she stammered then, swallowing hard, "why do you kill innocent white people? Do you take pleasure in it now when you say you did not then?"

Quanah continued studying her intently. "White people now come, take our food, shelter," he said, his voice sharp and challenging. "The white man does not keep his word. He says peace, but then he take our land, our buffalo. We fight now to live...even to death!"

"I waited eight years to kill you," Joanna insisted, as if he owed her something more. Yet, she knew that he had done a great thing, beyond his role as an Indian chief, to try to make that past right. "Only God knows how I missed you at Adobe Walls, grazing your horse instead and only nicking you."

Quanah said nothing, his eyes slowly turning away from her to stare into the fire.

"I—I think I better get out of here," she said to Brainerd.

He stood with her. "There's a tepee next door for you. You will be safe there."

"Are you staying here? With your...brother?" she asked.

He led her to the tepee entrance, leaned over with her as she moved to go out, his face close to hers.

"Be ready at sunup," he whispered. "We will move then. I still have Davison to take care of."

She nodded, then glanced over her shoulder at Quanah still staring stone-faced into the fire. Then she left.

• • •

Joanna awoke with a start. She blinked against the early morning sun stabbing through the tepee opening. Tom Brainerd stood over her and it was strangely silent. She pushed the buffalo robe off her and took the hand he extended to her.

When they stepped outside, there was little sign of the Indians—a few smoking ashes from the camp fires the previous night, a few travois poles. That was all.

She followed Brainerd as he walked slowly across the camp site, his head down, as if he were mourning the loss of his brother, Quanah. As they walked, Joanna saw Davison sitting down, his back to the same post to which she had been tied the previous day, his arms bound behind him with ropes. A few feet away Amos Chapman stood by the pile of ashes that had once been the council fire.

Tom stopped and glanced up to the hill overlooking the camp from the north. Joanna looked up too.

He was sitting on his pony, tall and straight, a repeater rifle in his right hand. He remained in that pose a long time, looking down at his brother, Tanna. Then he slowly lifted his rifle and held it high above his head. Tom took off his hat and lifted it in response.

The moment would be frozen forever in the memories of both men, Joanna knew. They would probably never see each other again except perhaps on a field of battle. Then Quanah turned his horse and disappeared over the crest of the hill.

Joanna glanced at Brainerd. "I'm sorry," she offered, knowing something of what he had to be feeling.

He stared a long time at the place where Quanah had sat his horse. Then he slapped his hat against his leg and put it back on his head.

"Get Davison mounted up, Chapman," he said to his scout. "Time to move." Joanna watched him walk toward his own horse, his step quick, catlike, his legs moving in easy strides. His reunion and mourning had come together in so short a span. But he would not mention it again, she knew. Captain Tom Brainerd was that kind of man—one who knew the sorrows of previous loss. And he would let time have its way in the healing.

13

Joanna lay under the wagon on top of her bedroll. The Temple camp was quiet now. The celebration that Jeremiah had insisted on having in honor of her and Captain Brainerd's safe return had been one of feasting, music, and Jeremiah's special commentary from the Good Book.

They had returned that afternoon, only two days after leaving the Temple camp. Even though it was after midnight, it was still very hot. No breeze stirred under the full moon and the air smelled of the parched land, an odor of dust mingled with burned grass. Joanna felt the ache in her legs and across her back where the Indian women had struck her. Her body throbbed in almost rhythmic beat, reminding her of all the shocking scenarios she had witnessed.

Staring up at the moon, she still tried to piece the events all

171

together. All of her eight years of waiting had come down into a few hours of climactic events, spinning away from her into new shapes that she could not fit into a congruent whole. With it had come a feeling of emptiness. There was nothing left to do. None of what she planned had ended correctly. Though the deep, nagging need for vengeance had dissipated within her, there was nothing to replace that wheel that had propelled her for so long.

Jeremiah had summed up her own feelings earlier around the fire, just before the troopers of Company L were to share in the Temples' homemade banquet.

"I started this journey," he said to all of them, "with a word from the Book, a promise of God. It says, 'When a man's ways please the Lord, He maketh even His enemies to be at peace with Him.' We now have arrived safely to this promised land with not a hair of our heads singed...close, yes! God has fulfilled His promise to us all. Only He can quiet the savage heart in His own way. I sweat a lot of fright myself coming on this journey, but no one can tell me how we got by that band of renegades that was after us the other side of the Canadian. And no one can explain how you men of Company L came on us at the right minute when those hundred braves were gathering up on the slopes to run us over.

"I can only explain it in God. God works in mysterious ways to deliver His own. And before we partake of this food, song, and fellowship, I want to thank you for your help and being God's instrument in our deliverance. I trust you will know His continuing safety as you go on. Now let us pray..."

The "savage heart" Joanna remembered well. In the past, even until the last day or two, she would have argued with Jeremiah about how much God could tame the lion in the heart of an Indian like Quanah. Now she knew that it could happen. Perhaps it was only for a moment, but in that moment, she had seen a fierce Indian chief demonstrate a touch of human compassion beyond which she thought he could ever be capable. It confused her some now as all shattered, preconceived notions usually did. The peace she longed for in the fulfilling of her vendetta had come in an entirely different way, far less violent. She needed time, however, to appreciate it fully.

"Joanna?" Marcella asked in a low tone of half-sleep from beside her.

"Hmmmmm?"

"I'm so glad you're back. I was sure I'd never see you again...
ever."

"I'm glad, too, Marcella. I thought for a while I would never see
you either."

There was a long pause. Then Marcella rose on her elbow and
leaned toward Joanna, that familiar pose Joanna had known for
so long.

"I heard Pa talking with Captain Brainerd just before supper," she said, keeping her voice low, like a child sharing a secret. "You know that dispatch rider who was here from Dodge
when you arrived back today? Well, he had messages for Captain Brainerd..."

"Oh?" Joanna replied, keeping her eyes on the full moon. She
had slept for four straight hours after returning to the Temple camp
earlier and had not seen Brainerd until the celebration feast a few
hours previous, but he hadn't spoken to her.

"Pa asked Captain Brainerd when he was leaving," Marcella went
on. "And Brainerd said the dispatch rider carried orders from
General Pope at Leavenworth that he, Tom Brainerd, was replac-
ing General Brook at Camp Supply. General Brook was being
reassigned to Colonel McKenzie's Fourth Cavalry in Texas who is
moving in a big campaign against Quanah Parker's Comanches. And
Captain Brainerd is taking his Company L with him! Isn't that
marvelous?"

Joanna felt a stillness come over her. "How soon is Brainerd going?" she asked, trying to sound indifferent.

"Tomorrow morning. I'm going to miss him," Marcella said with
a sigh. "But," and her voice rose, excited, "Brainerd also told Pa
that Captain Billingsley is coming here with two companies of
troopers on his way to join McKenzie as well. He will leave twenty
men here for a month to make sure the area is patrolled and kept
safe. Won't it be grand to see Captain Owen Billingsley, Joanna?"

Joanna did not reply immediately. Then, "Strange that Colonel
McDonnel would order a patrol in here all of a sudden..."

"Joanna," Marcella insisted, ignoring her remark, "I said, isn't
it great that Captain Billingsley—"

"Yes, of course, Marcella," Joanna replied quickly. "It will be
grand. I hope Billingsley will be here long enough for you two to
get more sociable."

"Three days!" Marcella responded in a voice too loud, and she clapped her hand over her mouth.

"Then you know what to do," Joanna said, shifting painfully on her bedroll. "Don't let him ride away south until you've got him properly hog-tied."

"Joanna!" Marcella exclaimed, astonished. "I won't do any such thing! Captain Billingsley will choose in his own good time!"

"A military man needs someone to come back to," Joanna advised. "Just remember that."

"How do you know that?"

"Just remember..."

Marcella sighed and put her head back on the pillow. After a few minutes of silence, she said, "Joanna?"

"What?"

"What did those Indians do to you...out there?" Joanna felt Marcella push herself up on an elbow again to lean toward her. "I mean...what *did* they do to you?"

"Not much. Captain Brainerd came into their camp before they could do much. Brainerd faced Parker down." Joanna hesitated about how much to reveal concerning the incident. She decided to keep it to herself as Brainerd would expect. But she told Marcella about the box she had brought back and Quanah's part in that.

After she finished the telling, there was a long pause.

"Joanna!" Marcella said in awe. Joanna turned her head to look at her. Her face was aglow in the flood of moonlight, picking up her big blue eyes, larger now in the wonder of what she had been told. "Joanna!" she went on, still finding the story hard to believe. "I never knew an Indian could—"

"Could be so civil or do anything like that? I know," Joanna finished for her. "It's like your Pa said: 'Only God can tame the savage heart.' Or maybe there isn't as much savage in them as we think...or maybe we think they were born savage like I always thought."

Marcella's face remained frozen in her pose of disbelief and wonder. "Joanna, I—"

"Don't think too long on it. Time you got some sleep anyway if you want to look right for Captain Billingsley."

Marcella remained leaning over Joanna, however. "What about Captain Brainerd?"

"What about him?"

"You've been with him two days—"

"Marcella," Joanna said with a sigh.

"There's so much I don't know!" Marcella protested. "What did you talk about? He saved your life! He went straight into an Indian camp and got you out! Any man that does that—"

"Marcella, you are a hopeless romantic!" Joanna scolded her in a voice that snapped and was too loud. "Now put your head down and get some sleep! I mean it!"

Marcella reluctantly put her head back down on her pillow and gave a long, trembling sigh. "Every military man wants someone to come back to," she repeated then. "*You* said that, Joanna." And Marcella turned over and put her back to Joanna as if to say that she had the last word.

· · ·

Joanna could not find sleep. She waited a little longer, listening to Marcella's easy breathing. Then she got up slowly and pulled on a light green cotton dress. It was too hot for anything else. She fluffed out her long, dark wavy hair to get the kinks out. Then she walked through the sleeping camp.

She stopped by one of the pools of water, watching the moon's reflection in it for a long time. There was a growing uneasiness in her, along with a weight of sadness around her heart—sadness for Quanah Parker and for Captain Tom Brainerd, forever divided now by uniforms and codes of honor and war. Then, oddly, sadness for herself, because there wasn't much left to keep her pushing on. Being here with the Temples was natural in a way. She loved them all as family. But now that her mission was finished, there was no sense of permanence here. What should she do? Go back to Northfield? Be a schoolmarm all the rest of her life, like all the "dignified" single ladies there? What future was here? It was Jeremiah's dream-come-true, not hers. Moreover, Joanna had no more dreams, no more visions, now that her journey to hunt down Quanah Parker was complete.

"Can't sleep?"

She turned her head at the sound of his voice. He was sitting on an old cottonwood tree limb, twenty feet away, tossing pebbles into the muddy creek bed.

"Not very well," Joanna replied, feeling a quickening of the pulse in her throat but not knowing why. She was not ready for any conversation with him. Yet, he would be gone in the morning.

Through the corner of her eye she saw him get up and walk toward her. She kept her eyes on the moon's smiling reflection in the pool. He was dressed in his blue uniform dress jacket, the one he had worn at the celebration. The white epaulets on the shoulders looked even brighter in the luminous mist of the moon.

"Smells like rain in the air," he commented idly, and he jiggled some pebbles in his right hand as if trying to make up his mind what to do with them.

"Congratulations on making major," Joanna began suddenly, making her conversation polite but friendly. After all, she owed him her life!

"How did you hear?"

"Marcella has ears for everything within a mile of her."

He chuckled, a light tone of amusement bubbling up into his throat. "I should have known, I guess. Actually Jeremiah asked what my plans were, so I told him."

"You are off in the morning?"

"That's what my orders read."

"What about Jack Davison and Colonel McDonnel?"

He tossed a pebble out into the dry creek bed and walked closer toward her, stopping a few feet away. "Well, the dispatch rider from Dodge brought two messages. One was from Colonel McDonnel. His wife suffered a mental breakdown two days after we left Dodge. McDonnel explained that she had carried the burden of his lie about not sending Davison as a courier that day five years ago to Fort Morrow. He also added that he suffered a relentless deterioration of his honor as an officer and a gentleman in the knowledge of what he had done, both to me and my wife. The colonel relieved himself of command at Dodge and had already telegraphed General Pope at Leavenworth asking to give testimony that would clear my name in the massacre. I have a copy of his telegraph message. By now the colonel and his wife are in Leavenworth. In the other message, General Pope restored my rank pending the colonel's testimony."

"So what about Corporal Davison?"

"He'll go to Camp Supply with me, wait out the court's decision at Leavenworth after McDonnel confesses it all. I expect he'll be set free. After all, he only followed orders from McDonnel that day, not knowing that McDonnel was out to defame me if he could. Anyway, it's up to the court now..."

She sensed he was a bit tired now in the retelling of what had been in his mind a long time, or maybe he was a bit impatient to get on to other things.

"Do you feel cheated?" she asked quietly. "I mean in not being able to deliver Davison to McDonnel and get your satisfaction?"

He picked up a few more pebbles, stood, glanced at her as if he weren't sure yet. "Sure...I guess so. I waited five years to do just that...but it's done now anyway. How do you feel now that you didn't get to kill Quanah?"

She hadn't expected the captain to counter with that question. She took her time, not quite sure either how to express it. "It was a long time to wait for me too...but now I'm glad I didn't kill him, of course."

"Right," and he jiggled the new pebbles in his right hand. "I lost my taste for making McDonnel crawl in front of me. Maybe it happened when I faced Quanah, my brother, out there...I dunno. More so, I think my childhood upbringing sank in finally. Something in the Book says, 'In wrath remember mercy.' You know something about that?"

She hesitated, not knowing why he should ask her to respond to that. "I've heard and was taught the Scriptures all my life," she replied simply. But there was more. She knew something had shifted within her as to the importance of the Scriptures in the light of all that had happened here. "But I never really listened much after my parents were killed," she added.

"The same with me after I lost my wife," he said. "How do you feel now?"

"Does it make that much difference to you?" she said, not wanting to be terse about it, but not sure how to explore this ground now.

He tossed another pebble out to the pool ten feet or so in front of them. "Well...just curious, I guess, if my feelings are anything like yours. You have to admit, events in the last few days can't be charged up to happenstance...my father would call it a matter of divine intervention. I think Jeremiah Temple would agree. You of all people would understand the vengeance that ate at me for five years...and now to feel nothing really but a certain quietness inside. Well, I don't want to sound like a Bible-beater working up a camp meeting...but I feel I've got to give credit where it is due..."

He left it hanging there. But his question to her was still alive, demanding. She sighed then, looking up at the full moon, trying to form the words.

"For eight years I listened to Jeremiah Temple read the Scriptures after supper every night," she went on then, feeling for the words that would properly express her closure with it all. "But I heard little of it...I had one thing on my mind, and God had no place in any of it. But tonight Jeremiah talked about 'God taming the savage heart' and something—maybe a revelation—struck me then. There is no way to explain how we came through hostile Indian territory and lived to see this place. There is no way to account for what happened in Quanah's village, that with death so near to me you should ride in and bring peace. And the fact that two men, you and Quanah, unknown to each other, enemies to the death by virtue of the different flags you both ride under, should come together at that precise moment is beyond human comprehension." She paused, picking her way slowly along. "But the capper for me was when Quanah produced that black sewing box of my mother's. Right then it seemed that the word 'mercy' in the midst of 'wrath' took hold. I've been thinking about all that since then...and tonight I realized the quietness after a storm...a long storm in my life..."

She paused, unable to add more. He said, "Yes...I saw something of that storm in you back at Dodge...and even in Quanah's camp you didn't want to sit down with him in his tepee...even in peace."

She glanced quickly at him. "As far as Dodge is concerned, I won't be manhandled like that again," she replied with finality. "God has tempered the storm and brought peace instead of vengeance...but I won't be shoved around either. There is justice as well as mercy, Major Tom Brainerd, and the Book teaches that too!"

He smiled and lifted his hands as if in surrender. "I could not imagine you in any other way," he said with a lightness in his voice.

He tossed another pebble that dropped into the pool with a light splash. She felt they were both waiting for the other to close with something that seemed illusive to them.

Then she said, "Why didn't your white parents in Colorado tell you that you were an adopted Indian?"

"Well," he began, looking down at the pebbles in his hand, "I figure they didn't want me to know I wasn't theirs. My father probably knew I was a lost Indian kid...probably had long black hair down around my face and the gold-eagle chain around my neck. My father was wise in understanding those things...and they probably didn't want me to know I was a breed..."

"Breed?"

"Part Indian. Breeds have a tough time making it in white society. Take Amos Chapman. He's good enough to be in command of a troop. Instead, because he's a breed, he's scouting." He paused. "Bother you I got some Indian blood in me?"

The question took her by surprise. Joanna glanced at him, and his gaze was intent on her. "Why should it?" she replied uncertainly because the beat in her throat had picked up again. "I—I have come to know you fairly well, after all..."

His laugh was musical in the delight he felt. "Fairly?" he inquired, and his teeth flashed brightly in the moonlight. "Well...yes, I guess 'fairly' is a decent way to put it."

She felt a flush to her cheeks for the inadequacy of her answer. "What will Quanah do now?" she asked, turning away from any more talk of his lineage. "What will happen to him?"

Tom took his time answering, perhaps not wanting to speculate. "Well, three regiments of the U.S. Army are moving out to box him in over there in the Staked Plains." His voice sounded heavy as he contemplated the battle that was to come. "I hope he takes to the reservations before it all falls in on him."

He shook the pebbles in his right hand again. It made a sound like mocking laughter. "Will—will you ever be back this way again?" she ventured, staring at the moon-kissed pool in front of her.

"Never know what the army has in mind. Maybe, maybe not." The officer paused, and she felt his gaze on her. "I'm going to miss you, Joanna. Kind of seems like we've shared a big piece of life together already." She felt the air getting closer, warmer, and she thought of going back to the wagon.

"You know," he began again, "my father in Colorado taught me something about little pebbles and water. Look here now..." Joanna watched him as he moved to the edge of the pool that was beyond a small hump of sand about six feet in front of them. "Come here, Joanna," he said. She hesitated, yet felt an overpowering sense of his presence then; it was both confusing and frightening to her. Still, she was curious now.

She walked up to stand beside him. Then he opened his hand and showed the pebbles. "My father said that when two people want to—to remain friends, they each throw a pebble into the water . . . and if the ripples cross the pool and touch the other side, they will be friends."

Tom turned slowly and faced her then, a foot away perhaps. She glanced at him and saw those same shafts of light in his blue eyes, and something else—a serious, intent look as if he were begging her to take this ceremony seriously.

He extended one of the pebbles to her. She took it from his fingers, touching his skin briefly, setting off new ripples around her heart. "Oops," he said, "I don't have one to match." He reached down behind her and picked one up. Waiting with eyes on the pool, contrary tides of fear swelled within her—afraid that the pebbles wouldn't ripple far enough to the edges; afraid that if they did, the implication might be more than she was prepared to absorb.

"Okay," he said, "on three, we throw our pebbles into the center of the pool. Ready . . . one, two, three . . . go!"

She saw her pebble splash lightly in the center. Then his came on top. His hit with a loud, splashing sound and a boil of water came up to cover hers and rolled across the pool on both sides.

She turned and glared at him. "You threw a rock!" she accused, feeling a flush come up in her cheeks. "You picked up a rock behind me—"

"Now, Joanna—"

"You cooked that one up, Captain Brainerd!"

And she reached out and gave him a shove in his chest with both hands. He tottered backward, his heels on the edge of the pool, balancing precariously, flashing the half-grin of surprise. He made one desperate lunge toward her with his right hand and caught her by the right arm. As he went down, she was yanked off her feet after him.

As they hit the water together, Joanna felt the rich coolness of the spring water snap through her. She snorted against the water in her nose, hearing his laugh and whoop at the same time. She rubbed the water from her eyes and looked up. He was standing waist high in the water.

"I told you once never to treat my horse like you did!" she harangued him. "I told you then I'd put a bullet in you if you ever did! And, by Jiminy, I don't intend to let you treat *me* worse than a horse!"

She swung her right fist at his face. He caught it halfway and held it. His grip was firm but gentle as if he held a wounded bird. Frustrated, she swung her other hand and splashed water at him. He blinked as it hit him, but his smile remained, and he laughed again. He took the hand tightly in his. Then he held both of them to his chest. His hat was gone, lost in the slide into the pool. His dark hair was wet and outlined the strong lines of his face, the soft but even shape of his mouth below the water-slicked line of mustache. She felt his heart beating rapidly under her hands that he held to his uniform. She tried to pull them away, but he held them tight.

"Joanna Danforth Temple!" his voice rose to make sure that she understood him. "I've loved you ever since you chewed me out for not allowing you to kill that old Indian at Dodge. I've had you on my mind every mile over this dry prairie, around the fires at night and coming with the sun in the morning." She tried to pull her hands away again, fear now mixing with her flashing anger. And then he let her hands loose and put his hands on her hair softly, then cupped her face between them, tilting her face up to his.

She could hardly breathe now. Her eyes were fixed on his face. Then he leaned down to her and kissed her gently on the lips. She jerked back in the shock of it. Then an avalanche roared through the dry canyons of her soul, tearing away all of the barriers held in place there for so long! His arms went around her and held her, his lips remaining on hers...until her arms rose beyond her will and went around his neck. She did not feel the water now, only her heart running away in a wild stampede together with the rising melody in her mind.

"Tom Brainerd," she choked out, pulling back a little from his lips, feeling the soft touch of his breath on her cheek. But there were no more words.

"Joanna," he murmured to her, entreating, holding her close yet with that same soft and firm touch. "It was right from the start...way back at Dodge...in the fort dining room...at the punch bowl...out on the porch..."

The captain kissed her again and she felt the spinning once more so that she thought her breath would explode in her chest. Then he climbed out of the pool, reached down, and helped her out.

"Ever been kissed in a pool of water before?" he asked, smiling at her, his arms going around her waist.

"No..." she answered hoarsely and leaned against his chest as his right hand stroked her hair. "I've never been kissed..."

"Joanna," he said quietly, holding her close, "I know that living on an army post isn't the best for any woman. Too hot in the summer, too cold in the winter. But who knows, I might get out of the army one of these days and take to cattle ranching like Jeremiah... maybe we could come back here and settle down along the Wolf, be next to the Temples. Joanna, I'm asking you to marry me. You know I'm a breed...if that bothers you, well, I understand—"

"Hurray!" Joanna heard a chorus suddenly blast through the soft cushion of the mysterious, explosive night, puncturing Brainerd's proposal short. They both turned to look toward it and saw the torches come to the creek in front of them. Jeremiah and Elizabeth were out front, then Andrew, and the rest of the family. Behind them, crowding in, were the troopers of Company L.

"Hip-hip!" Jeremiah yelled.

"Hurray!" they all cheered back three times.

"Mister!" Joanna queried, as Jeremiah and Elizabeth walked toward them, the others following behind. "What's this all about?"

"Well, my darling girl," Jeremiah boomed back, stopping a few feet from them, "I am about to perform your wedding!"

A wild cheer broke out from the troopers. Joanna felt numb. She looked at Tom again. "Is this all your doing?"

He shrugged in innocence, but there were lights of amusement in his eyes.

"Am I to be shotgunned into this, Mister?" she protested. "I have a right to make up my own mind! Why—how did you decide we were to be married anyway?"

"Well," Jeremiah blustered, "your captain—excuse me—Major Tom Brainerd there asked me for permission to marry you right after the celebration feast tonight. And I said I'd be right proud!"

"I need to think about this. I need time—"

"Girl, in a few short hours it will be dawn," Jeremiah intoned. "And Major Brainerd will be off to Camp Supply. You might not see him again. Do you want him to ride away with his kiss on your lips and know it or him no more?"

The troopers clapped their hands in encouragement to her.

"Joanna," Elizabeth said quietly, bringing a sense of calm in the wildness of the moment, "we are sorry we came down here in the middle of Tom's proposal, really...and, Jeremiah," her voice took on a sharp edge as she spoke to him, "you won't push her!"

"Thunderation!" Jeremiah retaliated impatiently. "I figured Major Brainerd would have had everything done and ready by now! Now, Joanna, unless you know of some impediment to keep you from this man's offer of marriage, are you prepared now to exchange your vows?"

"Joanna," Elizabeth interjected in a precise tone of voice, "do you love Major Brainerd?"

Joanna looked up at Tom again, remembering the kiss, the explosion within her at his touch. She remembered him asking her if she minded that he was a breed, and she saw that question in his eyes now.

But that was not in her mind at all. She was still shaky from the kiss, there was weakness in her knees, the shortness of breath. The night grew quiet then with only the snapping of the torches as they all waited. "Well," she said, mesmerized by his eyes, "I...yes...yes, I—I truly—"

"Then join hands," Jeremiah said abruptly, turning the pages of the Bible to the marriage notes, peering at them in the glare of the torch light. "You want to change your mind, you can when it comes to your vows, girl..."

Then, before he could proceed, Andrew stepped forward and extended a bouquet of bluebonnets to her.

"Andrew?" Joanna responded, taking the flowers, looking up at him in surprise. "How—when did you get these?"

"Oh...when Pa said he was sure it would—it would be some time tonight, Marcella and I went out to the meadow and we picked what we could find..."

She reached up and kissed him on the cheek, "Oh, Andrew, I love you..." Then she turned and embraced Marcella, and Marcella began crying softly.

"Let's get on with it," Jeremiah urged impatiently. "The night is far spent. Join hands, please, Joanna..."

Tom reached out and took her right hand in his. She glanced at him, felt his hand gripping hers—strong, firm, caressing, an extension of himself.

"Now," Jeremiah went on, clearing his throat, "some marriages are made in heaven. . . and by all the saints this is surely one if I ever saw one. Tom Brainerd, do you take this woman, Joanna Danforth Temple, to be your wife, to love her, protect her, provide for her until death separates you both?''

''I do,'' Tom said evenly and strongly, and his troopers cheered again.

''Now, then, Joanna, in front of these witnesses and God Himself, I allow Elizabeth to lead you in your vows. . .''

Elizabeth took the Bible from Jeremiah and glanced at Joanna, her blue-gray eyes were misty, but her smile expressing joy. ''Joanna, darling,'' she began softly, her voice trembling, ''do you take this man—who has come sent of God to chase forever the shadows from your heart—to be your husband, to love him, obey him, bear his children, and bring order to his house, until death separates you?''

Joanna saw the tears on Elizabeth's cheeks. She looked up at Tom. She saw that little smile cross his mouth. And she once again envisioned him chasing her back to Dodge on that day that she almost took the blood of that old Indian. She saw him as a lonely officer standing against the wall at the reception at Dodge. She remembered his ride into Quanah's camp, facing death to save her, a man gentle in his quest for peace, yet strong enough to fight for what he believed if it came to that.

''I do,'' she replied in a subdued voice, caught up in the wonder of the moment. The cheer shot into the night again, rattling a crescendo of strange sound in the wild, barren land.

''Then,'' Jeremiah's voice boomed out in triumph, ''as an appointed ambassador of Jesus Christ, I pronounce you man and wife! Now the long, dry summer for you, Joanna, has passed. For you, Major Tom Brainerd, your loneliness is no more. As you sought to bring peace to this troubled land, even to the death, God has seen fit to reward you both with love, love enough to transform the deserts of your lives into a tender summer. May it endure to the blessing of you both!''

• • •

It was long into the night now. A mourning dove in anticipation of the coming dawn cooed softly. Not many in Company L were asleep.

''Rutledge?'' Willie said. ''It be happenin' too fast fer me. We begins as nobodies—phantoms, right, Jackson? Right. Now we's come to be heroes! Now we's a real troop at a fort unduh a real majah...we chases Injuns clear back to Oklahoma...den we sees our majah marry his woman. Never happen in Injun country...but it be! I's gettin' a little scared God's gonna drop somethin' heavy on us to balance it..."

Rutledge sighed and smiled slowly, feeling a deep satisfying warmth inside like the day his mammy told him that "President Lincoln says we don't have to be chained no more..."

"God's been preparin' ya, Willie...before dis long, hot summer be done, we all's gonna know some tough times mebbe. But right now...the good Lawd seen fit to grow a rose in dis heah dust. I be smellin' it and enjoyin' it long's ah can. Guh-night, Willie, Jackson..."

"Rutledge, I don' feel like no sleep," Willie complained.

Then as the full moon slowly crawled its way across the heavens, and the stars blinked signals to a scorched earth lying quietly in the gentle squeeze of the ongoing night, a voice lifted to sound the benediction over the quiet land:

> Ere we reach the shining river,
> Lay we every burden down;
> Grace our spirits will deliver,
> And provide a robe and crown.
>
> Yes, we'll gather at the river,
> The beautiful, the beautiful river,
> Gather with the saints at the river
> That flows by the throne of God.

And Private Willie Dunkerton fell fast asleep.

EPILOGUE

There are many historical sources that establish the events of 1874, particularly the Indian uprising in the Panhandle area of Oklahoma and North Texas that is the focus of this novel.

For instance, Quanah Parker, chief of the Quahadi Comanche, is a person of record along with his white mother, Cynthia Parker. There was a battle between buffalo hunters and the Indians, Quanah's tribe among them, at a real place called Adobe Walls. The struggle of the Indian against the encroachment of white buffalo hunters into South Texas is documented as well. References to Billy Dixon, Amos Chapman, Generals Phillip Sheridan and Pope are real names drawn from that period. All other characters cast in this book are fictional.

Quanah Parker did surrender with his Quahadi tribe of Comanches in the spring of 1875 after several years of fierce battle against all whites, the army included, who ventured into the Indian treaty lands south of the Arkansas and Cimarron rivers.

Why he finally did choose to give in, when he resisted the "prison" on the reservation with such vehemence for so long, is attributed to the fact that he was outgunned and outmanned by the U.S. Army. This is unquestionably true in large part.

But some of the "old-timers," many of them aging Indians, who still remember the oral folklore of those days, still like to spin stories about the "legend of Quanah." In those legends, they refer to the "other brother" of Quanah, here in this novel referred to as Tanna. While there is no historical basis for this tale, these storytellers claim that Tanna, more white than Indian, was part of the reason for Quanah's surrender. Tanna, an Indian seeking peace, as the story goes, sought to influence Quanah to give up his bloody war against the whites.

In the spring of 1875 legend has it that Quanah Parker became more and more convinced that his long, lost brother, Tanna, had returned from the dead to deliver his message of peace. Because of that reasoning, Quanah finally decided to yield and turn himself and his tribe over to the U.S. Army and the reservation.